Mistletoe Mysteries

Mistletoe Mysteries

COLLECTED BY

CHARLOTTE MACLEOD

THE MYSTERIOUS PRESS

New York • London
Tokyo • Sweden • Milan

The Mysterious Press, 129 West 56th Street, New York, N.Y. 10019

Printed in the United States of America
First Printing: November 1989
10 9 8 7 6 5 4 3 2 1

Library of Congress Cataloging-in-Publication Data

Mistletoe mysteries / [edited by] Charlotte MacLeod.
   p.   cm.
  ISBN 0-89296-400-6
  1. Detective and mystery stories, American. 2. Detective and mystery stories, Canadian. 3. Christmas stories, American. 4. Christmas stories, Canadian.   I. MacLeod, Charlotte.
PS648.D4M57   1989
813'.08720833--dc20

                                               89-12475
                                                    CIP

Contents

Mistletoe Mysteries

CHARLOTTE MACLEOD

A COZY FOR CHRISTMAS

Sarah Kelling and her husband Max Bittersohn are old friends of mine. Back when they were first married, I wrote a book called The Convivial Codfish, *which takes place at Christmastime. Some of Sarah's loyal readers expressed displeasure because I let Max do most of the work in solving the mystery and slighted, as they thought, their heroine by sending her off to holiday shop for her newly augmented family. At the time, I believed that I was in fact assigning to Sarah the more difficult and important task. I welcome at last an opportunity to explain why I thought so then and I think so still.*

"**S**o Max has gone off with another woman?" Cousin Brooks Kelling appeared to find the circumstance highly entertaining.

"Wearing false whiskers and great-uncle Nathan's Prince Albert coat." Sarah Kelling Bittersohn didn't think it was funny at all. "He looked so handsome it made me sick."

"Men are all brutes." Cousin Theonia Kelling, wife to Brooks, gave her own particular brute a smile of total adoration. "Whatever possessed Max to do a thing like that?"

"He alleges it's in aid of that insane business about our somewhat beloved relative and the Great Chain of the Comrades of the Convivial Codfish," Sarah told her. "I suppose it's all my own fault for having helped Uncle Jem nag him into tracking it down, which doesn't make me feel any better about being left to pine alone and desolate." Sarah, like all the Kellings except Cousin Mabel, was a Gilbert and Sullivan aficionado. "You don't mind my inviting myself over?"

1

This time, Theonia's smile was for Sarah. "My dear, how could we?"

Aside from the fact that both Brooks and Theonia would have welcomed Sarah's company under any circumstances, there was the added point in her favor that she owned the house. During the lean years after the death of her first husband, the Tulip Street brownstone on Boston's historic Beacon Hill had been virtually Sarah's only asset, and a heavily mortgaged one at that. To keep herself afloat, she'd turned it into an ever-so-elite boarding house.

Now she was married to one of her former boarders, the handsome and affluent Max Bittersohn, a private detective who'd been a specialist in recovering vanished art objects when she met him but had lately developed a sideline in dragging beleaguered Kellings back from the brink. The newlyweds were living next door in a small apartment while their new house on the North Shore was being built. Brooks and Theonia had taken over the running of the boarding house, an arrangement that suited them all just fine.

"You'll stay to dinner?" Brooks was urging.

"Of course she'll stay," said Theonia. "It's quite all right, Sarah. Our top floor back has gone to Denver for the holidays."

Numbers were always a consideration at the boarding house, its lovely antique dining table could only seat eight in the elegant comfort the Kelling establishment demanded. Elegance had been Sarah's watchword from the start. Right now they were getting an early start on the customary predinner ritual by being served elegant little glasses of rather inelegant sherry from an extremely elegant Waterford decanter by a white-gloved butler who was the absolute epitome of elegance now that he'd had his missing tooth bridged in.

So as not to lower the tone, Sarah had come over in a full-skirted green velvet dinner gown and her second-best diamonds. Theonia was in deep crimson and pearls. The two were sitting together on the library sofa, against a backdrop of greens obtained at no expense from the North Shore property. Flickering lights from the open fire and soft gleams from the red candles on the mantelpiece fell benignly on Sarah's soft brown hair and Theonia's piled-high raven tresses, highlighting the one's delicate youthful beauty and flattering the other's middle-aged opulence.

"Well, if you two ladies aren't the very spirit of Christmas!"

Mrs. Gates, their all-time favorite boarder, had emerged from her first-floor suite and was making her careful way into the library. She herself made a charming picture in a long black gown set off by a fleecy white woolen shawl and an old-fashioned parure of gold and garnets. Charles the butler hastened to pull the old lady's favorite Queen Anne chair a little closer to the fire while Brooks gallantly escorted her to it.

"Thank you, dear boy."

She smiled up at Brooks, the firelight doing wonderful things to her spun-silver hair. "Just hang my work bag on the arm of the chair here, where I can get at it easily. You'll all forgive me if I go on with my sewing, won't you? I promised last February to make some tea cozies for this year's Holly Fair at St. Eusapia's. Now here it is the night before the fair and I'm still trying to finish the last one."

"Oh, it's exquisite!" Sarah exclaimed as Mrs. Gates drew out the cozy cover she was working on. This was a confection of blue moiré taffeta, embellished in the more-is-better Victorian mode with garlands of creamy satin ribbon, ruchings of lace, flirtings of fringe, plus a scattering of sewn-on pearls and an occasional sprig of embroidery to reassure the purchaser that no avenue had been left unexplored. "You must have spent ages. How many have you done?"

"Six counting this one and I must say I'm glad it's the last. If you'll thread my needle for me, my dear, I'll let you tidy my work bag. When my granddaughters were small, they used to think that was the greatest treat in the world."

"And so shall I."

As Theonia went to make sure everything was under control in the kitchen, Sarah perched on a footstool beside Mrs. Gates's chair, taking a childlike pleasure in sorting out the bits and pieces. "There's enough of the blue taffeta left to do another," she remarked. "Do you think you will, sometime? They must be great fun."

Mrs. Gates sighed. "I thought so when I started last spring. By now I'm so sick of them that I recoil at the mere thought. Take the taffeta and trimmings if you'd like to try one yourself."

"Do you mean it? May I really?"

Sarah had been wondering about a tea cozy for Max's mother. Herself a Wasp of the Waspiest, she was having a hard time reconciling this year's holiday observances between what she'd been brought up to and what might be acceptable to her recently acquired Jewish in-laws. Max thought they ought just to forget the whole thing, but Sarah was far too thoroughly schooled in how easy it was to start family feuds among the multitudinous Kellings to risk one with the Bittersohns. Family relations were desperately important, even if they did add to the agonies of holiday shopping.

Only that afternoon, she'd bought her new sister-in-law a soufflé dish and been rather badly mauled in the process. It would be lovely if she could manage to concoct an acceptable tea cozy rather than having to shop for one, though Sarah knew she'd never in the world come up with anything that compared to Mrs. Gates's. It would, of course, be possible to go over to St. Eusapia's tomorrow and buy this lovely thing if somebody else didn't beat her to it and if she could bring herself to pay the small fortune the church folk would undoubtedly be asking. And why shouldn't they? It would be criminal to let workmanship like this go for a pittance. St. Eusapia's was a wealthy parish, they'd find customers enough.

Sarah folded the oddments of fringe and ribbon inside the remnant of taffeta and stowed the small packet in the capacious side pocket, which was one reason why she'd chosen this particular gown. The other boarders were beginning to trickle in now, it was time to sit up and be a credit to the establishment.

Naturally the boarding house had seen some turnover in its clientele since Sarah had turned the keys over to Brooks and Theonia. The basement room that had for a while been Max Bittersohn's was now occupied by a flautist who looked melancholy and Byronesque but was in fact a jolly soul when he didn't have a concert to play. Since Mr. Snowfjord was performing tonight, he was saving his breath to swell his arpeggios. As far as the conversation was concerned, his silence wouldn't matter a bit; Mr. Porter-Smith could always be counted on to talk enough for two. One of Sarah's original six, Eugene Porter-Smith was a certified public accountant who worked for Cousin Percy Kelling. Tonight he'd given his familiar maroon dinner jacket a Christmassy touch with a bright green tie and a cummerbund to match.

Miss Jennifer Lavalliere, another of Sarah's holdovers, showed up wearing a brand-new two-carat diamond on her fourth finger left hand and little else worth mentioning. She was delighted to show off the ring to her former landlady and to tell her all about the young man who'd bestowed it, plus a few catty tidbits about the one who'd gone to Denver for the holidays.

Ms. Carboy, who shared the third floor with Miss Lavalliere, was a relative newcomer to Tulip Street: a long-boned, long-faced woman of forty-odd who reminded Sarah of Virginia Woolf. She had some sort of extremely high-powered job over at Government Center about which she tended to be inscrutable, possibly because the job was not in truth all that high-powered. She admired Mrs. Gates's handiwork at some length and made the gaffe of asking whether she might buy it then and there.

"I'm so sorry," Mrs. Gates replied a shade too sweetly. "I've committed myself to supplying six of these for my church fair, and that's all I've managed to do, assuming I get this done tonight.

If you really want one, I'm afraid you'll have to buy it over at St. Eusapia's between ten and four tomorrow."

Ms. Carboy sighed. "Then I'm afraid I'll have to do without it. I'll be tied to my desk all day and possibly far into the night. There's always so much paperwork to get through at the end of the year."

The sherry-sipping wound to its stately close, the butler announced dinner, Mrs. Brooks Kelling seated her guests. The flautist finished his soup, took two mouthfuls of the main course, excused himself, and rushed out into the night. The rest of the party partook of the excellent meal at their leisure and went back to the library for coffee.

Mrs. Gates picked up her work again and asked Sarah to rethread her needle. "I've just this last little bit to do. Then I'm finished, praise be!"

"What are the others like?" Sarah asked her. "Did you make them all the same?"

"Oh, no, each one is different, otherwise I'd surely have gone mad. I'd show you but they're all wrapped up and stowed away in a shopping bag for Charles to take to the church tomorrow morning."

Sarah would have been quite willing to repack them, but she knew better than to ask. She drank her coffee, said her good nights, and went home to try her hand with the leftovers.

She'd had no high hopes to start with; after a couple of hours she was quite ready to call a halt. The cozy cover she'd achieved looked only superficially like the one she'd tried to copy; it might do as a stage prop, but wouldn't do much to cement her somewhat tenuous diplomatic relations with Mother Bittersohn. Sarah was wondering whether to go to bed or sit and have a good pout when Max telephoned. The party had ended in catastrophe, he was stranded in the hinterlands, and would she drive out to pick him up?

They got to bed late, which meant a delayed start the next

morning. Sarah got Max off on his detectival rounds, then set off herself in quest of Mother Bittersohn's tea cozy. On a previous safari, she'd seen some attractive ones at reasonable prices in the shop she still thought of as the Women's Educational. By the time she got there today, though, the only cozies left were striped red and green and appliqued with saucy elves. Sarah didn't think Santa's elves would achieve their purpose in this particular instance.

The shop held lots of other delights, though. She wandered around for quite a while choosing trinkets for this one and that of her myriad relatives and buying herself a tote bag to carry them home in. After that, she popped into Bailey's to recruit her flagging energies with a hot fudge sundae and sat longer than she'd meant to, scooping up driblets of fudge sauce and trying to remember which of the Back Bay's many churches was St. Eusapia's.

Once reasonably sure of her goal, Sarah was faced with the problem of getting there. A taxi would be out of the question, traffic wasn't budging an inch. Outside Berkeley Street subway entrance she heard dire talk of a tie-up down below. They'd had snow earlier in the week, the sidewalks had been imperfectly cleared, drifts which the plows had piled up at the curbs were trodden into a lumpy mess. The wind had come up since morning, the skies were by now as muddy a gray as the frozen slush through which Sarah had to pick her way, along with far too many other gift-laden strugglers.

A Bostonian born and bred, Sarah accepted all this as a matter of course though she could hardly take it in stride, for striding under such conditions would have been dangerous if not impossible. Dressed for the weather in boots and a windproof storm coat with the hood pulled up, she didn't particularly mind the walk, but she did feel relieved when at last she reached the right church and entered the gaily bedecked parish hall.

What with one thing and another, she'd got here much later

than she'd meant to. The fair must have been a great success, the merchandise was pretty well picked over and the volunteer clerks looked ready to drop. Sarah found a fancywork table without any trouble, but only one of Mrs. Gates's tea cozies was left on display, and that one a bedizenment of red and green that featured a charming but hardly ecumenical Christmas tree worked in multicolored glass beads.

"Oh, dear," she moaned to the presiding angel, a Miss Waltham whom she remembered from one of her former late mother-in-law's civic committees, "is this the only cozy you have left? I watched Mrs. Gates finish up a heavenly blue one last night and was praying it might still be here."

"As a matter of fact, it still is."

Miss Waltham was a majestic lady with a determined chin and at the moment an even more determined set to her mouth. "The blue taffeta came with a note pinned to it saying 'Hold for W. J. Ronely' so naturally we set it aside. Needless to say, W. J. Ronely has failed to appear. People will do that, you know, make a great to-do about having merchandise put on reserve, then not show up, so we're stuck with a no sale and the church is out the money. I think we've been quite patient enough with W. J. Ronely, Mrs. Kelling. If you're willing to part with eighty dollars for a tea cozy, I'm more than willing to take it."

Sarah forbore to remind Miss Waltham that she was no longer Mrs. Kelling. However, she paid with a check that had her new name printed at the top, partly as a hint that she was no longer as she once had been and partly because she'd somehow managed to get through most of the generous sum Max had given her before he'd left. Miss Waltham accepted the check, took obvious pleasure in removing the "Hold for W. J. Ronely" note, and wrapped the cozy in many swaddlings of tissue paper.

"Thank you so much," said Sarah. "Don't bother about a bag, I have one."

She stowed her hard-won treasure carefully down inside her

tote bag and made a quick tour of the depleted tables. The White Elephants were by now a sick-looking herd, but she did find a charming little Staffordshire cat with a chipped but mendable tail that the bargain hunters had overlooked. The bakery table yielded a box of fudge and a bag of ginger cookies at closeout prices. At last Sarah wound up back at the fancywork table where Mrs. Gates's Christmas tree cozy was still displayed in lonely splendor. What could she do except stifle her Yankee conscience and say, "I'll take it."

By this time her tote bag was crammed. Miss Waltham wrapped the sumptuous gaud in all the tissue paper she had left, then slipped it into a crumpled brown grocery bag she fished out from under the counter.

"There's your cozy, Mrs. Bittersohn," she said in a good loud voice to let Sarah know she'd seen the error of her ways, "if that doesn't give somebody a Merry Christmas, I don't know what will."

Sarah thanked her and tucked the bag under her arm. As she turned to go, she was almost bowled over by a tall man in a dark overcoat who looked a bit like Virginia Woolf's brother.

"My name is Ronely," Sarah heard him bark at Miss Waltham. "You have a tea cozy put away for me."

"I'm sorry," Miss Waltham replied, "but we don't. You shouldn't have left it so late. We gave you up and sold the cozy to somebody else."

"But I got stuck on the subway!"

Sarah decided it would be rude to hang around and eavesdrop. She slipped out of the hall as fast as she could, buttoning her coat up to her chin and pulling her hood down over her forehead. The snow that had been threatening on her way over was coming down now: a mean, driving, sleety fall that obviously meant business. Sarah hoped Max didn't get snowbound in the exurbs, she herself would prefer not to be out in this storm much longer. She hurried up toward Arlington Street and was standing in front of the Ritz Carlton waiting for a break in the traffic so she could cross over and walk home through the Public Garden when she was whopped from behind and fell sprawling in the gutter.

The Ritz doorman was with her in an instant. He'd recognized her, of course; Max's clients were the sort of people who'd automatically put up at the Ritz.

"Mrs. Bittersohn, are you okay? That guy shoved you on purpose, I saw him. Did he get your pocketbook? Let me take that shopping bag. Do you want to come in the lobby for a while? Shall I call you a cab?"

"What did the man look like?" was all Sarah could think of to say.

"Tall, skinny guy in a dark overcoat. No use trying to catch him, he ran down the subway. He sure didn't look like a mugger. You just never can tell, can you? Here's your fudge."

"Thank you."

Sarah ought to know the doorman's name, but she was too flustered to recall it at the moment. At least the fudge was all right, the maker had packed it inside a plastic bag. Her handbag was safely hooked over her arm, its excellent clasp still closed. The only thing missing was the brown paper bag that held the tea cozy, the Christmas tree that had not been set aside for W. J. Ronely.

Eighty dollars down the subway. While she rubbed her bruises and straightened her coat, the doorman hunted between the ruts and under the nearest parked cars but didn't find her parcel. Sarah was not at all surprised. In a way she could even sympathize with W. J. Ronely. Christmas shopping was a desperate business; perhaps he, too, had a mother-in-law.

She tipped the doorman lavishly over his halfhearted protest, told him not to bother about a cab because she could make it to Tulip Street faster on foot, a statement he could hardly gainsay since the snow was snarling the traffic even worse than before, though that had hardly seemed possible, and set off across the Gardens.

She wasn't worried about being pursued again by W. J. Ronely. He'd got what he wanted, or thought he had. Even if he found out he'd snatched the wrong bag, he wouldn't know where to look for the right one. Unless he'd happened to overhear Miss Waltham or the doorman call her Mrs. Bittersohn. Bittersohn was not a common name. Max's was the only one in the Boston phone book.

Sarah tried not to look over her shoulder, but she did wish the walking weren't so beastly treacherous. She was astonishingly relieved to reach Beacon Street and cross over to the Hill. Tulip Street was only a matter of minutes now, and she'd be in the lee of the storm most of the way.

Still, when she reached the purple-paned townhouse where great-uncle Frederick's old army buddy General Purslane and his wife still lived, she decided to pop in and say hello. She'd give them the fudge, they both loved sweets.

The Purslanes were delighted to see her and the fudge. "Weren't you a dear to think of us!" Mrs. Purslane exclaimed. "Leave your coat and boots right here by the door, you're just in time for a cup of tea. What else did you buy at the fair?"

"One of Mrs. Gates's lovely tea cozies. Let me show you."

No use lamenting the cozy she'd loved and lost, Sarah was happy enough to show off the one she had. "Can you imagine how much work she put into this? You can barely see the stitches."

Mrs. Gates had constructed her cozies on the usual pillow-pillowcase principle: a decorated cover and a padded double semicircle of plain muslin underneath that did the actual work of retaining the heat in the teapot. Sarah slipped off the cover so that Mrs. Purslane could appreciate the perfection of the stitchery even on the underside. As she did so, she noticed a small incongruity.

Mrs. Gates had formed the padded underpart the natural way, by stitching the four pieces that made up the double semicircle together on the wrong side, then turning them right side out so that the seams would be hidden after the stuffing was in. The bottom seams were then slipstitched together so meticulously that the joining could barely be discerned without a jeweler's loupe. For some reason, however, about an inch and a half of the seam at the top had been ripped out, then sewn up from the outside with apparent care but little expertise.

"Mrs. Gates never did that!" Sarah squeezed gently below the stitches. "I think I feel something. Mrs. Purslane, do you have a pair of manicure scissors?"

"Here, use this."

Mrs. Purslane fished in her sewing box and handed Sarah a dainty but efficient seam ripper. Sarah picked gingerly at the clumsy stitches, then poked the slender tool through the opening she'd made.

"It's there, all right. I felt it. Can you find me some tweezers?"

"Certainly, just a second."

Tweezers in hand, Sarah fished around a bit and drew out a tiny transparent envelope. The general took one look and sprang from his easy chair.

"Microfilm, by gad! The woman must be a spy!"

"Mrs. Gates is eighty-nine years old and a bishop's widow," said Sarah. "She'd have had no reason to rip out the seam, she could have put the film inside while she was making the cozy. If she did rip the seam, she'd have sewn it up so you'd never have known. I could have done a better job than that myself. What are they of? I wonder."

"We'll soon find out," said the general. "Come into my study, I have a microfilm viewer there. For my book, you know."

The general was, needless to say, engaged in writing his memoirs. He'd been at them for the past twenty-five years or so, to the best of Sarah's knowledge. She and Mrs. Purslane watched with what patience they could muster while he tweezered the mysterious strip of blackness into place and switched on the light.

"What is it, George?" his wife asked impatiently.

"Wait till I adjust the—great Scott! Ladies, I shall have to ask you both to leave this room immediately. And please close the door behind you. I must get on the phone to the secretary of defense immediately. Sarah, you've done your country a service today. Now go straight home and forget all about it. That's an order."

"Yes, General," said Sarah. "But I'm taking my tea cozy with me."

She thanked Mrs. Purslane for the tea, wished her a Merry Christmas, was assured that she'd just given the general one, and faced what was by now a fairly convincing blizzard. Luckily she didn't have far to go. She entered her apartment with somewhat exaggerated circumspection.

Once inside, Sarah told herself not to be silly and started making a business of hanging up her wet storm coat and unpacking her tote bag. Her purchases might as well stay on the kitchen table, she could gift wrap them there once she'd decided which was for whom. As for the blue tea cozy, she got a needle and thread and mended the place she'd ripped out, exploring first with a thin-bladed knife to make sure nothing else was concealed in the stuffing and wondering who'd been at it before her.

The microfilm couldn't possibly have been inserted before Mrs. Gates finished her work. An expert like her couldn't have missed seeing those clumsy stitches while she was putting the cover over the padding. The job must have been done after she'd gone to bed, leaving the packed bag outside her door for Charles to pick up in the morning.

Brooks would have locked the house up tighter than Fort Knox as soon as Mr. Snowfjord got back from his concert and everybody else was safely inside. Nobody would have dared tamper with the bag while others were still about. Assuming that it would have been possible for an outsider to secrete himself anywhere in the house, it would have been impossible for the intruder to depart in the early hours without leaving some chain, bolt, or bar unfastened to give the fact away. Whoever did this thing had to be somebody who'd come in, stayed in, or gone out, if at all, in the accustomed way; confident that Charles would deliver the altered package to the place where it was supposed to go and that church folk would honor the message pinned to the doctored cozy.

There was, Sarah realized, the outside chance that Charles himself had stopped somewhere on the way to St. Eusapia's and waited while someone else did the dirty work. Charles was an actor when he got the chance; like some other actors, he might not always distinguish between what was good theater and what was bad business. If he'd entered knowingly into any such plot, though, Charles must have been involved in some advance planning. Sarah couldn't imagine his not spilling the secret to Mariposa, the housekeeper, with whom he was on what Cousin Theonia sedately described as close terms. And there was no way Mariposa would have let him go through with such a caper.

Theonia could sew as well as Mrs. Gates. Brooks probably could, too, if he tried; he was incredibly deft with his hands. Assuming they could have stooped to treason, which was unthinkable, neither of them would have made so clumsy a faux pas.

Sarah wished General Purslane hadn't been so desperately hush-hush about those films. If they had something to do with figures, such as a proposal for a defense contract, Sarah supposed Eugene Porter-Smith might conceivably be the culprit, assuming Cousin Percy had the sort of client who could get into this kind of trouble. If he did, Percy would probably do their books himself, though, rather than expose an employee to temptation.

If she'd had any idea what that important job at Government Center was, Sarah wouldn't have minded suspecting Ms. Carboy. As she didn't, the question would have to remain moot for now. That anybody would entrust a featherhead like Jennifer Lavalliere with a subversive microfilm seemed insane, but she did have that new fiancé and, as the doorman at the Ritz had so pertinently observed, you just never knew.

Mr. Snowfjord seemed an unlikely prospect but again, you never knew. A musician much in demand must get to meet a great many diverse people; and flautists were of necessity nimble-fingered.

Sarah nipped off her thread, slipped the enchanting blue cover back over the mended padding, and supposed she might as well get Mother Bittersohn's present wrapped before it caused any more trouble. On second thought, she wrapped it in aluminum foil and stuck it in the freezer compartment of the refrigerator.

The cover she'd tried to fashion out of Mrs. Gates's leftovers was still lying where she'd left it last night. Sarah found the padding out of an old tea cozy that she'd been meaning to recover sometime, ripped a couple of inches along the top, and picked up a snapshot Cousin Mabel had sent in lieu of a Christmas card. It showed Mabel standing beside an alligator on a Florida key, Mabel always went away for Christmas so that she'd have an excuse not to buy anyone a present. The alligator had the pleasanter smile, Sarah thought as she stuffed the photo inside the padding. She sewed up where she'd ripped, slipped the padding inside her improvised cover, and dropped the finished cozy back on the table.

These were the shortest days of the year. It should have been pitch-dark by now but the fast-piling snow and the old-fashioned streetlights were keeping the cityscape a ghostly, shimmering charcoal gray. As a rule, Sarah would have been happy to stand looking out at the street, enjoying the play of light and shadow, the eerie beauty of car headlights approaching at a crawl, small as blurry flashlight bulbs, then looming bigger and brighter and blurrier, changing to ruby aureoles as the cars passed by and the taillights came into view, shrinking and shrinking and fading away into the blur. Tonight she pulled down the window blinds and shivered a little as she went back to the kitchen.

Brooks would be here in exactly fourteen minutes to put up the last of the curtain rods. Brooks was always punctual to the dot, but fourteen minutes seemed a long time to be waiting by herself. The upstairs neighbor was at home, Sarah had heard the dragging footsteps and the tap of the cane. Mrs. Levits would have been housebound all day, like the Purslanes. She put some of her bargain cookies on a little plate and ran upstairs, too impatient to wait for the antique elevator, which was the size of a phone booth and slow as molasses running uphill in January.

Mrs. Levits was pleased with the cookies and avid for a long winter's chat; Sarah had to explain that she couldn't linger because she was expecting her cousin. Not being a fool, she used Mrs. Levits's phone to make sure Brooks was on his way before she went back downstairs, and waited for him on the landing. When they went in together, she was not much surprised to feel the draft from a broken pane in the door that led to the fire escape, to discover melting snow on her clean kitchen floor, and to notice that her faked-up blue tea cozy was gone.

"Good Lord, you've had a burglar," Brooks exclaimed. "Check your valuables, Sarah, while I call the police."

"No, don't call them," said Sarah. "I know what he took."

She told Brooks her story. He wasted no time on questions, but whipped out his tape and measured the broken pane.

"I have window glass at home. It will take me roughly eight minutes to nip over, cut a piece to size, and bring it back. Do you want to come with me?"

Sarah shook her head. "I ought to be all right here for a little while, surely, now that Ronely thinks he's got what he's after. I'd better stay and report to General Purslane."

She stuck a folded newspaper over the broken pane to shut out some of the cold air and picked up the phone. She was still talking to the general when the doorbell rang. Assuming it was Brooks with the glass, she said good-bye and went to punch the button that released the downstairs catch. Somebody thumped up the stairs—certainly not Brooks, he walked like a cat—and pounded on the door.

"United Parcel. Package for Bittersohn."

"Just leave it by the door," Sarah called out.

"You have to sign for it."

"Sign my name yourself. I'm in the bathtub."

If this was a bona fide UPS delivery, the driver would be in a mad rush to get back to his truck, which would be blocking however much of the narrow one-way street was still passable, and would do as she'd said rather than face Tulip Street again in this weather. If the messenger was bogus, Sarah preferred not to find out the hard way. Brooks could pick up the parcel when he came, if there was one.

She wished the door had one of those modern peepholes so she could see what the man looked like. It did have an old-fashioned keyhole, though, not used any more since a modern chain and deadbolt had been installed. Sarah knelt, flipped aside the tiny metal flap that covered the hole, and squinted through.

All she could see was a pair of hands in black leather gloves, carefully lowering a brown paper package to the floor. Since the package was about the size of the box of fudge she'd given the Purslanes, this seemed a remarkably delicate way to handle it. Maybe there was a "Fragile" label but even so—she jumped as the messenger turned and leaped for the stairs, taking them three at a time from the sound of the thumps. She caught one fleeting glimpse of a black boot and something brown, but that was all.

Brooks had been gone a little over four minutes, she'd let the package sit there until he got back. Then Sarah remembered the absurdly cautious way those gloved hands had set the small thing down, and lame Mrs. Levits up above, and the pokey old elevator down below.

It was crazy, it was impossible. No matter, it was a risk she must not take. Sarah opened the door, bent her knees, and very, very tenderly picked up the package.

The box was neatly wrapped. Her name and address were clearly typed on what looked like a standard UPS label. The sender's name was obscured, the paper was not stuck down with tape, and the fancy red-and-green Christmas string holding it together was tied in a simple bow knot. In God's name, what did one do now?

Standing there with the box in her hands and her heart in her throat, Sarah glared frantically around the living room. Next to the gas fire sat a market basket she'd stuffed with greens and red alder berries as an apology for the tree they weren't going to have. As fast as she dared, she settled the box among the greens and carried it out to the fire escape.

On Tulip Street, the townhouses were set in a solid row with tiny backyards opening on a service alley. Across the alley stood the backs of the houses that faced on the next street over. Some previous tenant had rigged an endless clothesline on pulleys between Sarah's fire escape and the one opposite; surely not to hang out washing in this posh historic area, more probably to ferry small articles across to a friend.

With a piece of wide red ribbon she'd snatched in passing from among her gift wraps, Sarah tied the basket to the lower section of the filthy but still intact clothesline and pulled on the upper part to send it bobbing out into the empty space above the alley.

She could see the basket well enough in the glow from the street lamp beneath and the light streaming out from her own kitchen. It looked incongruously festive with its freight of greens and the perky red bow she must have tied, though she didn't remember doing so. An automatic reflex, everybody was tying bows this time of year. She stepped over to the telephone and rang the general again.

"This is Sarah," she told him. "Perhaps I'm overreacting, but somebody's just left a package at my door. The messenger said UPS, but the box is so insecurely wrapped they'd never have accepted it. No, of course I didn't open the door. I peeked through the keyhole. The messenger set the box down much too carefully and dashed off in a terrible hurry. No, I've hung it out on the clothesline. I just hope whoever lives across the way doesn't think—oh, I must have waked a pigeon. Shoo! Shoo!"

Boston pigeons do not shoo easily. This one settled on the edge of the basket, causing it to tilt a little, to Sarah's horror, and began picking off alder berries in a methodical and businesslike fashion. Sarah kept an eye out while the general asked questions she couldn't answer.

Now the pigeon had tired of alder berries and gone to work on the package. It had the red-and-green string in its beak, tugging with all the weight and expertise a tough, street-wise bird might reasonably be expected to possess. The pigeon braced against the handle and jerked harder. The knot gave way. The basket exploded with only a muffled pop, but the huge ball of flame lit up the whole area. Just for a moment, then charred fragments began drifting down, vanishing into the enveloping grayness.

She was supposed to be a fragment.

"Never mind the bomb squad, General," she said dully. "The pigeon set off the incendiary. I'm glad he got the alder berries."

She hung up on the general and was still standing there with her arms dangling limp when Brooks came back. Opening the door took all the nerve she had.

"Sorry I took longer than I meant to," he apologized. "Ms. Carboy was just coming in and waylaid me on the steps."

Sarah came alive again. "What was she wearing?"

"Eh? Oh. Black boots and gloves, brown coat, and a brown fur hat." Brooks was a birdwatcher, he noticed details. He wouldn't be wrong.

"I have to call the general again," she said. "This will mess up your sherry hour."

"Why? Sarah, what's happened? You're white as a sheet."

"Just a minute, Brooks. General Purslane, are those secret service men still with you? Wonderful! Have them come immediately to the Kelling house on Tulip Street and pick up a woman named—what's her first name, Brooks?"

"Virginia."

"Naturally, what else? Virginia Carboy. Tall, thin, long-faced, about forty-five. She's the one who put the negatives in the tea cozy, attached the note, and delivered the bomb. Now, please. She may try to bolt once she realizes she hasn't set this house afire."

Sarah reconfirmed the address, broke the connection, and dialed again. Charles answered, fortunately.

"Charles, this is Sarah. Don't so much as lift an eyebrow, but you and Mariposa make absolutely sure Ms. Carboy doesn't get out of the house. Somebody's on the way to pick her up, she has to be there when they arrive. Knock her out and tie her up if you have to, but do it quietly."

Evidently violence had not been necessary. Watching out the front window while Brooks reset the glass in the door, Sarah had seen the secret service men rush to the house, seen Charles let them in with precisely the right blend of unruffled dignity and patriotic cooperation. She'd seen Ms. Carboy being led from the house in handcuffs and stowed safely away in the unmarked vehicle that had managed during its brief stay to fill the lower half of Tulip Street with a Yuletide medley of honking horns and drivers' curses.

"I can't imagine it was Cousin Mabel's photograph that turned Ms. Carboy into a homicidal maniac," said Sarah. "It must have been Mr. Ronely who broke in and took the blue tea cozy, don't you think? Ms. Carboy wouldn't have had time to commit a robbery, then rush back for an incendiary bomb, even if she'd had one kicking around her bedroom where Mariposa would be apt as not to set it off when she cleaned."

"I quite agree," said Brooks. "They wouldn't have had time to liase, as General Purslane would no doubt describe the action. Anyway, the reason for that elaborate rigmarole with the tea cozy has to have been that they couldn't afford to be seen together.

Otherwise, she could simply have walked up and handed him the negatives."

"So the bomb was a preplanned attempt to kill me," said Sarah. "Because Ronely, or whatever his real name happens to be, got the wrong tea cozy the first time around, I suppose. He may have thought I knew what he was up to and tricked him on purpose. Or else he was simply afraid I'd be able to identify him as the man who mugged me in front of the Ritz. Somehow or other he must have got word to Ms. Carboy that she was to deliver the fire bomb instead of just shooting or stabbing me because they didn't want it known I'd been deliberately murdered. If the arson squad had managed to detect signs of the bomb afterward, I suppose a story would have been gently leaked to the effect that Sarah Kelling Bittersohn was a known terrorist. Ugh!"

"Here," said Brooks, "you'd better have a nip of your own brandy. I don't know but what I might have one myself. What do you say we light the gas log?"

"You do it," Sarah replied. "I lit the last fire, I and the pigeon. It burned to death, poor thing."

"Better the pigeon."

That was a major concession from Brooks, who was normally on the side of his feathered friends. "Sit down and warm yourself, Sarah. I'd better start fixing that broken window."

While Sarah was finishing her brandy and Brooks was puttying the window, Charles snatched a moment from his service in the library to telephone that Ms. Carboy had been only too willing to rat on Mr. Ronely as soon as she realized the jig was up. Even now the secret service men must be closing in on him at a secluded rendezvous where he was trying to peddle Cousin Mabel and the alligator to a clandestine representative of an unfriendly foreign power. And Mrs. Brooks desired to ascertain whether Mr. Brooks would be back in time for dinner.

Brooks said Theonia had better not count on him because he still had Mrs. Sarah's curtain rods to hang. He then went on with his carpentry while Sarah roused herself from the gas log and began wrapping presents including Mother Bittersohn's tea cozy, which she now felt safe enough to take out of the freezer. Not to rock the boat, she used plain white paper and noncontroversial blue ribbon.

Max came home exhausted from tracking down clues and battling the storm, sorely in need of wifely consolation. She got him a drink and settled him down by the fireside with her and Brooks to discuss the case he'd been working on, which was a particularly intriguing one with many ramifications of interest to the analytic mind. Then Max got a telephone call that made him realize he'd inadvertently set up Sarah's uncle, of whom for some reason she was fond, to be the killer's next victim. Thereupon, all three of them charged off into the blizzard to ward off yet another disaster.

By the time they'd rescued the uncle, got the murderer safely jugged, and floundered their way back to Tulip Street, none of the three wanted to do anything except crawl into bed and stay there. Sarah had all but forgotten her own adventure until Max, warming his cold nose against the back of her neck, asked sleepily, "How did the shopping go?"

"All right," she replied. "I bought your mother a tea cozy."

"That's nice," he said, and fell asleep.

After a moment's reflection, Sarah did the same.

PETER LOVESEY

THE HAUNTED CRESCENT

Few mystery writers feel more comfortable and secure in the past than Peter Lovesey. This often charming, always fascinating British author thoroughly enjoys researching and creating the sense of an earlier time . . . not always the same time, for his stories have spanned many decades. Peter lives near Bath and often walks past the Royal Crescent, entertaining himself by imagining things that might have gone on and perhaps might still be going on there.

A ghost was seen last Christmas in a certain house in the Royal Crescent. Believe me, this is true. I speak from personal experience, as a resident of the City of Bath and something of an authority on psychic phenomena. I readily admit that ninety-nine percent of so-called hauntings turn out to have been hallucinations of one sort or another, but this is the exception, a genuine haunted house. Out of consideration for the present owners (who for obvious reasons wish to preserve their privacy), I shall not disclose the exact address, but if you doubt me, read what happened to me on Christmas Eve, 1988.

The couple who own the house had gone to Norfolk for the festive season, leaving on the Friday, December twenty-third. Good planning. The ghost was reputed to walk on Christmas Eve. Knowing of my interest, they had generously placed their house at my disposal. I am an ex-policeman, by the way, and it takes a lot to frighten me.

For those who like a ghost story with all the trimmings—deep snow and howling winds outside—I am sorry. I must disappoint you. Christmas, 1988, was not a white one in Bath. It was unseasonably warm. There wasn't even any fog. All I can offer in the way of atmospheric effects are a full moon that night and an owl that hooted periodically in the trees at the far side of the sloping lawn that fronts the Crescent. It has to be admitted that this was not a spooky-looking barn owl, but a tawny owl, which on this night was making more of a high-pitched "kee-wik" call than a hoot, quite cheery, in fact. Do not despair, however. The things that happened in the house that night more than compensated for the absence of werewolves and banshees outside.

It is vital to the story that you are sufficiently informed about the building in which the events occurred. Whether you realize it or not, you have probably seen the Royal Crescent, if not as a resident, or a tourist, then in one of the numerous films in which it has appeared as a backdrop to the action. It is in a quiet location northwest of the city and comprises thirty houses in a semielliptical terrace completed in 1774 to the specification of John Wood the Younger. It stands comparison with any domestic building in Europe. I defy anyone not to respond to its uncomplicated grandeur, the majestic panorama of 114 Ionic columns topped by a portico and balustrade; and the roadway at the front where Jane Austen and Charles Dickens trod the cobbles. But you want me to come to the ghost.

My first intimation of something unaccountable came at about twenty past eleven that Christmas Eve. I was in the drawing room on the first floor. I had stationed myself there a couple of hours before. The door was ajar and the house was in darkness. No, that isn't quite accurate. I should have said simply that none of the lights were switched on; actually the moonlight gave a certain amount of illumination, silver-blue rectangles projected across the carpet and over the base of the Christmas tree, producing an effect infinitely prettier than fairy lights. The furniture was easily visible, too, armchairs, table, and grand piano. One's eyes adjust.

It didn't strike me as eerie to be alone in that unlit house. Anyone knows that a spirit of the departed is unlikely to manifest itself in electric light.

No house is totally silent, certainly no centrally heated house. The sounds produced by expanding floorboards in so-called haunted houses up and down the land must have fooled ghost-hunters by the hundred. In this case as a precaution against a sudden freeze, the owners had left the system switched on. It was timed to turn off at eleven, so the knocks and creaks I was hearing now ought to have been the last of the night.

As events turned out, it wasn't a sound that alerted me first. It was a sudden draft against my face and a flutter of white across the room. I tensed. The house had gone silent. I crossed the room to investigate.

The disturbance had been caused by a Christmas card falling off the mantelpiece into the grate. Nothing more alarming than that. Cards are always falling down. That's why some people prefer to suspend them on strings. I stooped, picked up the card, and replaced it, smiling at my overactive imagination.

Yet I had definitely noticed a draft. The house was supposed to be free of drafts. All the doors and windows were closed and meticulously sealed against the elements. Strange. I listened, holding my breath. The drawing room where I was standing was well placed for picking up any unexplained sound in the house. It was at the center of the building. Below me were the ground floor and the cellar, above me the second floor and the attic.

Hearing nothing, I decided to venture out to the landing and listen there. I was mystified, yet unwilling at this stage to countenance a supernatural explanation. I was inclined to wonder whether the cut-off of the central heating had resulted in some trick of convection that gave the impression or the reality of a disturbance in the air. The falling card was not significant in itself. The draft required an explanation. My state of mind, you see, was calm and analytical.

Ten or fifteen seconds passed. I leaned over the banisters and looked down the stairwell to make sure that the front door was firmly shut, and so it proved to be. Then I heard a rustle from the room where I had been. I knew what it was—the card falling into the grate again—for another distinct movement of air had stirred the curtain on the landing window, causing a shift in the moonlight across the stairs. I was in no doubt anymore that this was worth investigating. My only uncertainty was whether to start with the floors above me, or below.

I chose the latter, reasoning that if, as I suspected, someone had opened a window, it was likely to be at the ground or basement levels. My assumption was wrong. I shall not draw out the suspense. I merely wish to record that I checked the cellar, kitchen, scullery, dining room, and study and found every window and external door secure and bolted from inside. No one could have entered after me.

So I began to work my way upstairs again, methodically visiting each room. And on the staircase to the second floor, I heard a sigh.

Occasionally in Victorian novels a character would "heave" a sigh. Somehow the phrase had always irritated me. In real life I never heard a sigh so weighty that it seemed to involve muscular effort—until this moment. This was a sound hauled up from the depths of somebody's inner being, or so I deduced. Whether it really originated with somebody or some *thing* was open to speculation.

The sound had definitely come from above me. Unable by now to suppress my excitement, I moved up to the second-floor landing, where I found three doors, all closed. I moved from one to the other, opening them rapidly and glancing briefly inside. Two bedrooms and a bathroom. I hesitated. A bathroom. Had the "sigh," I wondered, been caused by some aberration of the plumbing? Air locks are endemic in the complicated systems installed in these old Georgian buildings. The houses were not built with valves and cisterns. The efficiency of the pipework depended on the variable skill of generations of plumbers.

The sound must have been caused by trapped air.

Rationality reasserted itself. I would finish my inspection and prove to my total satisfaction that what I had heard was neither human nor spectral in origin. I closed the bathroom door behind me and crossed the landing to the last flight of stairs, more narrow than those I had used so far. In times past they had been the means of access to the servants' quarters in the attic. I glanced up at the white-painted door at the head of these stairs and observed that it was slightly ajar.

My foot was on the first stair and my hand on the rail when I stiffened. That door moved.

It was being drawn inward. The movement was slow and deliberate. As the gap increased, a faint glow of moonlight was cast from the interior onto the paneling to my right. I stared up and watched the figure of a woman appear in the doorway.

She was in a white gown or robe that reached to her feet. Her hair hung loose to the level of her chest—fine, gently shifting hair so pale in color that it appeared to merge with the dress. Her skin, too, appeared bloodless. The eyes were flint black, however. They widened as they took me in. Her right hand crept to her throat and I heard her give a gasp.

The sensations I experienced in that moment of confrontation are difficult to convey. I was convinced that nothing of flesh and blood had entered that house in the hours I had been there. All the entrances were bolted—I had checked. I could not account for the phenomenon, or whatever it was, that had manifested itself, yet I refused to be convinced. I was unwilling to accept what my eyes were seeing and my rational faculties could not explain. She could not be a ghost.

I said, "Who are you?"

The figure swayed back as if startled. For a moment I thought she was going to close the attic door, but she remained staring at me, her hand still pressed to her throat. It was the face and form of a young woman, not more than twenty.

I asked, "Can you speak?"

She appeared to nod.

I said, "What are you doing here?"

She caught her breath. In a strange, half-whispered utterance she said, as if echoing my words, "Who are you?"

I took a step upward toward her. It evidently frightened her, for she backed away and became almost invisible in the shadowy interior of the attic room. I tried to dredge up some reassuring words. "It's all right. Believe me, it's all right."

Then I twitched in surprise. Downstairs, the doorbell chimed. After eleven on Christmas Eve!

I said, "What on earth . . . ?"

The woman in white whimpered something I couldn't hear.

I tried to make light of it. "Santa, I expect."

She didn't react.

The bell rang a second time.

"He ought to be using the chimney," I said. I had already decided to ignore the visitor, whoever it was. One unexpected caller was all I could cope with.

The young woman spoke up, and the words sprang clearly from her. "For God's sake, send him away!"

"You know who it is?"

"Please! I beg you."

"If you know who it is," I said reasonably, "wouldn't you like to answer it?"

"I can't."

The chimes rang out again.

I said, "Is it someone you know?"

"Please. Tell him to go away. If you answer the door he'll go away."

I was letting myself be persuaded. I needed her cooperation. I wanted to know about her. "All right," I relented. "But will you be here when I come back?"

"I won't leave."

Instinctively I trusted her. I turned and descended the two flights of stairs to the hall. The bell rang again. Even though the house was in darkness, the caller had no intention of giving up.

I drew back the bolts, opened the front door a fraction, and looked out. A man was on the doorstep, leaning on the iron railing. A young man in a leather jacket glittering with studs and chains. His head was shaven. He, at any rate, looked like flesh and blood. He said, "What kept you?"

I said, "What do you want?"

He glared. "For crying out loud—who the hell are you?" His eyes slid sideways, checking the number on the wall.

I said with frigid courtesy, "I think you must have made a mistake."

"No," he said. "This is the house all right. What's your game, mate? What are you doing here with the lights off?"

I told him that I was an observer of psychic phenomena.

"Come again?"

"Ghosts," I said. "This house has the reputation of being haunted. The owners have kindly allowed me to keep watch tonight."

"Oh, yes?" he said with heavy skepticism. "Spooks, is it? I'll have a gander at them meself." With that, he gave the door a shove. There was no security chain and I was unable to resist the pressure. He stepped across the threshold. "Ghost-buster, are you, mate? You wouldn't, by any chance, be lifting the family silver at the same time? Anyone else in here?"

I said, "I take exception to that. You've no right to force your way in here."

"No more right than you," he said, stepping past me. "Were you upstairs when I rang?"

I said, "I'm going to call the police."

He flapped his hand dismissively. "Be my guest. I'm going upstairs, right?"

Sheer panic inspired me to say, "If you do, you'll be on film."

"What?"

"The cameras are ready to roll," I lied. "The place is riddled with mikes and tripwires."

He said, "I don't believe you," but the tone of his voice said the opposite.

"This ghost is supposed to walk on Christmas Eve," I told him. "I want to capture it on film." I gave a special resonance to the word "capture."

He said, "You're round the twist." And with as much dignity as he could muster he sidled back toward the door, which still stood open. Apparently he was leaving. "You ought to be locked up. You're a nutcase."

As he stepped out of the door I said, "Shall I tell the owners you called? What name shall I give?"

He swore and turned away. I closed the door and slid the bolts back into place. I was shaking. It had been an ugly, potentially dangerous incident. I'm not so capable of tackling an intruder as I once was and I was thankful that my powers of invention had served me so well.

I started up the stairs again and as I reached the top of the first flight, the young woman in white was waiting for me. She must have come down two floors to overhear what was being said. This area of the house was better illuminated than the attic stairs, so I got a better look at her. She appeared less ethereal now. Her dress was silk or satin, I observed. It was an evening gown. Her makeup was as pale as a mime artist's, except for the black liner around her eyes.

She said, "How can I thank you enough?"

I answered flatly, "What I want from you, young lady, is an explanation."

She crossed her arms, rubbing at her sleeves. "I feel shivery here. Do you mind if we go in there?"

As we moved into the drawing room I noticed that she made no attempt to switch on the light. She pointed to some cigarettes on the table. "Do you mind?"

I found some matches by the fireplace and gave her a light. "Who was that at the door?"

She inhaled hard. "Some guy I met at a party. I was supposed to be with someone else, but we got separated. You know how it is. Next thing I knew, this bloke in the leather jacket was chatting me up. He was all right at first. I didn't know he was going to come on so strong. I mean I didn't encourage him. I was trying to cool it. He offered me these tablets, but I refused. He said they would make me relax. By then I was really scared. I moved off fast. The stupid thing was that I moved upstairs. There were plenty of people about, and it seemed the easiest way to go. The bloke followed. He kept on following. I went right to the top of the house and shut myself in a room. I pushed a cupboard against the door. He was beating his fist on the door, saying what he was going to do to me. I was scared out of my skull. All I could think of doing was get through the window, so I did. I climbed out and found myself up there behind the little stone wall."

"Of this building? The balustrade at the top?"

"Didn't I make that clear? The party was in a house a couple of doors away from you. I ran along this narrow passageway between the roof and the wall, trying all the windows. The one upstairs was the first one I could shift."

"The attic window. Now I understand." The sudden draft was explained, and the gasp as she had caught her breath after the effort.

She said, "I'm really grateful."

"Grateful?"

"Grateful to you for getting rid of him."

I said, "It would be sensible now to call a taxi. Where do you live?"

"Not far. I can walk."

"It wouldn't be advisable, would it, after what happened? He's persistent. He may be waiting."

"I didn't think." She stubbed the cigarette into an ashtray. After a moment's reflection she said, "All right. Where's the phone?"

There was one in the study. While she was occupied, I gave some thought to what she had said. I didn't believe a word of it, but I had something vastly more important on my mind.

She came back into the room. "Ten minutes, they reckon. Was it true what you said downstairs, about this house being haunted?"

"Mm?" I was still preoccupied.

"The spook. All that stuff about hidden cameras. Did you mean it?"

"There aren't any cameras. I'm useless with machinery of any sort. I reckoned he'd think twice about coming in if he knew he was going to be on film. It was just a bluff."

"And the bit about the ghost?"

"That was true."

"Would you mind telling me about it?"

"Aren't you afraid of the supernatural?"

"It's scary, yes. Not so scary as what happened already. I want to know the story. Christmas Eve is a great night for a ghost story."

I said, "It's more than just a story."

"Please."

"On one condition. Before you get into that taxi, you tell me the truth about yourself—why you really came into this house tonight."

She hesitated.

I said, "It needn't go any further."

"All right. Tell me about the ghost." She reached for another cigarette and perched on the arm of a chair.

I crossed to the window and looked away over the lawn toward the trees silhouetted against the city lights. "It can be traced back, as all ghost stories can, to a story of death and an unquiet spirit. About a hundred and fifty years ago this house was owned by an army officer, a retired colonel by the name of Davenport. He had a daughter called Rosamund, and it was believed in the city that he doted on her. She was dressed fashionably and given a good education, which in those days was beyond the expectation of most young women. Rosamund was a lively, intelligent, and attractive girl. Her hair when she wore it long was very like yours, fine and extremely fair. Not surprisingly, she had admirers. The one she favored most was a young man from Bristol, Luke Robertson, who at that time was an architect. In the conventions of the time they formed an attachment which amounted to little more than a few chaperoned meetings, some letters, poems, and so on. They were lovers in a very old-fashioned sense that you may find difficult to credit. In physical terms it amounted to no more than a few stolen kisses, if that. Somewhere in this house there is supposed to be carved into woodwork the letters *L* and *R* linked. I can't show you. I haven't found it."

Outside, a taxi trundled over the cobbles. I watched it draw up at a house some doors down. Two couples came out of the building, laughing, and climbed into the cab. It was obvious that they were leaving a party. The heavy beat of music carried up to me.

I said, "I wonder if it's turned midnight. It might be Christmas Day already."

She said, "Please go on with the story."

"Colonel Davenport—the father of this girl—was a lonely man. His wife had died some years before. Lately he had become friendly with a neighbor, another resident of the Crescent, a widow approaching fifty years of age by the name of Mrs. Crandley, who lived in one of the houses at the far end of the building. She was a musician, a pianist, and she gave lessons. One of her pupils was Rosamund. So far as one can tell, Mrs. Crandley was a good teacher and the girl a promising pupil. Do you play?"

"What?"

I turned to face her. "I said, do you play the piano?"

"Oh. Just a bit," said the girl.

"You didn't tell me your name."

"I'd rather not, if you don't mind. What happened between the colonel and Mrs. Crandley?"

"Their friendship blossomed. He wanted her to marry him. Mrs. Crandley was not unwilling. In fact, she agreed, subject to one condition. She had a son of twenty-seven called Justinian."

"What was that?"

"Justinian. There was a vogue for calling your children after emperors. This Justinian was a dull fellow without much to recommend him. He was lazy and overweight. He rarely ventured out of the house. Mrs. Crandley despaired of him."

"She wanted him off her hands?"

"That is what it amounted to. She wanted him married and she saw the perfect partner for him in Rosamund. Surely such a charming, talented girl would bring out some positive qualities in her lumpish son. Mrs. Crandley applied herself diligently to the plan, insisting that Justinian answered the doorbell each time Rosamund came for her music lesson. Then he would be told to sit in the room and listen to her playing. Everything Mrs. Crandley could do to promote the match was done. For his part, Justinian was content to go along with the plan. He was promised that if he married the girl he would be given his mother's house, so the pattern of his life would alter little, except that a pretty wife would keep him company rather than a discontented, nagging mother. He began to eye Rosamund with increasing favor. So when the colonel proposed marriage to Mrs. Crandley, she assented on the understanding that Justinian would be married to Rosamund at the same time."

"How about Rosamund? Was she given any choice?"

"You have to be aware that marriages were commonly arranged by the parents in those days."

"But you said she already had a lover. He was perfectly respectable, wasn't he?"

I nodded. "Absolutely. But Luke Robertson didn't feature in Mrs. Crandley's plan. He was ignored. Rosamund bowed under the pressure and became engaged to Justinian in the autumn of 1838. The double marriage was to take place in the Abbey on Christmas Eve."

"Oh, dear—I think I can guess the rest of the story."

"It may not be quite as you expect. As the day of the wedding approached, Rosamund began to dread the prospect. She pleaded with her father to allow her to break off the engagement. He wouldn't hear of it. He loved Mrs. Crandley and his thoughts were all of her. In despair, Rosamund sent the maidservant with a message to Luke, asking him to meet her secretly on the basement steps. She had a romantic notion that Luke would elope with her."

My listener was enthralled. "And did he come?"

"He came. Rosamund poured out her story. Luke listened with sympathy, but he was cautious. He didn't see elopement as the solution. Rather bravely, he volunteered to speak to the colonel and appeal to him to allow Rosamund to marry the man of her choice. If that failed, he would remind the colonel that Rosamund could not be forced to take the sacred vows. Her consent had to be freely given in church, and she was entitled to withhold it. So this uncomfortable interview took place a day or two later. The colonel, naturally, was outraged. Luke was banished from the house and forbidden to speak to Rosamund again. The unfortunate girl was summoned by her father and accused of wickedly consorting with her former lover when she was promised to another. The story of the secret note and the meeting on the stairs was dragged from her. She was told that she wished to destroy her father's marriage. She was said to be selfish and disloyal. Worse, she might be taken to court by Justinian for breach of promise."

"Poor little soul! Did it break her?"

"No. Amazingly, she stood her ground. Luke's support had given her courage. She would not marry Justinian. It was the colonel who backed down. He went to see Mrs. Crandley. When he returned, it was to tell Rosamund that his marriage would not, after all, take place. Mrs. Crandley had insisted on a double wedding, or nothing."

"I wouldn't have been in Rosamund's shoes for a million pounds."

"She was told by her father that she had behaved no better than a servant, secretly meeting her lover on the basement steps and trifling with another man's affections, so in future he would treat her as a servant. And he did. He dismissed the housemaid. He ordered Rosamund to move her things to the maid's room in the attic, and he gave her a list of duties that kept her busy from five-thirty each morning until late at night."

"Cruel."

"All his bitterness was heaped on her."

"Did she kill herself?"

"No," I said with only the slightest pause. "She was murdered."

"*Murdered?*"

"On Christmas Eve, the day that the weddings would have taken place, she was suffocated in her bed."

"Horrible!"

"A pillow was held against her face until she ceased to breathe. She was found dead in bed by the cook on Christmas morning after she failed to report for duty. The colonel was informed and the police were sent for."

"Who killed her?"

"The inspector on the case, a local man without much experience of violent crimes, was in no doubt that Colonel Davenport was the murderer. He had a powerful motive. The animus he felt toward his daughter had been demonstrated by the way he treated her. It seemed that his anger had only increased as the days passed. On the date he was due to have married, it became insupportable."

"Was it true? Did he confess to killing her?"

"He refused to make any statement. But the evidence against him was overwhelming. Three inches of snow fell on Christmas Eve. It stopped about eight-thirty that evening. The time of death was estimated at about eleven P.M.. When the inspector and his men arrived next morning no footsteps were visible on the path leading to the front door except those of the cook, who had gone for the police. The only other person in the house was Colonel Davenport. So he was charged with murdering his own daughter. The trial was short, for he refused to plead. He remained silent to the end. He was found guilty and hanged at Bristol in February, 1839."

She put out the cigarette. "Grim."

"Yes."

"There's more to the story, isn't there? The ghost. You said something about an unquiet spirit."

I said, "There was a feeling of unease about the fact that the colonel wouldn't admit to the crime. After he was convicted and condemned, they tried to persuade him to confess, to lay his sins before his Maker. A murderer often would confess in the last days remaining to him, even after protesting innocence all through the trial. They all did their utmost to persuade him—the prison governor, the warders, the priest, and the hangman himself. Those people had harrowing duties to perform. It would have helped them to know that the man going to the gallows was truly guilty of the crime. Not one word would that proud old man speak."

"You sound almost sorry for him. There wasn't really any doubt, was there?"

I said, "There's a continuous history of supernatural happenings in this house for a century and a half. Think about it. Suppose, for example, someone else committed the murder."

"But who else could have?"

"Justinian Crandley."

"That's impossible. He didn't live here. His footprints would have shown up in the snow."

"Not if he entered the house as you did tonight—along the roof and through the attic window. He could have murdered Rosamund and returned to his own house by the same route."

"It's possible, I suppose, but why—what was his motive?"

"Revenge. He would have been master in his own house if the marriage had not been called off. Instead, he faced an indefinite future with his domineering and now embittered mother. He blamed Rosamund. He decided that if he was not to have her as his wife, no one else should."

"Is that what you believe?"

"It is now," said I.

"Why didn't the colonel tell them he was innocent?"

"He blamed himself. He felt a deep sense of guilt for the way he had treated his own daughter. But for his selfishness the murder would never have taken place."

"Do you think he knew the truth?"

"He must have worked it out. He loved Mrs. Crandley too much to cause her further unhappiness."

There was an interval of silence, broken finally by the sound of car tires on the cobbles below.

She stood up. "Tonight when you saw me at the attic door you thought I was Rosamund's ghost."

I said, "No. Rosamund doesn't haunt this place. Her spirit is at rest. I didn't take you for a real ghost any more than I believed your story of escaping from the fellow in the leather jacket."

She walked to the window. "It is my taxi."

I wasn't going to let her leave without admitting the truth. "You went to the party two doors along with the idea of breaking into this house. You climbed out onto the roof and forced your way in upstairs, meaning to let your friend in by the front door. You were going to burgle the place."

She gasped and swung around. "How did you know that?"

"When I opened the door he was expecting you. He said 'What kept you?' He knew which house to call at, so it must have been planned. If your story had been true, he wouldn't have known where to come."

She stared down at the waiting cab.

I said, "Until I suggested the taxi, you were quite prepared to go out into the street where this man who had allegedly threatened you was waiting."

"I'm leaving."

"And I noticed that you didn't want the lights turned on."

Her tone altered. "You're not one of the fuzz, are you? You wouldn't turn me in? Give me a break, will you? It's the first time. I'll never try it again."

"How can I know that?"

"I'll give you my name and address, if you want. Then you can check."

It is sufficient to state here that she supplied the information. I shall keep it to myself. I'm no longer in the business of exposing petty criminals. I saw her to her taxi. She promised to stop seeing her boyfriend. Perhaps you think I let her off too lightly. Her misdemeanor was minor compared with the discovery I had made—and I owed that discovery to her.

It released me from my obligation, you see. I told you I was once a policeman. An inspector, actually. I made a fatal mistake. I have had a hundred and fifty years to search for the truth and now that I found it I can rest. The haunting of the Royal Crescent is at an end.

DOROTHY SALISBURY DAVIS

CHRISTOPHER AND MAGGIE

How did Grand Master Dorothy Salisbury Davis happen to write this particular story? She lived it. Part of it, anyway.

When she got out of college, she became a traveling magician's assistant simply because that was the only job she could find.

Come Christmas, Dorothy put her aged car up for sale to finance a trip home for the holidays. The man who'd been going to pay her thirty dollars for it got drunk on the money instead, so she and a friend decided to drive the whole way. It was a long trip and a tough one. They had three flats and a gummed-up motor, spent part of a night in a railroad roundhouse that was cold as banished hope, finally got to the friend's house after thirty-six hours with no sleep, parked on the street, and went to bed. When Dorothy woke, her car had been towed away for violating the overnight parking rules. When she went to the police station to get it back, she found a man wanting to buy the car. He paid her a hundred dollars in cash. Dorothy bought the new coat she so badly needed, spent the rest on Christmas presents, and decided the traveling life was not for her. So she became a mystery writer instead and here's her memory-laden Christmas present to you.

"**A**nd now, my grown-up friends and all my little pals, our revels are almost over, as Shakespeare said." The magician turned to his assistant who wasn't much help at magic, an encumbrance really, but he liked to have her on stage. She added class. "Isn't that what Shakespeare said, Miranda?"

Miranda, whose real name was Maggie, drew herself up to her full five feet one and a half inches. She was a pretty girl with shining brown eyes and a quick smile. She looked wholesome where Christopher would have preferred a sly, seductive woman. Miranda was about as mysterious as a duck. But since she was personable and the partner at hand, Christopher the Great used her to the limits of his imagination. Miranda intoned:

> *"Our revels now are ended. These our actors,*
> *As I foretold you, were all spirits, and*
> *Are melted into air . . . "*

Christopher, one hand under his chin in the manner of a popular vaudeville comedian, mugged amazement as Miranda roundly mouthed the words. A few lines more and he interrupted her and asked the audience, "Ain't a college education wonderful?"

The audience of eighteen men and seven women sat with the same mute patience they accorded a dull sermon on Sunday morning. The twenty children were restless. The drafts kept gusting through the hall. The flag quivered in its stancheon. The lights flickered on the Christmas tree. The steam pipes hissed and rattled. At a signal from Christopher, Miranda gave a great whang to a Chinese gong. The audience jumped. They were alive.

Christopher announced as the finale the most dangerous feat in his repertoire. The act, he said, had made him famous the world over. He was a dapper man, slight, with hollow cheeks, a sharp nose, pale blue eyes, a thin mustache, and an unmistakable midwestern accent although he claimed to have grown up in Budapest, Hungary. His hands were graceful and quick and his whole body had a squirrellike agility. For this trick, however, he stood severely straight and still. He seemed to feed himself, one by one, an entire packet of needles. He grimaced in pain at every swallow. The folding chairs squeaked as his audience sat forward, finally alert. The children's eyes were popping.

"Hush," Miranda said to a house already hushed.

Christopher balled a length of thread and stuffed it into his mouth. In his display of agony, he resembled a Christian martyr often featured on funeral cards. His audience belonged to him. The hundred or so empty chairs no longer mattered. Then, with a silent prayer, he extracted an end of thread from between his tongue and his teeth and carefully drew out a chain of neatly threaded needles. He skipped down the steps and invited a youngster in the front row to look into the cavern of his mouth.

Maggie didn't know how he did it. Nor did she care. It seemed mighty unhygienic. In fact, she hated magic, but she had the only job she could get. The country was in a depression—dust bowls and soup kitchens, Father Coughlin and John L. Lewis, the latter revered in Bluefield, West Virginia, the coal and rail town they were about to pull out of, to head home for Christmas. Home for Maggie was a small town in Michigan, for Christopher it was Fort Wayne, Indiana. Christmas was two days away.

It was ten past twelve when they hit the highway in Christopher's sedan. It was custom-packed, floorboards to roof, the back seat removed to accommodate his magic, livestock, and luggage. Maggie's luggage consisted of an imitation leather suitcase and a canvas bag of books for which the only room was at her feet. Two spare tires were strapped to the running boards. Those on the car were as bald as the liners inside them. The car gave a thud at every tar-filled crack in the pavement. There was a strong odor of bird dung in the car—Maggie didn't think rabbit droppings smelled—but stronger was the smell of the half onion Christopher had at the ready in case the windshield frosted. It was a cold night and grew colder the higher they went into the mountains. An oval moon rode high. It silvered the hills, etched telegraph poles, slag heaps, and occasional cottages in which the lights were long out. Far down in the valley the railroad tracks shone in the moonlight.

Their red, green, and yellow signals were cheery. "Isn't it beautiful?" Maggie observed.

"What I wish—I wish there was more traffic," Christopher said. "If we were to break down . . . "

Maggie cut him off. "We won't."

"That's the difference between you and me," Christopher said. "I look for the worst to happen, you the best."

"Might as well," she said.

Christopher sniffed. "Do you smell alcohol?"

"I smell onion," Maggie said.

"If she boils dry we're in trouble. She was already overloaded without those books of yours. What do you need with all those books? Why didn't you sell *them*?"

"You know why," Maggie said. What she had sold was her car—for thirty dollars on the spot when Christopher arrived in town and offered her a ride almost all the way home. The booking of Christopher the Great out of Fort Wayne called for a minimum of five performances a week; they were promoted, in the name of the sponsoring local charity, by five women, each working a town a week in advance of Christopher, and moving on the day after the performance. There were towns like Glens Falls, N.Y.; Oil Town, Pa.; Pittsfield, Mass.; and Bluefield that Maggie wasn't ever going to forget.

Christopher took off his mitten and groped for her hand where it was snuggled in her pocket. "I love you, Maggie, books and all. I love you the best of all my girls."

"I love you, too," she lied—or half lied—and gave him her hand to keep him from groping any farther.

The road soon demanded both his hands on the steering wheel. He started to sing, "You tell me your dreams, I'll tell you mine . . . "

Maggie sang harmony, a strong alto to his quavering tenor.

They were almost an hour into their journey when a thump, thump, thump signaled a flat tire. Christopher cursed philosophically and pulled to the side of the road. It took all his wirey strength to jack up the overloaded Chevy, a rock wedged under the other rear wheel. While he removed the loosened bolts by moonlight, Maggie went behind a billboard to pee. The billboard featured Santa Claus, a Coca-Cola in his hand: "The pause that keeps you going." Christopher was blowing on his hands. A vast silence surrounded them. Then from inside the car came the cooing of his doves. Maggie laughed.

"It ain't funny, Maggie," the magician said. "They never coo at night."

Then came another sound in the far distance, the fluted whistle of a train. Maggie wished she were on the train, but didn't say so. She needed all her money to buy a few family Christmas presents and a warmer coat. If she had told her dream it was that she could get a job teaching history. She adored history. She was carrying twelve volumes of English history that had belonged to her grandfather, along with several volumes of poetry. An English major, a minor in history, she was overeducated for the jobs available.

A car went by so fast it almost sucked her with it. Christopher shouted curses after it. An echo made them resound. "Hel-loooooo," Maggie called and her voice bounced around the hills. "Go to hell!" Christopher shouted. Hell, hell, hell, hell . . . A few minutes later he eased the car down, strapped the flat tire into place, and put his tools in the trunk. He went behind the billboard. Maggie warmed her hands on the radiator.

"I should've saved it," he said, returning. "Did I ever tell you about the time in Iron Mountain when the radiator went dry?"

"You did, you did!" One night every week after the show they would find a friendly tavern, drink beer and eat fried fish, French fries, and cole slaw. They'd play the jukebox and dance until the place closed up. Christopher had told her several versions of his life story. She still didn't know his last name unless it was Christopher. In which case she didn't know his first name. One of his stories made her cry the first time she heard it—how he had wanted to be a pianist when he was a kid. His mother stole from the family food allowance to get him lessons and then somehow managed to buy a piano. His father made him play for him one day while he sat beside him on the piano bench. All of a sudden, without any warning, he slammed the lid down on the boy's fingers. Three of them were broken. It was the doctor who got him doing magic tricks to make the fingers nimble again.

Maggie climbed back into the front seat, kicked her heels against her books, and tried to rub warmth into her arms. There was a heater but it leaked engine fumes and Christopher was afraid they might kill his doves or the rabbit.

According to a road sign they were forty miles out of Bluefield. Maggie said she was getting hungry. Christopher offered her a Milky Way. She had given up mushy chocolate in high school.

"How about half an onion?"

"No thank you," Maggie said and started to sing "Stormy Weather," her all-time favorite song.

They had almost made it to the top of a long climb when the car began to chug. The smell of alcohol grew stronger and stronger. Steam was escaping from the radiator. Christopher kept coaxing the hiccoughing car, "Come on, gal, I'm your pal . . . " He managed to pull off the road before the engine gave out. The "sealer" hadn't worked, he said and cursed the garage man who had sold it to him with a money back guarantee—in Bluefield.

They searched the roadside, Maggie on one side, Christopher on the other, for a promising-looking house, then for just any house. There didn't seem to be one. Christopher worried about his props, his twenty thousand dollars' worth of equipment, more or less, a priceless white rabbit, and a pair of turtle doves.

Below them and running roughly parallel to the road was the railway track, even more sparsely traveled than the highway. Christopher was carrying a two-gallon milk can he hoped to fill with water. He waved it overhead and shouted as a pickup truck went by. It didn't stop.

A metallic glow appeared ahead, illusive at first as a will-o'-the-wisp. It turned out to be a mailbox. They followed the rutted road that wended downhill from it. The road soon divided and still they could see no buildings. But from where they then stood they saw a railroad crossing and the crossing guard's house. The light in it was like a beacon of civilization. Christopher figured that it had to be where the highway they were on crossed the tracks. If they could get the Chevy to the top of the hill they could coast all the way down. A raucous shriek shattered the stillness. It hit Maggie like a bolt of pain.

"It's a goddamn jackass," Christopher said. And to prove itself the animal gave several long hee-haws. That started a dog barking nearby. "Let's get the hell back to the car," Christopher said.

He talked to the car and patted the radiator before getting in.

"I'm praying," Maggie said when he put his foot on the starter. "Can't hurt."

The motor turned over, sputtered between life and death, took more gas, and when Christopher shot the car into gear it leaped ahead. Alongside the mailbox it began to chug again. "You can make it, baby. I know you can." When it was on the verge of conking out, he threw it out of gear, revved the motor, and thrust it into gear again. It leaped a few yards more. They made it, cheering, to the top and began the long, winding descent. "Now you better pray we can stop," he said.

The first thing Christopher noticed when they pulled off the road a few feet their side of the tracks was a well pump, a cup hanging on a chain alongside. The light in the crossing guard's house seemed dimmer close up than it had at a distance. In fact, there was no window this side, what they were seeing was reflected light. "You go in and ask him if we can get warm and have some water," the magician ordered. "But just in case he's ornery, I'm going to fill her up right now." He left the engine running and took off his scarf to muzzle the steam when he removed the radiator cap.

Maggie approached the little house through the stubble of a railside garden. The guard's STOP sign hung beside the door. She wondered why women couldn't be railway guards: all that time to read and a cozy rabbit hutch of a house. She rapped on the door and observed in the reflected light trackside that there was also a coal bin there. No one answered her knock. Sleep, she decided, must be a terrible temptation. Christopher was pumping. No water yet. The pump sounded a little like the donkey. She knocked again and thought of the poem, "The Listeners."

"Eureka!" Christopher cried and she heard the splash of water.

She did not like to try the door. The guard might be doing God knew what. She went around to the window. It was bleary with dust. A halo surrounded a naked light bulb hanging from the ceiling. She rapped on the glass and cleared a place to look in. A gray-haired man was slumped in a rocker, his legs sprawled toward the stove, his back to the door. His chin was on his breast and a newspaper lay on the floor at the side of his chair. A fire glowed in the potbellied stove. She rapped again on the window, this time with her class ring. He made no move. She ran back to where Christopher was lugging the can of water.

"There's something wrong with the old man in there. I think maybe he's dead."

"Dead asleep," he said. "Get in the car."

"We can't just drive off and leave him."

"Why not? That's what people have been doing to us all night," Christopher shouted, pulling back from a burst of steam. "I'm going to get another can of water and move on."

"Chris, I'm going back and see what's wrong with him."

"What do you think you are, a doctor? And don't call me Chris."

Maggie ran back to the house. This time she opened the door. The big railway clock over the desk said 3:10. Every tick sounded as though it was going to be the last. The old man was in the same position as he was when she'd seen him from the window. "Mister . . . " She approached him tentatively and touched his hand. It was terribly cold although the room was warm.

Christopher came in muttering about putting a beggar on horseback. "Holy Christ," he then said reverently. He walked slowly around the chair, stepping carefully over the old man's feet. He stopped and pointed a trembling finger to where a thin trickle of blood dribbled from the man's ear onto his shoulder. "That means he was hit in the back of the head. Have you got a mirror?"

"In the car," she said. "Should I go get it?"

"Never mind." Christopher went to the desk and picked up the phone. It was dead. He hung up and tried it again. Quite dead. A telegraph signal began to rap out of the apparatus on the desk. They just looked at one another. Neither of them understood Morse code, but the staccato transmission made the message sound urgent.

"If there's a train coming through we can flag it down," Maggie said.

"Like we did the cars," Christopher said.

"Look, this can't have happened long ago. If we saw the light from way up there it had to be through the open door, right?" She hurried outdoors in time to see a change in the colored signals alongside the northbound track, green off, yellow on. The train gave a long series of whistles and the automatic warning lights began to blink at the roadway crossing, the bell to ring furiously although there was not a car in sight. Maggie caught up the guard's sign from alongside the door. The great white eye appeared from the south; clouds of steam billowed up and fell back over the engine to shroud the cars behind. The track signal switched from yellow back to green. For just an instant Maggie caught sight of an automobile parked on the other side of the northbound track. The oncoming engine blocked it out. Then, a man jumped out of the darkness nearly opposite to where she had seen the car. He stood on the southbound track and waved at the oncoming train. Someone in the cab threw a sack down to him. Maggie lost sight of him in a billow of smoke.

"Christopher?" She called out as though he might do something.

He was right behind her. "No!"

The engine came abreast of them. Maggie waved the sign and shouted, "Man dead, man dead!" and pointed at the house.

The trainman waved at her, but heard nothing, she was sure, what with the grind of the wheels, the warning whistle, and the accelerating *chu-chu-chu-chu—chu-chu-chu-chu* . . . The train plowed on leaving them, too, in a spray of smoke.

She turned her back to the smoke and saw the man again, running toward the rear of the train; he had to get around it to get to the car. She started after him. Christopher brought her down with a flying tackle. Struggling to get up she saw the lights go on in the car on the other side of the train. "They'll get away," she shouted.

"You're damn right they will!" Christopher headed for the Chevy.

Maggie took a last look down the tracks. Now the man was running toward her alongside the train. A few yards before he reached her he jumped for the ladder on the side of a boxcar, caught it, and swung himself onto the steps. For just an instant she thought of trying to grab hold of him but he was too soon past. The train picked up speed. Between the passing boxcars she saw the other automobile drive along the tracks as far as the road and then turn north. She caught sight of the man with the packet in the light of the crossing. He was clinging like a barnacle to the side of the boxcar.

Maggie looked into the flagman's house from the door. He seemed more dead, as if that were possible, and she didn't even know the telegraph code for S.O.S. She galloped back to Christopher's car and clambered in. The caboose was rolling by.

"You kicked me in the teeth," Christopher said. "I think you've ruined my needle act."

"Sorry," she said, although she wasn't. The needle act was disgusting. "Christopher, could we try and catch up with that other car and see where it goes?"

"What about getting help for that poor old man back there?" Pure sarcasm.

"We can send it. And if he's dead, he's dead, isn't he?"

A snowball had a better chance in hell than they had of catching the other car, so Christopher said he'd try.

Maggie studied the road map under the flashlight. "You know what? We'll be coming into Williamson soon. I'll bet the train stops there and that's where they'll meet up. I'll bet I'm right."

"And what if you are? What do we do then?"

"I wish we had a gun," she said.

"What?"

"I told you once, my father's a deputy sheriff. He's a farmer, but he's also a deputy sheriff."

"I don't like guns and I don't like deputy sheriffs," Christopher said. "Process servers, that's all they are."

"All the same," Maggie said. Then: "I'll bet that was a mailbag they snatched. The way he waved his arms—that could be how the old man did it every night."

"Okay, tell me something if you're so smart," the magician said. "Why bump the old guy off first? Why not grab the mailbag from him after the train's gone through and nobody's around? If it was a mailbag."

"Because . . . " Maggie said slowly, "they didn't mean to kill him. He was asleep and they just wanted to make sure he stayed that way and didn't see who they were. I'll bet they live around here. It's Christmas and they're broke. There was bound to be money in the mail. Christopher, can't we go any faster?"

"You make me nervous every time you say Christopher. We got about five miles left before she boils dry again."

"There could be a reward, you know, and we'd split it," Maggie said. "Hey! Where's your stage gun, the one you shoot the rabbit with?" It was another of his tricks that Maggie didn't like. She was pretty sure he had a deaf rabbit because of it.

"It's in the green metal box with the silks," he said. "Just don't upset the goddamn livestock."

Maggie, her knees on the seat, flashlight in hand, began the search for the green box. A car passed, going the opposite direction.

"That's your guy going back to pick up his buddy on the tracks."

"No," Maggie said. Through a small space between boxes she saw the train running parallel to them, sometimes quite close. She prayed they wouldn't have to cross the tracks again before Williamson. They'd never make it to the crossing first. She also prayed she could find the green box. She shone the flashlight into the sad, pink eyes of the rabbit where he stared out the window of his case.

"Williamson's a ghost town since the Depression," Christopher said. "The train won't stop there."

"Want to bet?" She spotted the green metal box on the floor. It was underneath three suitcases and the Chinese Head Chopper. She had to change places with the rabbit to get to it. Talk about Alice in Wonderland. It took a long time but she got the box out. By then her fingers were numb.

"Williamson, three miles," Christopher read a road sign.

"Any sign of their car?"

"I can see a taillight if that's what you mean."

"It's theirs," she said with conviction, changing places again with the rabbit. She got out the gun and four blank cartridges, wedged the box between the rabbit and the cage of turtle doves, and loaded a cartridge. That was all the starter's pistol would take at a time.

"I must be crazy to give you that," Christopher said. "What do you think you're going to do with it?"

"Just have it."

They were losing ground to the train, running even at the moment with the caboose.

"Try and keep up, Christopher. Maybe I'll catch sight of him."

Christopher swore at damnfool women who thought they were Annie Oakleys.

Williamson *was* a ghost town, to judge by the outskirts. The streetlights were dead—empty, broken globes. Houses were boarded up. Even the billboards were bare. But the train was slowing down, its whistle sharp and measured, a distinct signal. A trainman came out onto the caboose platform and began to work what seemed to be levers. A noisy shudder ran the length of the train.

"It's stopping," Maggie said, and they were passing car after car now. Between two of the cars she glimpsed a figure with a great hump on his back. "I see him!" she cried. "I'll bet he jumps before they stop."

"He'll kill himself if he does. He must be frozen stiff."

Suddenly they lost complete sight of the train where the road made a hairpin turn, going steeply downhill. When they saw it again it was dead ahead, stopped across the tracks.

A thin row of high-slung lights lined the station platform. Light shone from the stationmaster's office, but the rest of what once was an elegant gabled building was in spooky darkness. The car Maggie convinced herself they had followed was parked next to the platform. Christopher wouldn't drive near it.

"Okay, park and we'll walk," Maggie said. "Just pretend we're going to report the old man to the stationmaster."

"I'm not pretending. That's all I am going to do." He turned the Chevy around and parked facing the highway which continued parallel to the tracks. Main Street crossed the tracks down into the town. "If anything happens run like hell back here. They'll find that old man without us."

Maggie trudged to the platform, passing close to the parked car. She didn't go right up to look but she couldn't see anyone in it. Maybe it wasn't their car at all. The train let out an enormous sigh, every car simultaneously. Down the platform, on the other side of the office a man in a railway cap and a sheepskin coat was handing up bags from a Railway Express wagon. Behind Maggie the crossing bell was clanging furiously as though it could waken a dead town. More than half the train stretched out of sight beyond the Main Street crossing.

She looked around to see where Christopher was. He had cut over in front of the parked car and was striding along the platform toward where the baggage was being loaded. She'd be willing to bet he wouldn't even mention the man they'd seen jumping the train. She ran to catch up with him but cast a glance over her shoulder every few steps. The magician and the stationmaster were talking when she looked back and saw two men running alongside the tracks, their figures caught for the moment in the crossing light. They were headed for the parked car.

She shouted, "Christopher!" He paid no attention. She ran back. The men separated, one on a beeline to the car and the other headed, stiff-legged, for the highway. No, she realized, he was heading for Christopher's car. She dug the pistol out of her pocket and fired its single shot. A pop. A mere pop. Another cartridge might be louder but she was too shaken to reload. Her heart felt like it was beating itself to death, but she ran full speed for the Chevrolet. The other car roared into motion behind her. Its lights circled her: the driver meant to run her down or scare her off the road. She flung herself toward the bushes and kept rolling over and over. By the time she was safe and recovered her senses, both cars were heading onto the highway and on back the way they'd come. Christopher was running from the station, shouting "Stop! You thieving bastards, stop!"

Maggie picked herself up and made it to where the magician was sobbing with rage.

"He almost ran me over," Maggie said.

"They've got my rabbit! They've got my whole goddamn life! What have you done to me, Maggie?"

She didn't say anything until the lights of both cars disappeared. Then her mind began to work again. "What do they want with your car anyway? They won't take it far. All they want is a head start so we can't follow them again. Come on, Chris," she coaxed. "Take one more chance on me. Let's hike as far as the turn in the road." She hooked her arm through his and pulled him forward.

"Don't call me Chris," he muttered.

As they neared the turn, the whole valley below them seemed swathed in a shimmering mist, a few pinpricks of light showing through. It was like an upside-down sky. "Isn't it beautiful?" Maggie exclaimed.

"Shut up," Christopher said.

But when they rounded the curve he cried out, "By God, you're right! There she is!"

The Chevy sat in stubborn majesty, her radiator against the guardrail of the overlook.

Christopher turned the car around and refilled the radiator from the milk can. Maggie got in and thought about how long it had been since she'd got out of bed the previous morning. She had pawned her watch in Danbury, Connecticut, in October and lost the ticket in Framingham, Massachusetts, but she had a Baby Ben alarm clock in her book bag. She reached for it and knew at once that what was at her feet was not her book bag.

She sat very still and didn't say a word until they were about to pass the Williamson station. "Christopher, you'd better stop."

"No, ma'am," he said.

"My book bag is gone. They've taken it."

"Hurray for them."

She pulled the bag at her feet up onto her lap.

"What's that?" he said, and then, "Oh, my God."

He slammed on the brakes and even by what was left of the moonlight they could read the marking, U.S. MAIL.

"I reckon we'll get your books back for you, ma'am," the sheriff of Mingo County said, "but I can't guarantee it'll be by noon." Noontime was the hour at which the best garage repairman in Tug River Valley had promised a mended radiator and two new tires. The sheriff figured that in due time the Norfolk and Western Railway might just pay for them. "But you'll be yonder by a long ways then."

The magician and Maggie had had a few hours' sleep at opposite ends of an old leather sofa in the sheriff's office. His wife had brought them a wonderful breakfast of ham, fried cornmeal mush, and eggs, with coffee enough to keep them awake all the way to the Michigan state line. The rabbit nibbled carrots from the woman's root cellar, the doves traveled with their own supply of bird seed. Christopher took a five-dollar gold piece out of the sheriff's wife's ear and put it in her apron pocket—to give her kids for Christmas.

"I knew when I heard your story," the sheriff summed things up, "it had to be the McCoy brothers. They weren't ever known to do anything the easy way if they could find a hard one. And folks got to thank the good Lord that most times they're just plain unlucky. Like your turning up tonight. A couple of years back they aimed to rob the local bank. They squeezed themselves through the ventilating system during the night and was inside waiting for the manager to open up the next morning. Only trouble, that was the day President Roosevelt closed every bank in the country. Nobody opened up. Some people round here blamed it on the McCoys at first. Dang near lynched them. They'd've saved us a pack of trouble since if they had."

The sheriff took off his hat, scratched his head, and put his hat back on again. "It may turn out the best luck they ever did have was you finding the old man. They could hang for that if he don't pull through. But that old man is tougher than all the McCoys put together. It won't surprise me none if he lives to be state's witness."

Maggie and Christopher looked at one another. Then Maggie asked the question: "What's the old man's name, Sheriff?"

"Smith. Just plain Willie Smith."

ERIC WRIGHT

KAPUT

Canadians are great storytellers, and two-time Arthur Ellis Award winner Eric Wright is one of the best. Like all good yarnspinners, he takes his inspiration where he finds it and doesn't always realize right away what he's found. Back in 1952, Eric worked for a year in Churchill, Manitoba. Some thirty-seven years later, it occurred to him that he might get a story out of his experience and here it is.

Ten years ago, this versatile Torontonian began writing detective fiction. By now, mystery readers know Eric Wright best for his Charlie Salter novels, but he's no new hand at writing short stories. He sold the first one he ever wrote to The New Yorker *in 1959. Eric is a founding member and a past president of Crime Writers of Canada and on the executive committee of the International Crime Writers League.*

"**L**oneliness was bad," he said. "It could do terrible things to people. But there was worse. I knew two fellas up here once— they worked a trapline near Mile 42—well, I tell you, they got to hate each other, those two, like one of them marriages where the husband and wife is exchanging notes all the time, not speaking. These two got like that. They couldn't agree on anything after a while. Never mind, though, they had to stick it out to the spring.

"What they did to avoid arguments, they had a deck of cards, d'ye see, and they cut 'em to see who was to do the chores. They cut for everything. It worked out pretty well for a while. One of them would have a run of luck and he would have a nice time watching the other work, then it would swing back. Some of the chores was worse than others, of course, like going out to see why the dogs are restless in forty below in a snowstorm that fills your tracks behind you. That's a bad one, because maybe you've got to scare off a pack of wolves, or a bear. Still, that's how they worked it.

"Then one of them got cute. He picked up a book somewhere, probably from the mission or the Hudson's Bay store, on how to be a conjuror. There was a bit in it on how to do card tricks and one of them showed you how to cut any card you wanted. This fella took the book and hid it and practiced when his partner was away on the trapline and he got so he could cut any card he wanted. Pretty soon his partner was doing all the dirty hard jobs and he was doing the easy ones, like making the coffee in the morning. His partner never tumbled to it, just waited for his luck to turn.

"Then he found the book when the other fella was away. He didn't say anything at first, just waited. Then one night they thought they had a bear outside so they cut the cards and the poor fella lost again. What he did then was interesting. He took his gun and got dressed like he was going after the bear and went out the cabin and started to holler. His partner came out with his own gun and the fella who was being cheated shot him as he stood in the door.

"Then he fired off three or four rounds of his partner's gun, laid him on the floor of the cabin with his gun in his hands, closed the place up, harnessed up the dogs, and three days later turned himself in at the Mountie post. He told the Mounties he'd shot his partner in self-defense. Said his partner had gone crazy and suddenly started shooting at him while he was out seeing to the dogs. Lucky, he said, he had his gun with him so there was only one thing to do. He tried to talk him out of it, but the fella just shot at him. The Mounties accepted that. They had no choice. It happens."

Duncan Bane swallowed his beer in a long smooth slide and I signaled the beer parlor waiter for more. I figured we had a while to go before I got what I wanted.

I was in Churchill, Manitoba, collecting material for what I hoped would be an oral history of the north. My idea was to find some of the old people who were still around who had been there in the thirties, the old trappers, the missionaries, perhaps the odd Hudson's Bay factor who had decided to stay after retirement.

So far I hadn't had much luck. I had started in Flin Flon, then moved on to The Pas, and now I was in a beer parlor in one of the oldest settlements on the Hudson's Bay. Churchill is a grain port for a few weeks a year, a year-round railhead for the twice-weekly train, and, as I was finding out, a tourist town. Duncan Bane was the chief tourist attraction.

I was staying at the hotel above the beer parlor and the waiter, hearing of my mission, had insisted that Duncan Bane was the man I should talk to. He was a trapper, now retired, who had come up north as a young man during the Depression. Now in his seventies, he spent his days in the beer parlor at his own table in the corner. I introduced myself to him, bought him some beer, and he started to talk. He had been talking now for half an hour and none of it was any use to me.

My experience of this kind of thing is that sometimes you have to wait a long time to get what you want. It's like being an antique dealer who calls in at a remote farmhouse on the off chance that the owner will have something whose value he is unaware of. First you have to admire everything the farmer is proud of—the dishwasher, the microwave, even the VCR; then, down in the basement, while he is showing you his new furnace, you stumble over the hundred-year-old dry sink he is using for a woodbox. Oral history is like that. What you want to hear is the stuff they are slightly ashamed of.

I was beginning to think, though, that Duncan Bane was a waste of time. He certainly looked the part: old work pants held up by suspenders, a much-washed check shirt, and, best of all, a huge tangle of beard beneath a blue-veined bald head. He had cast himself in the role of "old trapper," and he made his living, or his beer money, sitting in the parlor telling stories for tourists, and probably allowing them to take his picture, for a consideration.

So far he had told me three stories. The story about the two trappers and the deck of cards I had heard years ago in Winnipeg, then again twice on this trip, in Flin Flon and Cranberry Portage. Bane told it well from long practice.

First he'd told me the story of the miner who had struck gold in the north and gone to Winnipeg, hired three whores, then, to acclimatize them, filled the hotel suite with two feet of corn flakes so that he could teach them how to walk on snowshoes. This has always been one of my favorite stories. Bane claimed to have known the miner.

His next story had concerned the pregnant Eskimo woman who had been left to die by her band, but who had appeared out of the blizzard two months later with a healthy baby dressed in the skins of animals she had trapped, and whose flesh she had survived on, as well as devising needles and thread from the bones and sinews to sew the skins for clothing. This one goes back to Samuel Hearne's diaries, where Wordsworth probably heard of it to write his version. Bane claimed to have met the Mountie who took her in when she appeared at his post.

I knew what was going on from the beginning. The table he sat at was clearly where he regularly held court. The few drinkers at other tables glanced our way occasionally, grinning—obviously at old Duncan conning the tourist. Nevertheless, he *had* been a trapper, and he had lived in the north for fifty years, and I figured that once Bane had run through his party pieces I might still get something. He seemed to be winding down now, and I signaled the waiter for more beer.

"How did you find out what really happened between those two partners?" I asked, quasi-skeptically. It was an obvious

question and if I didn't challenge him a little bit he might get
bored.

"He told me," Bane said. "On his death bed," and looked
expansively around the room.

I decided that acting as if I believed him was wrong. There was
something about the way he made his last ridiculous statement
that implied the further comment, "And if you believe that you'll
believe anything."

"Now you're bullshitting me," I said, laughing, choosing a level
of gullibility that could be a challenge to him.

His mouth opened, his eyes widened, and he looked around the
room again, in mock protest. Then he laughed. "You're a smart
one," he said. "That's a story that was told to me. I can't testify to
it."

"And the others?"

"Oh, no," he protested. "Them are true enough."

Now what? I needed something personal, something he might
not have polished into a story. "What did you do for entertainment?" I asked. "Did you work alone?"

"I did, yes. About once a month I'd find me way to the mission
and have a drink or two with the priest, or up to the post and the
same thing with the factor there. Once a year I went into town."

"Winnipeg?"

"That's right. I'd have a whoop and a holler and get me oil
changed and a couple of teeth pulled. That was enough for me.
People talk about being bushed if they stay up here too long at a
time. I been bushed for fifty years. I'm bushed now, I suppose,
but I couldn't live in town now, not me."

The tape stopped and I changed it over. Now I was getting
somewhere. "What about Christmas?" I prodded.

"How d'ye mean?"

"Didn't you get lonely at Christmas even?"

"Only once. In the city. I'd broke me hand setting one of me
traps and I couldn't get it straight, so I went into town to the

hospital. They wrapped it in plaster, but so I could use it. One of the furriers I dealt with made me a good mitt which would go over it. I was all set to come back when I noticed it was the twenty-third, two days before Christmas, so I stayed where I was, to celebrate. Well, let me tell you, I've never been so down in me life. Christmas in the Winnipeg Hotel. The city was deserted—Winnipeg downtown always looks deserted these days, have ye noticed?—and an empty city is a lot lonelier than a cabin, where you can hear your dogs outside and the crack of the lights in the sky at night. I never did that again. If I didn't go to the mission or the post I'd save meself a mickey of rye for the day. I wouldn't do any work, just sit in me cabin until the whiskey was gone, then go to bed."

"Did you drink much, by yourself, at other times?"

"Never." Now he was serious. "Never. I've seen it kill a few, not the drink but what it can bring. Fella gets to drinking and falls asleep outside. He don't last long. I've seen a few of them, whites *and* Indians. Matter of fact, there was one up at the fort here, one Christmas Eve. Call that waiter and I'll tell you about it."

Not quite what I wanted, but it sounded better than his tales for tourists. He was more relaxed now—I calculated that he must be on his eighth beer—and he had stopped orating. The waiter loaded us up, and Bane started in.

"Back in the early fifties, it was. There was a big military base there then, Army, Navy, Air Force, even a couple of sailors. There was Americans as well as Canadians. I think they were supposed to stop the Russians when they came over the top of the world. They was training in arctic warfare, learning how to survive and fight at forty below. I don't think they ever got to the fighting bit; they was learning that it took them twenty-three hours out of every twenty-four just to take care of surviving which only left them one hour for fighting. Somebody asked them once if they would have to get an agreement with the Russians about which hour they would use for the fighting. Anyway, there were hundreds of them and I worked with them for a while. They hired me to show them the country and I used to go out with them in their Caterpillars when they were mapping the area. I got to know some of them pretty good, one especially, a big sergeant from somewhere down in the south. He wanted a polar bear skin real bad to take back and I got him one. You wasn't supposed to shoot polar bears but one of them attacked me one day and I had to kill it in self-defense." He stuck his tongue in his cheek and gave me a grotesque, owlish look to make sure I understood. "So Sergeant Vivaldi was very grateful and he insisted I come up to the sergeants' mess on Christmas Eve, to the dance, and stay over a couple of days." He shook some salt into his beer and took a swallow. "I didn't want to go but he insisted and so did some of the others so I went and it was quite a night I can tell you. They made a bit of a pet of me, found me a coat and tie, you had to wear a coat and tie in the mess, and they give me a nice room. I used my team to come as far as the mission where I staked my dogs out, and they came in a Caterpillar and fetched me the rest of the way.

"The American sergeants was the hosts for Christmas Eve. They used to compete in showing each other a good time on the holidays, which they celebrated all of, Canadian and American both. So the Canadians was the hosts on our Labor Day and the Americans on theirs and on Sadie Hawkins' Day. They'd divided up Christmas so the Americans got Christmas Eve and the Canadians looked after New Year's Eve.

"As I say, it was quite a night. The mess was all decorated like a night club. 'White Nights' Lounge' they called it, with fancy lights and balloons and such, and a bottle of champagne on every table, free. I don't like the stuff meself, but there it was, one for every table. And they had a band. The Yanks had flown up a band from Washington just for the night and they were really letting her rip. I hadn't danced, me, for twenty years and I wasn't planning to try even if I could've done their dances, but Sergeant Vivaldi kept getting the girls to ask me—I could see what he was up to and I didn't mind, but I couldn't do those dances. The girls? There were some, a few wives and secretaries and such. There was enough if they shared themselves around. There was a Mrs. Caruso at out table, her husband was a sergeant away in Washington and she was sharing herself around a bit with an accountant for one of the construction companies, but I'll come to that. So I told Vivaldi to stop it. I'd only ever danced the polka, none of this jitterbugging stuff, and I told him, but the next thing you know he's over talking to the band and I'm up there dancing a polka with a girl named Lucy from St. Boniface. French girl. Round we went, all by ourselves with the crowd clapping and a big cheer at the end. I reckon it was the champagne. I don't like it, but nothing else would have got me up. Afterward I recited a poem through the microphone which I'd made up when I was alone in me cabin, and that got a big hand."

This was what I wanted. "Can you remember it? Could you recite it now?"

"Sure I can. I'll do it for ye later. Let me get on with me story. The band got louder and louder and at one point the trombone player took off his shoes and played the instrument with his bare foot. That was the kind of evening it was. Then, about midnight, they served lunch."

"Supper?"

"We always call it lunch in this part of the world. Where are you from? Anyway, they served the food. Now here is where it started. Some of the civilians had asked the Americans if they could lend a hand. There was about twenty civilians who was part of the mess, honorary sergeants sort of, construction foremen, the accountant, people like that, and they wanted a chance to show their gratitude, as I was told, but there wasn't enough of them to put on their own evening so they asked to join in with the Americans. They was responsible for the lunch. So now, about midnight the lights dimmed and there was a roll of drums and then a strange thing happened. The door to the kitchen opened and out came the camp barber, running, pushing one of them steel trolleys they use in hotel kitchens, loaded with plates of spaghetti. After him came another fella with a trolley, and after *him* came a fella called Figge, all of them running. Figge crashed into the other two, upsetting them, fighting the barber, rolling over and over in the spaghetti which was all over the floor. Well, the band was pretty tanked up by now and they started to play galloping music and we got up on the tables to watch and cheer. Of course, Sergeant Vivaldi wasn't about to let his evening be spoilt—it wasn't being spoilt, we was having a fine time—but him and three or four others separated Figge and the barber, and some others cleaned up the floor, and then we lined up in the kitchen for our spaghetti just as they always did on Saturday night. We heard afterward that the fight had started in the kitchen. That fella Figge was a nasty piece of work, he'd been by the table earlier during the dancing and he'd had a few. He asked our girls but they wouldn't dance with him and the last time he came by he shouted to Vivaldi that he couldn't keep it all to himself."

"All what?"

"He used a word suggesting the female gender as only a fella like Figge would use in mixed company. Even I knew that. Anyway, it had been Figge's idea that the civilians should dress up as waiters and they was supposed to all enter together and form a ring on the floor, in the dark, and when the lights went up there they would be, with their trollies of spaghetti. Sean the barber thought it was a bad idea. He thought they would all bump into each other and they was still arguing when they heard the roll of drums, and Sean the barber took off before the lights was dimmed or any of the others was ready. We saw what happened next. Figge smashed into the barber on purpose. That wasn't the end of it, either. A little while later they had to separate Johnson—the plumbing foreman—and the barber, and then Figge and Johnson were at each other. It was like a brushfire. But that's what it can get like up here. These fellas weren't used to the life and they took it out in drinking and fighting more than you'd see in town. Fact is, a lot of them were up north because they'd run out of places to go. A lot of alcoholics came up here when the work started on the Distant Early Warning line; alcoholics, fellas skipping out on their wives, running away from debts. For some of them, the north was the last place they could get a job. And like I told you, they got into feuds with each other. There's lots of time during the winter for that kind of thing to fester, because they couldn't get away from each other. Figge and Johnson, for example. There was bad blood there because Figge had won Johnson's parka in a poker game one night. That was a beautiful coat that Johnson had brought with him from his last job on the Gaspé peninsula. Made of summer caribou hide—the winter hides are no good for clothing—and it was Johnson's pride, but he was losing heavy and finally he bet his coat against the pot and lost. Figge should have took that coat and put it away, but he liked to dress up in it sometimes just to make Johnson feel bad. Fact is, just about all of the civilians had had a falling out with each other at one time or another over the winter, but I mention the coat because it was the cause of what happened later. Let's have another beer."

When the waiter came, he took two glasses and swallowed one in a gulp. He continued. "The dance went on until one o'clock or thereabouts and then it happened. Everyone went to bed; I had a room in the mess, but most of the construction fellas was staying in their own camp, a couple of hundred yards away, far enough on a night like that. Did I tell you? Outside it was like walking around the inside of a milk bottle. They went off home in twos and threes and when I went to bed there were only two parkas and a pair of mukluks left in the cloakroom. Mukluks. Boots. Take note of that. It's a clue."

"A what?"

"A clue. I won't say any more. The next morning was Christmas and I wasn't feeling up to much, nobody was, I reckon, but I went down to the mess for a cup of coffee and when I walked in I thought the war had started. The place was full of people all talking at once. Eventually somebody broke off to tell me what had happened. Johnson, the construction foreman, had been found in the snow the night before, beaten up, unconscious, and now he was in the camp hospital. The word was he wasn't expected to live. His sub-foreman—his close pal, Claud Dupuis— had gone looking for him because he'd said goodnight to Johnson and had a last drink himself but when he got home Johnson wasn't there. They shared a room, you see. Dupuis went back to the mess to look for him but it was all quiet by now so he raised the alarm and they—the construction fellas—went to look for him in case he'd fallen asleep in the snow. They found him soon enough, he hadn't gone far, but he was a bit of a mess. As I say, unconscious, nearly frozen, and lots of blood about.

"They was all talking and jumping to conclusions in the mess but there wasn't anyone could say he knew anything. Dupuis had seen him set off, at least. Johnson had told Dupuis he was going home and Dupuis had one last drink and followed him.

"Now there was a captain in the Canadian army in charge of security and he took over. It was a military camp but they had never sorted out whether a civilian crime should be investigated by the military or the Mounties, but since no one could get to town in the storm, Captain Blood—I forget his real name—he took charge. And take charge he did. When he interviewed me late in the day he'd set up what he called an investigations room in the office behind the bar, and he had drawn a map of the area where it had happened with a cross where they found Johnson. All this in colored crayon on a big sheet of paper pinned to the wall. On another sheet he had a sort of time chart of the before and after, all broken up into quarter hours, and on another sheet he had the names of all the people in the mess that night, mostly in black with the fellas who had to walk to the construction camp in red. They was the chief suspects. It looked like a hell of an operation and that was when I realized that poor old Johnson was going to die.

Captain Blood was having a fine time himself, you could see that. It was like the war room of the Pentagon.

"Lots of the names was already crossed off, and after he'd done me, he crossed me off, too. Most of the people he had questioned could account for each other so he'd crossed them off. They'd gone home in twos and threes, and they could testify for each other. I couldn't, of course, I'd just gone to bed, so he asked me for me keys and give them to a sergeant to search my room while he kept me there. Looking for clothes with blood on them he was, though he didn't say. When the sergeant came back, the captain crossed my name off his list as if he'd accomplished something and I left. There was a few names not crossed off yet. Sean Brady, the barber, was one, so was Figge, and two or three others.

"Christmas dinner that day wasn't very jolly, I can tell you. Everyone had an idea who had pounded Johnson, most of them different, and we got a lot of talk about what would happen to him when they caught him, if ever. Claud Dupuis didn't say much, but you could see he'd want a hand in anything that was done to the man who had assaulted his friend.

"Johnson died the next day. The sergeant hospital orderly was telling us at supper that he croaked a couple of words, then gave up. As the orderly heard it, all he said was 'Kaput,' and we all knew what that meant. I did, anyway, and I saw Claud Dupuis look up sharp."

"It means 'finished,'" I said.

Bane looked at me in triumph and took a long swallow. "Ah. That's what they all thought. Let's just say it's another clue. I'll explain in a minute.

"The storm was letting up a bit and the next morning I got permission from Captain Blood to go to town to see after my dogs. One of the Americans took me in on a Caterpillar, and while I was there I had a chat with the French priest at the mission to confirm an idea I'd had, and when I came back I told the captain what I'd found out. He got very excited about it and organized search parties to go over every inch of the area. They found what he was looking for under a building pushed out of sight, and the captain took Figge in and he and the Mountie corporal questioned him for the rest of the day."

"Why Figge?" I asked, as I was supposed to. "What did they find?"

"What did they find?" he asked with an air that made me want to pour my beer over him. "What d'ye think they found?"

"I don't know. What?"

"Figge's parka. Or rather, Johnson's parka. The caribou one that Figge had won off Johnson. Covered in blood."

"So Figge did it?"

"Looks like it, don't it?"

"How did you know? What did you hear from the priest?"

"I'll tell you that at the end if you haven't figured it out. Now the next surprise everyone got, after they got over their relief that it was Figge, was that the accountant at our table, Spenser, was involved somehow. He spent three hours with the captain and the Mountie, and after he came out he started to pack his clothes, ready to leave, and Figge was released. They didn't let him loose, of course. Claud Dupuis would have killed him, just on the chance that they were right in the first place, so they took him into town and locked him up in a little Mountie jail for his own protection. Did you figure out why yet?"

"No."

The old man looked pleased. "It came out later that Figge could prove he was in the billiard room all night, on one of the couches, because the accountant was there, too, for a lot of the time, certainly when Johnson was attacked."

"With Figge?"

"No, no. With Mrs. Caruso, the American wife whose husband was away in Washington. The accountant had to give him an alibi because Figge could give a blow by blow account of how they'd spent the night while he was up at the other end of the room, pretending to be asleep. I told you he was a nasty piece of work. They'd locked themselves in, too, which the mess sergeant could testify to. He'd found the door locked when he made his rounds. The accountant left right away, before Sergeant Caruso came back. They wanted to keep it secret but there was too many people in the room when Figge was talking so we heard enough.

"Now Captain Blood gets an idea. First he'd figured that it was Figge because of the parka, but now he figures that it must have been someone wearing Figge's parka who had it in for Johnson *and* Figge. I thought that was pretty smart of him. Now he wanted laboratory tests done on the clothes of all those on his list because those caribou parkas shed a bit, and it should have left some hair. The Defense Research Board had a few botanists and biologists up there—one of them come to me one day and asked if he could get a blood sample from one of my dogs and I said sure, take as much as you like and the fella advanced on my lead dog with a needle in his hand before I caught him back. I was just teasing him. Another ten feet and he would have got his sample, all right, and so would they. These scientists had a bit of a laboratory but what Captain Blood wanted would have taken six months, I reckon, still, they started in. Meanwhile the Mountie started questioning us all again to find out who had it in for Johnson and Figge, the two of them, and they came up with a name. You know who?"

"Sean Brady, the barber."

"That's right. Well done. I could have told them that's who they'd come up with."

"Why didn't you?"

"Because by now I could see they was sucking up swamp water, and I had my own ideas which I wanted to confirm for meself. I'd had enough of Captain Blood rushing off half cocked. So they settled on Sean, as I knew they would, and they went through his room with a magnifying glass, and checked him for bruises, all the time the laboratory was trying to find caribou hairs on his best suit. I knew they wouldn't find anything, but as for Sean Brady, he would have done it if he'd had the guts, so I didn't mind if they gave him a bit of a going over. They didn't find anything but I told them they'd better keep Brady under protective custody, too, because Dupuis was looking to batter anyone to get even for his friend. While they were interviewing Brady I walked over to the hospital to pay my last respects to Johnson, and I offered to take his things back to Dupuis who was packing them all up in a box to send to his wife. Poor old Claud was in a hell of a state, so I stayed and had a long talk with him and calmed him down, and the next day he left on the train. And that was it. They never did figure out who was impersonating Figge. I did, though."

"Claud Dupuis, his friend."

"How did you figure that out?" One side of his mouth had dropped, in wonder apparently. You could see his right bottom canine.

"I was just guessing," I said, though it was more than that. Everybody was accounted for except Dupuis. "I don't know how you figured it out, but I think I know why Dupuis did it."

"Why is that?"

"The story of the two trappers. Dupuis and Johnson had been sharing a room for six months. They hated each other, and Dupuis hated Figge, like everyone else. So he put on Figge's parka and went after Johnson, killing two birds with one stone."

The old man stared at me, forgetting even to drink. He looked stunned. "What are you talking about? Did you know these fellas? No? Well, I did. They were blood brothers, let me tell you."

I have never seen a man so angry. The vein running down the center of his skull looked ready to burst. In some way I had attacked the heart of his story and he needed to dispose of me before he could continue.

"This is *not* the story of the two trappers," he spat out. "What I'm telling you is true. Do you understand me? I knew them fellas." He waited to see if I was properly cowed.

I made conciliatory gestures. "So tell me. How did you figure it out?"

He still said nothing for a long while, then he collected himself and took a swallow of beer. "Let's start with 'kaput,'" he said. "You don't speak French? I thought we was all supposed to be bilingual these days. I do, and Ojibway, and Eskimo. You have to up here. Did I tell you Johnson was French? It wasn't 'kaput' he said. I knew he wouldn't be speaking German and the look on Dupuis's face triggered me off, so I went to town and had a word with the priest, like I said, and sure enough the word is 'capote.' French. It means a special kind of parka, like Johnson's. So I thought it was Figge meself, then, but when Figge came up with his alibi, I sorted it all out. As you say, only one fella was not quite accounted for, and when Captain Blood wanted to test everyone's clothes, he gave me an idea. Of course, the two parkas and the pair of mukluks in the cloakroom helped."

"Why?"

"Where was the other pair of boots? You couldn't go out in weather like that in dancing shoes. Somebody had his boots on but not his parka."

"Dupuis? Took Figge's parka and went after Johnson?"

"That's what an outsider might think, who didn't know these fellas." Once more he stared me down before he continued. "Not me, though. What I did realize right away is why Dupuis looked so strange when he heard the word 'kaput.' He knew what Johnson had really said and if he'd been innocent he'd have jumped in quick. But it was no surprise to him and he didn't know how to react."

"So why did he go after Johnson?"

"You haven't figured it out? He didn't. There was no way he would have gone after Johnson." He looked at me fiercely. "No way. He went after Figge."

"But Figge was in the billiard room, listening to . . . "

"So he was, but Dupuis didn't know that. When he saw a fella

going through the door wearing Figge's coat he decided to settle a
score, for himself and for his friend. Johnson had stolen back his
own coat. They was all pretty drunk, remember. He beat up
Johnson before he got a good look at him."

"Why didn't he leave it at that? He could still discover him a bit
later and watch the whole camp look for someone who had it in for
Figge. Besides, he didn't know that Figge had an alibi. It could
have looked like a fight between Johnson and Figge over the coat.
Why didn't he leave it?"

"Because of the blood. I told you there was a lot of blood on his
parka. They wasn't all that drunk, the others. Someone would
have noticed. So he swapped parkas on Johnson and hid Figge's
parka where it could be found. Then he slipped back and got
Johnson's regular parka out of the cloakroom, where Johnson had
left it when he decided to steal back his capote. So now Johnson
was wearing an ordinary parka with blood on it and Dupuis
wasn't."

"You couldn't prove it."

"That's why I went to pay my last respects to Johnson in the
hospital. When they left me alone with him, I found his suit,
covered with caribou hair. Then I looked in his parka. It was an
army surplus parka; the Canadian army had sold them to a lot of
the construction workers so it was pretty well identical to a lot of
others, and that's why everyone put his name in them on a little
white tag they put in for the purpose. Johnson's had been torn
out."

"Why didn't you tell the police?"

"Because of the way Captain Blood was talking. He was
wanting to charge someone with attempted murder or manslaugh-
ter but that wasn't the way it was. Dupuis wasn't a murderer. He
just wanted to loosen a few of Figge's teeth. It was a mistake. I felt
sorry for him, so I told him what I knew, told him there being no
name tag wouldn't signify because the police would have ways of
proving it was his coat. So he left. He didn't have to. I wouldn't

have said anything. Like I said, it was a misunderstanding. You take my point? He killed his friend by mistake."

I saw now why my easy comparison of his story with the tale of the two trappers had make him so angry.

"I did tell the Mountie, though," he said suddenly. "I waited a year, then I told him. You know what he said?"

"What?"

"He said considering I'd had a year all to myself in the cabin he'd have thought I could make up a better story than that. He didn't want to be bothered, ye see, and besides, Dupuis had taken all the evidence with him. Now catch that waiter before I die of thirst."

"What about the poem?"

"The one I recited? Are you staying at the hotel? Meet me here tomorrow, then, and I'll tell it to you. I'm all talked out now. There's the waiter now. Quick before he looks away."

I left him then, but I did come back next day to record his poem. I waited for an hour but he never appeared. The waiter told me to hang on, Duncan Bane was *always* there, he said, but I had a feeling that Bane would just as soon not talk to me anymore.

JOHN LUTZ

THE LIVE TREE

John Lutz says he identifies with the grinchy dad in this story. He doesn't really hate Christmas, but he's irked by the fuss and bother of getting ready for it. His kids always used to demand a real tree but now that they're grown up and in college, he's fulfilled a long-held ambition and bought an artificial one.

There's nothing artificial about the tree in this story; but it's certainly not the sort you'd pick up at your neighborhood farm and garden stand.

John Lutz writes straightforward detective novels, but when it comes to the short stories he loves to do—and for which he's won an Edgar Award—he's full of surprises. In this holiday tale, we find out that even a fine upstanding Christmas tree can have an awfully curious twist to it.

Clayton Blake was tired of Christmas, and it was still five days away. His four-year-old son, Andy, was curled on the sofa pouting, making Clayton feel about as small as one of Santa's elves. But damn it, he was *right* about this.

His wife, Blair, said, "You're wrong about this, Clay. What would it hurt to buy one more real Christmas tree? It's a big thing to Andy, and he's still so young. He doesn't understand how you feel about Christmas."

Clayton's argument with Blair and Andy had left his nerves ragged. But he was still determined to buy a small artificial tree this year, keep god-awful Christmas fuss to a minimum. "How Andy feels doesn't change what Christmas really is," he said.

"Nothing but a major marketing blitz that starts sometime in October. You know the retail stores make half their profits during the Christmas season?" He peaked his eyebrows in indignation. "*Half!* I mean, it's reached the point where how well they can con us at Christmas determines how the entire economy's gonna go. The *world* economy! Goddamn governments rise or fall on it."

Andy said, "Wanna weal tree." It came out as a pitiful bleat.

Blair looked as if she were suffering physical pain. Then she shook her head, her long blond hair swaying. A beautiful woman still in her thirties. Slightly myopic blue eyes. Bedroom eyes. "Tell Andy about the economy," she said. "He'll understand your position once the two of you have talked about gross national product and the trade imbalance."

There was a clatter on the porch. Stomping footsteps. The mail being delivered. Clayton was grateful for the interruption.

He and Blair both strode to the front door to get the mail. When she saw what was happening she stopped and let Clayton step out onto the porch to collect it. As he pushed outside, the winter wind seemed to slice to his bones like icy razor blades.

He was still cold after he came back in. Just those few seconds outside had chilled him to the quick. Temperature must be near zero. He really hated not only Christmas, but this time of year in general. Gray skies and gloom.

"Twee," Andy insisted.

Clayton hardened his heart and ignored his son. Said with disappointment, "Looks like nothing but Christmas cards." He dropped the stack of mail on the table in the foyer. Laughed without humor at the one envelope he was still holding. It was a longer envelope than the others, and he recognized the return address. The state penitentiary. This would be the yearly Christmas card from his brother Willy, who was serving time for mail fraud. Clayton said, "The usual card from Willy," and tossed the envelope in with the unpaid bills piling up from Christmas shopping. *'Tis the season to be indebted.*

Blair said, "Even in prison, Willy's got the Christmas spirit."

"Even in prison, Willy's got you conned," Clayton said. "Willy can con anybody he wants to, and from any distance."

"He might be a con man," Blair said petulantly, "but he's also a decent person." Left hanging heavy in the air was the implication that Clayton was *not* a decent sort; he was the kind of miser who wouldn't even let his family have a genuine Christmas tree. That irritated him. Wasn't he an excellent provider? A faithful and sober husband? A good father to their son, if perhaps a stricter one than Blair would have liked? And how was Willy—a convicted criminal—a decent person? Wasn't that just what a con artist needed you to believe—that he was basically decent?

Blair began opening the Christmas cards, using a long red fingernail to pry beneath envelope flaps. "Well, when are you going to buy this *artificial* tree?" she asked resignedly, without meeting his gaze.

"In a little while."

Still not looking up, she said, "Andy was looking forward to picking out a real one with us over at the lot on Elm Avenue."

Clayton didn't answer. He actually didn't even want to go to the trouble of buying and setting up even an artificial tree. Some of them were complicated and the branches didn't fit right. What he really wanted was a window shade with a picture of a tree on it. He could pull it down during the holidays, then roll it up sometime around the new year. Better not tell Blair about that idea, though.

Andy said, "Pweese, Daddy!" from the sofa.

"You can get up now, son," Clayton said just as the doorbell rang. "But behave. No more temper tantrums."

He took two steps to the door and opened it. Stood with his mouth hanging open, breathing in cold air.

His brother, Willy, was standing on the porch.

"Willy, how'd you—"

"I'm let out on a good behavior program till after Christmas,"

Willy said. "They're doing that now for trusties convicted of nonviolent crimes." He grinned. "Nobody'll skip. Not this time of year. That's why they call us trusties."

Clayton didn't know what to say. He wasn't actually all that glad to see his brother. They'd never gotten along well.

"Willy!" Blair said behind Clayton. "For God's sake, come on in!"

"Yeah!" Clayton said, pulling out of his shock. "Get in here, Willy. Cold out there."

Willy the master criminal smiled. He was a shorter, bulkier version of Clayton, but with a face that perpetually beamed and a nose red from hanging over too many highball glasses. While Clayton's features were lean and intense, giving him the look of a concerned headmaster, Willy resembled a life-coarsened department store Santa out of uniform and on his way to a bar. Clayton wondered if Willy had been drinking before coming here. *Did Santa's reindeer have antlers?*

Willy hadn't moved. He said, "I got something with me." Reached off to his left and tugged at an obviously heavy and resisting object.

A Christmas tree came into view.

Not only a tree, but a large one. Almost six feet tall and also big around.

Not only a large tree, but a live one. Its roots still surrounded by a massive clump of earth that was wrapped in burlap tied with twine.

What was going on here? Clayton wondered. Had Willy conned a tree from a nursery in the spirit of Christmas? He was capable of it, and that was sure how it appeared.

Blair almost screamed, "A *real* tree!"

"Weal twee!" Andy scampered across the living room and bounced off Clayton's leg.

Clayton cleared his throat and said, "This is your uncle Willy, son."

Andy said, "Wi-wee."

Willy was beaming down at Andy with an expression so tender it surprised Clayton. He'd been in prison since before Andy's birth. "Finally get to see you, little buddy."

Clayton said, "Leave the tree on the porch for now and come inside, Willy. You're so cold you're white." *Except for the drinker's nose.*

As Willy leaned the tree against the house and stepped through the door, Blair said, "You sure you're feeling okay, Willy? You *are* kind of pale."

"Oh, yeah. Pri—where I been does that to the complexion. You know me, always healthy. Never even a cold."

Germs slain by alcohol, Clayton thought, but he kept the opinion to himself.

Willy peeled off his coat. He was wearing a cheap blue suit. Scuffed black shoes. Prison issue.

Willy handed his coat to Clayton and glanced around. "Good. I was hoping you hadn't bought a tree yet. Wanted to surprise you. We gotta get it in a washtub with some water in it pretty soon. Then, after Christmas, you can plant it someplace in your yard. It'll grow tall and strong right along with Andy, here."

Clayton wasn't surprised to see that Andy, like all things warm-blooded, had taken an immediate liking to Willy. He was standing close and gazing up at him as if Willy were a life-size G.I. Joe. War toys, Clayton thought. At least Willy hadn't brought Andy war toys.

Blair bustled off to get Willy a cup of hot chocolate. Willy settled down on the sofa with Andy next to him. Old pals already.

Clayton said, "Where you staying, Willy?"

Willy waited until Blair had returned. He said, "Well, I thought maybe here. I gotta report back in right after Christmas."

Clayton had barely opened his mouth when Blair said, "Great, Willy. We've got a guest room."

Andy said, "Back in where, Uncle Wi-wee?"

"Uncle Willy meant he had to go back home," Clayton said quickly. "Soon as Christmas is over."

Willy sat back in the softness of the sofa and looked around. "Great place, Clayt. Great family. Great cup of chocolate. You know how lucky you are?"

Clayton said he knew.

They went out for supper at a family-style restaurant that served fried chicken and was decorated with holly and pine rope and red bows. Willy was his usual mesmerizing self and Andy behaved beautifully. Clayton was surprised to be enjoying himself. Actually glad to see Willy, the older brother of whom he'd always been so jealous. In high school Willy had stolen from Clayton the affections of Janet Gerinski, a cheerleader whose good looks transcended even the glinting metal orthodontic braces of the era. Janet had interested Willy for about two passionate weeks, and was now married to an insurance man and living in an even more expensive part of town than the Blakes.

Clayton knew he'd never really forgiven Willy, who, after dropping Janet, left school and hitchhiked to California. There Willy's intended career in rock music had quickly fallen through. That was when Willy began plying his charm in pursuit of illegal profits. From the record industry to telephone boiler rooms to plush hotel suites in Reno, Willy had bilked thousands of dollars from unsuspecting admirers and business associates.

Odd, Clayton thought, how nobody liked what Willy had done, but everybody seemed to like Willy. It was something Clayton had never understood.

The next morning was Saturday, and the three adults, with Andy's help, stood the live pine tree more or less straight in a washtub and decorated it. Clayton felt good watching Andy. Thought for the first time that maybe it hadn't been such a good idea to deprive the boy of a real Christmas tree at only four years old.

"Hey, Clayt!" Willy said that evening after Blair's home-cooked dinner. "Let's all drive downtown and show Andy the display windows. They got a train about a mile long in one of the department stores." He grinned over at Andy. "You sat on Santa's lap yet, buddy?"

"Not since he was a year old," Blair said, shooting a glance at Clayton Scrooge.

Willy shoved his chair back and stood up. "Well, we can fix that tonight. Stores are open late. C'mon, folks. I got some shopping to do anyway."

Clayton was surprised. "Where would you get money in—"

Blair raised a hand palm out to silence Clayton.

"Aw, you know me , Clayt," Willy said. "How I always been able to play cards."

Cheat at cards, Clayton thought. But again he kept his silence.

After Willy helped Blair load the dishwasher, they set off in the station wagon for the highway leading downtown. Willy suggested they sing. Clayton objected only briefly before being overruled. By the time they got downtown he was actually enjoying belting out Christmas carols, listening to Andy sing with lisping soprano gusto. Blair was smiling and looking—well, angelic.

Willy winked at Clayton in the rearview mirror. "Holiday spirit, Clayt."

Clayt. Clayton had always hated that nickname. And now only Willy called him that.

Andy was enthralled by the colorful display windows. Sat beaming on Santa's lap and asked for a model plane. Which amazed Clayton; he and Blair were giving Andy a simple plastic model plane for Christmas.

An hour before the stores were due to close, Willy told the rest of the family to drive home without him. He wanted to do some shopping and then he'd take a cab back to the house.

Clayton agreed, and they said good-bye and went outside to walk the short, cold two blocks to the parking lot.

No one said anything. Even Clayton thought the drive home was comparatively dull.

And during the drive he began to think. Why was Willy laying on the charm? Was he trying to work some kind of con? Clayton couldn't be sure, but he was determined to be careful.

Christmas morning was a delight. Clayton felt a warmth he hadn't thought possible watching Andy open the many presents placed under the tree by his uncle Willy. With the warmth was an unexpected melancholy yearning for Christmas mornings years ago when he and Willy had been held in check at the top of the stairs and then allowed to race downstairs and examine their own presents. He remembered the pungent scent of the real Christmas tree, the same scent that was now Andy's to remember. The years at home with Willy might not have been as bad as Clayton usually recalled them. Besides, shouldn't there be a time limit, a statute of limitations on ancient injuries?

It had snowed that morning, as if the weather knew one of Willy's gifts to Andy would be a sled. That afternoon, after a meal of ham and sweet potatoes, with apple pie for dessert, Willy suggested they all go to a hill in a nearby park and test the sled. Clayton was reluctant at first, but he went along and had a marvelous time even though he suspected three or four fingers might be frostbitten. He even soloed downhill with the sled, something he hadn't done since he was twelve. "Got carried away," he explained to a grinning Blair when he'd clomped uphill, snow-speckled and trailing the sled on its rope.

As they were trudging through the snow back to the car, Clayton and Andy fell behind Willy and Blair. Andy looked up at Clayton, his reddened face curious beneath his ski cap. "How come Uncle Wi-wee don't get cold?"

"He does get cold, I'm sure."

"Don't act cold."

Which was true, Clayton realized. Maybe Willy was fortified with alcohol, he thought, and then immediately felt guilty. As far as he knew, Willy hadn't touched anything alcoholic since he'd arrived for his Christmas visit.

That night, after an exhausted Andy had fallen asleep on the sofa next to Willy and then been carried upstairs to bed, Blair made some eggnog and the three adults sat around talking.

"I always envied you, Clayt," Willy said, wiping eggnog from his upper lip.

Clayton was surprised.

"Still do. The roots you put down early. You oughta take stock of what's yours in this world and appreciate it. I mean, nothing lasts forever, and you got this time with Blair and Andy . . . "

Now Clayton was astonished. For a moment it appeared that Willy might actually break down and weep. *Willy a family man?*

Then Willy sat up straighter and asked for a refill on the eggnog. The familiar Willy; there was alcohol in eggnog. He was again the charming con man who'd bilked thousands from people who strangely wouldn't count him among their enemies.

After Willy had gone to bed, Blair said, "He knows he's getting older, and he has to go back to prison tomorrow. I feel terrible about that, don't you? Clay?"

For the first time in years, Clayton said without reservation, "I pity him."

The morning after Christmas, Willy was gone.

They hadn't heard him depart.

He'd left no note.

His bed was made and there was no sign that he'd even visited them. When Andy woke up and asked about him, Clayton told him his uncle Willy had gone back to where he worked in another country. Peru, Clayton had finally said, when pressed. Andy didn't like it. Cried for a while. Then accepted this explanation and got interested in the array of toys he'd received yesterday.

Two days later Clayton was reading the morning paper when Blair said, "Clay!" Something in her voice alarmed him. He put down the paper and saw her standing by the table in the foyer, where she'd been sorting through the mail. Her face was pale and puzzled. "I found this still unopened," she said, and held out a white envelope and the letter that had been inside.

Clayton stood up and walked over to her. Saw she was holding the envelope that had come from the state prison. "Willy's Christmas card," he said.

He'd never before seen such a look in her blue, blue eyes. "But it's not a card. It's . . . " As he gently took the letter from her hand she said, " . . . a death notice."

Clayton stood paralyzed and read. Blair was right. The state penitentiary had written to inform Clayton as Willy's next of kin that one Willard Blake had died of pneumonia. They were awaiting word concerning the disposition of the body.

Clayton stood with his arms limp, the hand holding the letter and envelope dangling at his side.

"Look at the postmark," Blair said in a hoarse whisper, crossing her arms and cupping her elbows in her palms, as if she were cold. "Look at the date on the letter. It's three days before Willy's visit."

Something with a thousand tiny legs seemed to crawl up the back of Clayton's neck. He drew a deep breath. Exhaled. "A mistake, that's all. Some kind of mistake at the prison."

He looked again at the letterhead. Found a phone number. Strode into the kitchen and called the prison.

It hadn't been a mistake, the woman he talked to said. She told him she was sorry about his brother. Said, "About the remains . . . "

Clayton slowly replaced the receiver and sat staring at the phone. Blair walked into the kitchen and saw the expression on his face. Slumped down opposite him.

They stared at each other.

* * *

Andy helped Clayton plant the live tree in the backyard. Every Christmas they lovingly decorated it with strings of outdoor colored lights.

There was something—something he knew was absurd—that Clayton couldn't shake from his mind. In a place beyond lies, Willy had come face to face either with St. Peter or with the devil. Could Willy—even the magnificent faker Willy—con either of *those* two? Maybe.

Only maybe.

Which was what nagged unreasonably at Clayton. If Willy hadn't worked a con to buy his extra time on earth, had he worked a trade?

Even after Andy had grown up and left home for college, Clayton continued to decorate the stately pine tree every Christmas. And in the summer he'd unreel the garden hose and stand patiently in the glaring sun, watering the ground around its thick trunk. He'd thoroughly soak the earth beneath the carpet of brown dried needles.

It was impossible to know how deep the roots of such a tree might reach.

HOWARD ENGEL

THE THREE WISE GUYS

Jews don't celebrate Christmas, they only started it. So what's Jewish detective Benny Cooperman doing in a Christmas anthology? Howard Engel reminds us that Christmas is a time for getting together with good friends, and an author's favorite characters are not merely his creations, they're his pals. The only problem with characters like Benny is that they tend to wander off and make friends of their own who give nothing but trouble, which is how Benny wound up attending service in St. Mary's Church.

In addition to being a mystery writer, Howard Engel is a former radio executive producer for the Canadian Broadcasting Corporation and is now writer in residence at the library in Hamilton, Ontario. That's an extremely rare position, but then mystery writers, like their characters, often find themselves in unusual situations.

The visions of sugarplums dancing in my head stopped dancing and disappeared into the graveyard of interrupted dreams when the telephone rang.

"Hello?"

"Benny? I hope I didn't get you up?"

"Martha? What time is it?"

"How am I supposed to know? I haven't worn a timepiece since I lost the one my wicked old stepmother left me. I just phoned to wish you a merry Christmas, Cooperman." Martha sounded like she was on a tear and I was one of the people she shared the knowledge with by telephone. She knew I was no boozer, so I usually heard about her exploits after the fact.

"Merry Christmas yourself, Martha. Have you been up all night? I'm assuming that that gray stuff outside my dirty window is day."

"Oh, Benny, you can't be cross with me, not on Christmas. You're the only person in town I know who won't be up to his knees in wrapping paper and squalling brats this morning. Jews don't celebrate Christmas, they just started it."

"Martha, it sounds like you've been doing enough celebrating for Christian and Jew alike. Answer my question: have you been up all night?"

"Of course I have. I decided not to go down to my sister's in Bermuda. My brothers have all kicked the bucket except for Francis, and *she*, that wife of his, phoned to say that they were having an intimate inner-family celebration this year. Just sixty or seventy of her dearest and closest friends, but not her own husband's sister. There are getting to be fewer and fewer Tracys in the phone book, I said to her. *He*, Francis, wouldn't even talk to me. But I don't care, Benny. May the good Lord keep them childless, that's all. I'm not interrupting anything am I, Benny?" Martha paused here and I looked at the unslept-in half of my bed. It was as flat, clean, and un-mussed as it usually is.

"Nothing particular," I said.

"Good! I was just thinkin' about you, you little devil, and so I thought I'd give you a call."

"And so you just picked up the phone and called me at the break of day."

"Benny, it's broken, long ago. And I didn't see any russet mantle on yon high eastward hill either. Too many condos going up in Grantham, Benny. It's a bloody crime."

"Martha, who have you been celebrating with?" That stopped her for long enough for me to find my jacket with my cigarettes and get a Player's alight without actually touching a foot to bare linoleum. The fact that I upset a pile of paperbacks while doing it was only a minor catastrophe. Any day that began with a call from Martha was already separated from its fellows.

"Celebrating with?" she said, beginning to catch up with the drop in tempo. That was the only kind of drop that she would allow to escape her when she was flying high, as she obviously was this morning. I'd met Martha Tracy in 1980. She was working for a real estate tycoon, local variety, who had apparently just shot himself with a target pistol. That was when I still thought of myself as a specialist in divorce work. I guess that back then the penny still hadn't dropped that there was no more money to be made transom-gazing or standing under leaky eave troughs getting evidence of marital infractions for divorce lawyers. Don't get me wrong. When there was a buck to be made in divorce work, I was all for it. Nowadays I take what comes along and wait until it comes along, searching titles in the registry office for my cousin, Melvyn. Since our first meeting, Martha had helped me out in a few investigations. A couple of times she had put up a witness for me in her house over on Western Hill. Once she put me up when some heavies were looking for me.

Martha was almost as good on the phone as she was in person. Face to face, you saw the firm, Churchillian jaw and the solid, no-nonsense figure. At this hour in the morning, she was almost realer than real. This wasn't the first time she'd got me out of bed, it is true, but I had to remember the times when the shoe was on the other foot.

"I was celebrating with the celebrated Martha B. Tracy, that's who. I closed up the stores along St. Andrew Street and I had a little celebration that started at the Golf Club and I ended up where I always do, at midnight mass at St. Mary's, because it's just around the corner from my place."

"You caused quite a stir, I'll bet."

"It's not what your twisted little mind's thinking, Benny. I got caught in a fight with some young punks."

"During the service?"

"Sure. I hadn't gone to confession so I couldn't join in the line for Holy Communion. I was just sitting there next to the column with the poor box attached, over the left-hand side as you face the altar. Hell, you wouldn't know anyway. Have you ever been in St. Mary's?"

"Martha, I've even rung the bells." She didn't believe me, but I didn't want to slow down her story, if that's what it was planning to be. "Tell me what happened."

"I was sitting there, minding my own business, when three young punks came along and tried to grope me."

"They were after your maiden treasure, were they?"

"Don't be condescending. They were rude and violent, although in the end they ran away out the door in the transept."

"Seriously, were you hurt, Martha?"

"I'll last. I'll lay you out, Cooperman. You'll see. To be honest, they weren't after me, they were after a package wrapped in newspaper that was wedged into the corner of the pew I was in. Their interest in me was in removing an obstruction. But, Benny, how was I to know? They didn't say 'Move over,' they just started beating me up. That's what I thought they were doing. I thought they'd mistaken me for a drunk and were trying to roll me, get my purse."

"What happened to the package?"

"That's what I'm calling you about. What's the matter with your hearing? The package was full of plastic bags of a white powder, Benny. I think I scored a kilo and a half."

"You didn't score anything. They don't even say that on TV any more, Martha. Let me think. Ahnnn."

"Well?"

"I'm thinking. I'm thinking."

"You and Jack Benny. You're going to tell me to take it in to the cop shop, right?"

"It might make it easier to go to confession."

"I thought of that, when I thought about it, that's what I thought. But, cops and those young punks, Benny. They're just high school kids. Why send for the howitzers when we haven't even tried small-arms fire yet?"

"What am I in this, a BB gun? Martha, you have to tell the cops. See if you can talk to Sergeants Savas or Staziak. They won't thump those punks any more than is coming to them. Okay?"

"Now I'm thinking. It's hard, Benny, when you've been through what I've been through."

"Did anybody follow you when you left St. Mary's?"

"Yes . . . no. No, everybody'd left by the time I got up. I may have passed out from the shock of it all." There was another of her reflective pauses. "I think the service was over a good little while before I left the church. The altar candles had all been put out and there wasn't anybody hanging around the doors."

"Did anybody try to mess with you on your way home?"

"A couple of kids asked if I had any spare change. You know the way they do nowadays. They're all at it. But nobody tried to get the package from me."

"Martha, I've known you a long time, right?"

"A few summers. Yes. Why?"

"There's part of this you won't tell me. Come on, why don't you want to go to the cops? This is Benny, remember? Tell Benny."

"Aw, Benny, it's because I think I know the kids who did it. I've watched them grow up. They used to shovel the snow off my sidewalk and sell me chocolate bars I didn't need for their basketball teams. There has to be a gentler way than going for the heavy artillery."

"They could have cut your throat in church, Martha, and you're worried about getting somebody new to do your sidewalk. Come on!"

"Jason Abbott was always a nice kid. So was Lester Garvey and that other one, that Larry, whatever-his-name-is: Storchuck, I think. I think they were surprised to see me there, Benny. What am I going to do? You're the private detective."

"Private investigator. I'm not a detective. Look, Martha. This is a big drug drop. This isn't nickel and dime stuff. Those kids were making a big connection. Unless you were exaggerating about the size of that package."

"Well, I didn't actually weigh it. Maybe it's closer to a dozen ounces or so. Benny, if you'd seen their faces when they ran away—"

"You're breaking my heart, Martha. Tell me about the Little Match Girl."

"Tell me when you ever rang the bells at St. Mary's on St. Andrew Street West? That's not your local synagogue, is it?"

"I'll make this brief. Just long enough for me to check the number for Chris Savas at Niagara Regional Police. When we lived at 40 Monck Street, our neighbor, Jim O'Reilly, was a butcher until he retired. After that he was the bellringer at St. Mary's. When I was three or four, we were great pals. He used to take me on his shoulder into the church tower and I'd help him with the ropes."

"And I've lived in that parish all my life and I didn't know that, Benny. I guess the poet didn't go far enough when he said, 'Never send to know for whom the bell tolls, it tolls for thee.'"

"You can always toll a bell, Martha, but you can't tell it much. Let's get back to your problem. The solution is in calling Chris Savas at 555-6000." I repeated the number and she grudgingly wrote it down. I ended the conversation by telling her that I'd come over in about an hour. She was getting stubborn and fractious at her end of the line. She didn't want me sitting in her kitchen, she wanted the package of dope out of her house without having to send a couple of kids to jail on Christmas Day. But she agreed at last and I rolled out of bed, showered, shaved, and did all the things I didn't think I was going to do on Christmas, beginning with stepping out into the freezing world.

St. Mary's Church on St. Andrew Street West was cool and dim, the way churches should be. There was some light coming through tall pointed windows, glazed with small panes of window glass. The stained glass would come after the roof had been fixed and the steeple had been raised up to the height the architect had had in mind. There wasn't much light coming off the frozen streets anyway; even the best stained glass would have failed to inspire much in this light.

I found the column with the poor-box on the left-hand side of the church and checked the pew where Martha had been sitting. Somebody had carved a small recess in the angle of the seat, where it met the supporting plank. Long sermons and idle hands, I thought. As I was coming out, three teenagers were on their way in. They checked me out by pretending to show a keen interest in a statue of the virgin in a candle-lit side chapel. They looked about sixteen years old, maybe younger. The boy in the middle was a light-skinned black with his hair shaved close to his head up the sides. He wore it longer at the crown. The other two boys had similar cuts, except that one of them, the dark-haired one, had chevron-like cuts all the way up his skull, where the barber had cut closer to the scalp than elsewhere. They were all wearing black leather jackets and chewing gum. I stood behind them watching them and the elevated statue. As soon as I stopped, their attention was divided.

"What do you want?" asked the black kid.

"That was a royal screw-up. We heard what happened." I was trying on a part I rarely play. It might get me some information, it might get me shoved into the altar rail. "We're very cross with the three of you," I said with deliberate understatement. "What are you planning on doing about it?"

"The broad was starting to shout. We had to get away!" said the kid with the chevron haircut, who was now looking a little younger than the other two.

"You let that old bag make a monkey out of you! You know who she is at least?"

"She's—" began the black kid, then he stopped himself. "She's just somebody came to hear mass, is all. We don't know her from nobody."

"She was kicking up and making a racket. You gotta see it from our side," said the boy who'd been silent until now.

"We thought you kids could handle this."

"We told you we never done nothin' like this before. Nothin' this big."

"You never saw me before in your life and you better remember that."

"He means that's what we told Eddie Manion."

"Eddie didn't tell you to give the stuff away to women who get a little high on Christmas Eve."

"Look, mister, we didn't even want to take the stuff from Eddie."

"That's right, he twisted our arms. Said he'd tell Father Daeninckx on us if we didn't play along."

"And what did he tell you to do with it?"

"Just hold it over the long weekend and then give it back to the Dittrick Hotel."

"That's right. Now what are you going to do? Eddie's got a long memory and a short temper."

"Maybe you could explain . . ." The black kid let the words die on his tongue. The two others looked at him.

"You could do hard time getting mixed up with Eddie Manion in this."

"Yeah, we've been talkin' about that all night."

"Hey, who are you working for anyway, mister? Are you with Manion in this or what?"

"Listen you three. Manion is finished. He's all washed up, hung out to dry, and you've just had the escape of your lives if it happens. That's a big if, I'm tellin' you. You've been playing

Russian roulette with an automatic and you don't even know it."

"What the hell can we do about it?"

"If I were the three of you, I'd bury myself in homework over the holidays and forget about the street action for about six months for a start."

"Are you a nark or a cop or what?"

"Listen up, the three of you. The cops know who you are. You've been identified. Which one of you is Lester?" The two white boys fingered their black pal. "Everything depends on what you do from now on."

"Okay, okay, mister, we'll be cool, right?" The other two agreed with Lester and began backing away from me.

"Just a minute! Where can I get news to you if something should come up? I may need to get in touch over the weekend." The three huddled and when they came up for air one of them gave me the Storchuck phone number. I wrote it down and let the boys casually retreat down the aisle of the nave and through the felt-covered doors in the permanently temporary baffle that surrounded the front doors. In a moment, I heard the muffled slam of one of the three big front doors. On my own way out, I was tempted to set alight all of the candles that had gone out overnight, but I decided not to meddle in which prayers got answered and which were put on hold. I also avoided dipping my fingers into the scallop shell of holy water that stood near the entrance. I'd just spent more time in church than my whole family for the last thousand years.

When I got to Martha's, I could see that she was nursing an impressive hangover. On top of that, she seemed nervous. She reported that she had talked to a Corporal Harrow on the phone. From her face, I could see she hadn't been happy with the conversation. "Some cops ask you questions that make you feel that it's your own fault for being robbed, Benny, like you'd drawn a target on yourself and aimed the gun."

"Is he coming over?"

"That's what the man said."

"What's bothering you, Martha?"

"Does it show? I must be getting old, Benny." She was puttering about in her kitchen, wiping the perfectly clean counter with a blue cloth again and again. In the end, I managed to out-wait her and she told me about her doubts. "That Harrow fellow is convinced that the boys are part of a gang of dope peddlers."

"Well, if that package was full of dope . . ."

"I know, I know," she said, rinsing out the blue cloth. "But, Benny, he talked like they were the kingpins of the drug market. He said he'd get them if it cost him his badge."

"Excessive zeal, is that what you're complaining about?"

"Benny, look. Harrow scared me more than the kids did."

"Did you give him their names?"

Martha avoided my face. "They slipped my mind. That corporal is very intimidating. And I didn't want to get them in any more trouble than they're already in. You know what I mean?"

"Yeah," I said, watching Martha make a couple of cups of her specialty, instant tap-water coffee. "The corporal used to be a sergeant until he lost his spurs trying a fast one. I guess it's still eating him." Martha gave me a look with one of the cups. "We go back a long way together," I explained. "As a matter of fact, I don't think it will do those kids any good if Harrow finds out that I've been involved in this. I'll check back with you in a couple of hours. Okay?"

"M'yeah, I guess. Bring some pizza if you can find a place open. This town's got no consideration for single people."

I left, avoiding the broken front step, and went back home. Half an hour later, Martha called: "Benny, is it you?"

"No, it's Donner and Blitzen. What happened?"

"Well, he came over and grilled me about the whole thing, and managed to get me to give their names. Damn it, I knew I would under pressure. It's the way I'm made, Benny."

"Well, that settles their hash, I guess. Christmas in the cells. Hark the herald from the basement of the cop shop."

"It may not be as simple as that, Benny."

"You mean he still has to get you to pick them out of a lineup?"

"More than that. I opened the package before Harrow got here."

"And?"

"And I made up another package with the same sort of freezer bags. And I gave that to Harrow." Martha's voice was trailing off so that I could hardly hear her.

"What did you put in the bags, Martha?"

"Talcum," she whispered.

"Talcum!"

"Well, I had an extra supply from the time I had athlete's foot a year ago."

Martha never ceased amazing me, but I didn't tell her and I didn't bore her about tampering with evidence either. I was too busy with a scheme that was coming together in my own head. Over the phone I gave Martha the Storchuck boy's phone number. I briefed her on what to say to him. She mumbled agreement that with Martha often means the opposite and I went out to track down a very special pizza.

In the end, I had to settle for a run of the loom model that looked like it had collected the anchovies from at least fifty earlier jobs. When I got it to Martha's place, I checked the landscape for patrol cars. The coast was as clear as the night that was beginning to fall. I could count sharp, untwinkling stars overhead between the wisps of clouds. Lack of cloud cover let the cold in, or at least that's what I've always been told.

The broken step nearly undid my sore back, but I managed to get to her door without further injury. I could hear her coming before I laid a glove on the door. "Pizza!" I announced and handed in the cardboard box, which was beginning to sag. Martha carried

it to the porcelain-topped old-fashioned kitchen table and opened
the lid.

"Perfect," she said. "Help yourself to beer in the icebox." A lot
of people in Grantham still say icebox even though they've never
seen one. Martha had, so I made allowances as I took the tops off
two ales. Martha hated what she called the "play-beer" that was
advertised on television.

Martha and I toasted one another and helped ourselves to the
first of the gooey wedges of dripping cheese and pastry. Martha
was drinking her second beer by now, and telling me, as she often
did, about the time she came to her senses next to a provincial
cabinet minister in a roadhouse outside Fredericton, New Bruns-
wick, staring down into the remains of a congealed pizza. It must
have been the sad story of her life judging by the number of times
she recounted the tale.

"Do you think your scheme will work, Benny?"

"We won't know until we hear about it on TV or read about it
in the paper on the day after Boxing day," I said. "I can even see
the headline, Martha: DRUG KINGPIN NAILED WITH KILO OF COKE."

"Manion will be the most surprised guilty party the cops ever
pulled in in a raid," said Martha. "It took a twisted mind like yours
to think up such a diabolical plot."

"Martha, you did most of it when you made the fake package of
talcum. I mean the talcum was real, only—"

"I can read your mind. Don't bother to finish."

"Manion wanted the stuff out of his place, the Dittrick Hotel,
until after the long weekend. That meant he'd been tipped off that
the hotel was going to be raided."

"What better time than Christmas?"

"When it happens, he's going to get the surprise of his life. The
kid will know where to hide the stuff where even a dumb cop can't
miss it."

"And the three kids? Don't forget Harrow is hot on their trail."

"Yes, and when he catches them, he can arrest them for possession."

"No he can't. They are not in possession."

"Well, he could get them on conspiring to commit an indictable offense. Only, once the lab checks it out, Harrow will find his case against the guys has exploded in a puff of talcum powder."

"Even if they'd been caught with a ton of it, there's no law that says you can't own as much talcum as you want." Here Martha's face fell. If I hadn't been almost nose to nose with her across the table, I might have missed it.

"What is it, Martha?"

"I was just trying to remember. No. I'm *sure* it was the talcum I gave him. I'm eighty percent sure of it."

MARY HIGGINS CLARK

THAT'S THE TICKET

People like to dream of a white Christmas, but the chances are that a good many would settle happily for a green one. Who hasn't dreamed also of hitting the lottery? And who other than that kind and generous lady, best-selling author Mary Higgins Clark, would have thought of making one lucky player's dream come true? But collecting on a lottery ticket is like getting gold from a leprechaun—you mustn't let yourself be distracted for one single instant, or you may find Christmas green has turned to poison ivy.

If Wilma Bean had not been in Philadelphia visiting her sister Dorothy, it never would have happened. Ernie, knowing that Wilma had watched the drawing on television, would have rushed home at midnight from his job as a security guard at the Do-Shop-Here Mall in Paramus, New Jersey, and they'd have celebrated together. *Two million dollars!* That was their share of the special Christmas lottery.

Instead, because Wilma was in Philadelphia paying a pre-Christmas visit to her sister Dorothy, Ernie stopped at the Friendly Shamrock Watering Hole for a pop or two and then topped off the evening at the Harmony Bar six blocks from his home in Elmwood Park. There, nodding happily to Lou the owner-bartender, Ernie ordered his third Seven and Seven of the evening, wrapped his plump sixty-year-old legs around the bar stool, and dreamily reflected on how he and Wilma would spend their newfound wealth.

It was then that his faded blue eyes fell upon Loretta Thistle-bottom who was perched on the corner stool against the wall, a stein of beer in one hand, a Marlboro in the other. Ernie thought Loretta was a very attractive woman. Tonight her brilliant blond hair curled on her shoulders in a pageboy, her pinkish lipstick complemented her large purple-accented green eyes, and her generous bosom rose and fell with sensuous regularity.

Ernie observed Loretta with almost impersonal admiration. It was well known that Loretta Thistlebottom's husband, Jimbo Potters, a beefy truck driver, was extremely proud of the fact that Loretta had been a dancer in her early days and was also extremely jealous of her. It was hinted he wasn't above knocking Loretta around if she got too friendly with other men.

However, since Lou the bartender was Jimbo's cousin, Jimbo didn't mind if Loretta sat around the bar the nights Jimbo was on a long-distance haul. After all it was a neighborhood hangout. Plenty of wives came in with their husbands and as Loretta frequently commented, "Jimbo can't expect me to watch the tube by myself or go to Tupperware parties whenever he's carting garlic buds or bananas along Route 1. As a person born in the trunk to a prominent show business family, I need people around."

Her show business career was the subject of much of Loretta's conversation and tended to grow in importance as the years passed. That was also why even though she was legally Mrs. Jimbo Potters, Loretta still referred to herself as Thistlebottom, her stage name.

Now in the murky light shed by the Tiffany-type globe over the well-scarred bar, Ernie silently admired Loretta, reflecting that even though she had to be in her mid-fifties, she had kept her figure very, very well. However, he wasn't really concerned about her. The winning lottery ticket, which he had pinned to his undershirt, was warming the area around his heart. It was like having a glowing fire there. Two million dollars. That was one hundred thousand dollars a year less taxes for twenty years. They'd be collecting well into the twenty-first century. By then they might even be able to take a cook's tour to the moon.

Ernie tried to visualize the expression on Wilma's face when she heard the good news. Wilma's sister, Dorothy, didn't have a television and seldom listened to the radio so down in Philadelphia Wilma wouldn't know that now she was wealthy. The minute he'd heard the good news on his portable radio, Ernie had been tempted to rush to the phone and call Wilma but immediately decided that that wouldn't be fun. Now Ernie smiled happily, his round face creasing into a merry pancake as he visualized Wilma's homecoming tomorrow. He'd pick her up at the train station at Newark. She'd ask him how close they'd come to winning. "Did we have two of the numbers? Three of the numbers?" He'd tell her they didn't even have one of the winning combination. Then when they got home, she'd find her stocking hung on the mantel, the way they used to do when they were first married. In those days Wilma had worn stockings and garters. Now she wore queen-sized pantyhose so she'd have to dig down to the toe for the ticket. He'd say, "Just keep looking; wait till you see the surprise." He could just picture the way she'd scream and throw her arms around him.

Wilma had been a darn cute young girl when they were married forty years ago. She still had a pretty face and her hair a soft white-blond was naturally wavy. She wasn't a showgirl type like Loretta but she suited him just right. Sometimes she got a little cranky about the fact that he liked to bend the elbow with the boys now and then but for the most part, Wilma was A-okay. And boy, what a Christmas they'd have this year. Maybe he'd take her to Fred the Furrier and get her a mouton lamb or something.

Contemplating the pleasure it would be to manifest his generosity, Ernie ordered his fourth Seven and Seven. His attention was diverted by the fact that Loretta Thistlebottom was engaged in a strange ritual. Every minute or two, she laid the cigarette in her right hand in the ashtray, the stein of beer in her left hand on the bar, and vigorously scratched the palm, fingers, and back of her right hand with the long pointed fingernails of her left hand. Ernie observed that her right hand was inflamed, angry red and covered with small, mean-looking blisters.

It was getting late and people were starting to leave. The couple who had been sitting next to Ernie and at a right angle to Loretta departed. Loretta, noticing that Ernie was watching her, shrugged. "Poison ivy," she explained. "Would you believe poison ivy in December? That dumb sister of Jimbo decided she had a green thumb and made her poor jerk of a husband rig up a greenhouse off their kitchen. So what does she grow? Weeds and poison ivy. That takes real talent." Loretta shrugged and repossessed the stein of beer and her cigarette. "So how ye been, Ernie? Anything new in your life?"

Ernie was cautious. "Not much."

Loretta sighed. "Me neither. Same old stuff. Jimbo and me are saving to get out of here next year when he retires. Everyone tells me Fort Lauderdale is a real swinging place. Jimbo's getting piles from all these years driving the rig. I keep telling him how much money I could make as a waitress to help out but he don't want anyone flirting with me." Loretta scratched her hand against the bar and shook her head. "Can you imagine after twenty-five years, Jimbo still thinks every guy in the world wants me? I kind of love it but it can be a pain in the neck, too." Loretta sighed, a world-weary sigh. "Jimbo's the most passionate guy I ever knew and that's saying something. But as my mother used to say, a good roll in the sack is even better when there's a full wallet between the spring and mattress."

"Your mother said that?" Ernie was bemused at the practical wisdom. He began to sip his fourth Seagrams and Seven-Up.

Loretta nodded. "She was a million laughs but she told it straight. The heck with it. Maybe someday I'll win the lottery."

The temptation was too great. Ernie slipped over the two

empty bar stools as fast as his out-of-shape body would permit. "Too bad you don't have my luck," he whispered.

As Lou the bartender yelled, "Last call, folks," Ernie patted his massive chest in the spot directly over his heart.

"Like they say, Loretta, 'X marks the spot.' There were sixteen winnin' tickets in the special Christmas drawing. One of them is right here pinned to my underwear." Ernie realized that his tongue was beginning to feel pretty heavy. His voice sank into a furtive whisper. *"Two million dollars.* How about that?" He put his finger to his lips and winked.

Loretta dropped her cigarette and let it burn unnoticed on the long-suffering surface of the bar. *"You're kidding!"*

"I'm not kidding." Now it was a real effort to talk. "Wilma 'n me always bet the same number 1-9-4-7-5-2. 1947 'cause that was the year I got out of high school. 'Fifty-two, the year Wee Willie was born." His triumphant smile left no doubt to his sincerity. "Crazy thing is Wilma don't even know yet. She's visiting her sister Dorothy and won't get home till tomorrow."

Fumbling for his wallet, Ernie signaled for his check. Lou came over and watched as Ernie stood uncertainly on the suddenly tilting floor. "Ernie, wait around," Lou ordered. "You're bombed. I'll drive you home when I close up. You gotta leave your car here."

Insulted, Ernie started for the door. Lou was insinuating he was tanked. What a nerve. Ernie opened the door of the women's restroom and was in a stall before he realized his mistake.

Sliding off the bar stool, Loretta said hurriedly, "Lou, I'll drop him off. He only lives two blocks from me."

Lou's skinny forehead furrowed. "Jimbo might not like it."

"So don't tell him." They watched as Ernie lurched unsteadily out from the women's restroom. "For Pete sake, do you think he'll make a pass at me?" she asked scornfully.

Lou made a decision. "You're doing me a favor, Loretta. *But don't tell Jimbo."*

Loretta let out her fulsome ha-ha bellow. "Do you think I want to risk my new caps? They won't be paid for for another year."

From somewhere behind him Ernie vaguely heard the din of voices and laughter. Suddenly he was feeling pretty rotten. The speckled pattern of the tile floor began to dance, causing a sickening whirl of dots to revolve before his eyes. He felt someone grasp his arm. "I'm gonna drop you off, Ernie." Through the roaring in his ears, Ernie recognized Loretta's voice.

"Damn nice of you, Loretta," he mumbled. "Guess I chelebrated too much." Vaguely he realized that Lou was saying something about having a Christmas drink on the house when he came back for his car.

In Loretta's aging Bonneville Pontiac he leaned his head back against the seat and closed his eyes. He was unaware that they had reached his driveway until he felt Loretta shaking him awake. "Gimme your key, Ernie. I'll help you in."

His arm around her shoulders, she steadied him along the walk. Ernie heard the scraping of the key in the lock, felt his feet moving through the living room down the brief length of the hallway.

"Which one?"

"Which one?" Ernie couldn't get his tongue to move.

"Which bedroom?" Loretta's voice sounded irritated. "Come on, Ernie, you're no feather to drag around. Oh, forget it. It has to be the other one. This one's full of those statues of birds your daughter makes. Cripes, you couldn't give them away as a door prize in a looney bin. No one's *that* nutty."

Ernie felt a flash of instinctive resentment at Loretta's putdown of his daughter, Wilma Jr., Wee Willie as he called her. Wee Willie had real talent. Someday she'd be a famous sculptor. She'd lived in New Mexico ever since she dropped out of school in '68 and supported herself working evenings as a waitress at McDonald's. Days she made pottery and sculpted birds.

Ernie felt himself being turned around and pushed down. His knees buckled and he heard the familiar squeak of the boxspring.

Sighing in gratitude, in one simultaneous movement, he stretched out and passed out.

Wilma Bean and her sister Dorothy had had a pleasant day. In small doses Wilma enjoyed being with Dorothy who was sixty-three to Wilma's fifty-eight. The trouble was that Dorothy was very opinionated and highly critical of both Ernie and Wee Willie and Wilma could take just so much of that. But she was sorry for Dorothy. Dorothy's husband had walked out on her ten years before and now was living high on the hog with his second wife, a karate instructor. Dorothy and her daughter-in-law did not get along very well. Dorothy still worked part-time as a claims adjuster in an insurance office and as she frequently told Wilma, "the phony claims don't get past me."

Very few people believed they were sisters. Dorothy was, as Ernie put it, like one side of eleven, just straight up and down with thin gray hair which she wore in a tight knot at the back of her head. Ernie always said she should have been cast as Carrie Nation; she'd have looked good with a hatchet in her hand. Wilma knew that Dorothy was still jealous that Wilma had been the pretty one and that even though she'd gotten heavy, her face hadn't wrinkled or even changed very much. But still, Wilma theorized, blood is thicker than water and a weekend in Philadelphia every four months or so and particularly around holiday time was always enjoyable.

The afternoon of the lottery drawing day, Dorothy picked Wilma up from the train station. They had a late lunch at Burger King, then drove around the neighborhood where Grace Kelly had been raised. They had both been her avid fans. After mutually agreeing that Prince Albert ought to marry, that Princess Caroline had certainly calmed down and was doing a fine job, and that Princess Stephanie should be slapped into a convent until she straightened out, they went to a movie, then back to Dorothy's apartment. She had cooked a chicken and over dinner, late into the evening, they gossiped.

Dorothy complained to Wilma that her daughter-in-law had no idea how to raise a child and was too stubborn to accept even the most helpful suggestions.

"Well, at least you have grandchildren," Wilma sighed. "No wedding bells in sight for Wee Willie. She has her heart set on her sculpting career."

"What sculpting career?" Dorothy snapped.

"If we could just afford a good teacher," Wilma sighed, trying to ignore the dig.

"Ernie shouldn't encourage Willie," Dorothy said bluntly. "Tell him not to make such a fuss over that junk she sends home. Your place looks like a crazy man's version of a birdhouse. How is Ernie? I hope you're keeping him out of bars. Mark my words. He has the makings of an alcoholic. All those broken veins in his nose."

Wilma thought of the outsized Christmas boxes that had arrived from Wee Willie a few days ago. Marked *Do not open till Christmas*, they'd been accompanied by a note. "Ma, wait till you see these. I'm into peacocks and parrots." Wilma also thought of the staff Christmas party at the Do-Shop-Here Mall the other night when Ernie had gotten schnockered and pinched the bottom of one of the waitresses.

Knowing that Dorothy was right about Ernie's ability to lap up booze did not ease Wilma's resentment at having the truth pointed out to her. "Well, Ernie may get silly when he has a drop or two too much but you're wrong about Wee Willie. She has real talent and when my ship comes in I'll help her to prove it."

Dorothy helped herself to another cup of tea. "I suppose you're still wasting money on lottery tickets."

"Sure am," Wilma said cheerfully, fighting to retain her good nature. "Tonight's the special Christmas drawing. If I were home I'd be in front of the set praying."

"That combination of numbers you always pick is ridiculous! 1-9-4-7-5-2. I can understand a person using the year her child was born but the year Ernie graduated from high school? That's ridiculous."

Wilma had never told Dorothy that it had taken Ernie six years to get through high school and his family had had a block party to celebrate. "Best party I was ever at," he frequently told her, memory brightening his face. "Even the mayor came."

Anyhow, Wilma liked that combination of numbers. She was absolutely certain that someday they would win a lot of money for her and Ernie. After she said good night to Dorothy and puffing with the effort made up the sofabed where she slept on her visits, she reflected that as Dorothy grew older she got crankier. She also talked your ear off and it was no wonder her daughter-in-law referred to her as "that miserable pain in the neck."

The next day Wilma got off the train in Newark at noon. Ernie was picking her up. As she walked to their meeting spot at the main entrance to the terminal she was alarmed to see Ben Gump, their next-door neighbor, there instead.

She rushed to Ben, her ample body tensed with fear. "Is anything wrong? Where's Ernie?"

Ben's wispy face broke into a reassuring smile. "No, everything's just fine, Wilma. Ernie woke up with a touch of flu or something. Asked me to come for you. Heck, I've got nothing to do 'cept watch the grass grow." Ben laughed heartily at the witticism that had become his trademark since his retirement.

"Flu," Wilma scoffed. "I'll bet."

Ernie was a reasonably quiet man and Wilma had looked forward to a restful drive home. At breakfast, Dorothy, knowing she was losing her captive audience, had talked nonstop, a waterfall of acid comments that had made Wilma's head throb.

To distance herself from Ben's snail-paced driving and long-winded stories, Wilma concentrated on the pleasurable excitement of looking in the paper the minute she arrived home and checking the lottery results. 1-9-4-7-5-2, 1-9-4-7-5-2, she chanted to herself. It was silly. The drawing was over but even so she had a *good* feeling. Certainly Ernie would have phoned her if they'd won but even coming close, like getting three or four of the six numbers, made her know that their luck was changing.

She spotted the fact the car wasn't in the driveway and guessed the reason. It was probably parked at the Harmony Bar. She managed to get rid of Ben Gump at the door, thanking him profusely for picking her up but ignoring his broad hints that he sure could use a cup of coffee. Then Wilma went straight to the bedroom. As she'd expected, Ernie was in bed. The covers were pulled to the tip of his nose. One look told her he had a massive hangover. "When the cat's away the mouse will play." She sighed. "I hope your head feels like a balloon-sized rock."

In her annoyance, she knocked over the four-foot-high pelican that Wee Willie had sent for Thanksgiving and that was perched on a table just outside the bedroom door. As it clattered to the floor, it took with it the pottery vase, an early work of Wee Willie's, and the arrangement of plastic baby's breath and poinsettias Wilma had labored over in preparation for Christmas.

Sweeping up the broken vase, rearranging the flowers and restoring the pelican, now missing a section of one wing, to the tabletop stretched Wilma's patience to the breaking point.

But the thought of the magic moment of looking up to see how close they'd come to winning the lottery and maybe finding that this time they'd come *really* close restored her to her usual good temper. She made a cup of coffee and fixed cinnamon toast before she settled at the kitchen table and opened the paper.

Sixteen Lucky Winners Share Thirty-Two Million Dollar Prize, the headline read.

Sixteen lucky winners. Oh to be one of them. Wilma slid her hand over the winning combination. She'd read the numbers one digit at a time. It was more fun that way.

1-9-4-7-5

Wilma sucked in her breath. Her head was pounding. Was it possible? In an agony of suspense she removed her palm from the final number.

2

Her shriek and the sound of the kitchen chair toppling over caused Ernie to sit bolt upright in bed. Judgement Day was at hand.

Wilma rushed into the room, her face transfixed. "Ernie, why didn't you tell me? *Give me the ticket!*"

Ernie's head sunk down on his neck. His voice was a broken whisper. "I lost it."

Loretta had known it was inevitable. Even so, the sight of Wilma Bean marching up the snow-dusted cement walk followed by a reluctant, downcast Ernie did cause a moment of sheer panic. "Forget it," Loretta told herself. "They don't have a leg to stand on." She'd covered her tracks completely, she promised herself as Wilma and Ernie came up the steps to the porch between the two evergreens that Loretta had decked out with dozens of Christmas lights. She had her story straight. She had walked Ernie to the door of his home. Anyone knowing how jealous Big Jimbo was would understand that Loretta would not step beyond the threshold of another man's home when his wife wasn't present.

When Wilma asked about the ticket, Loretta would ask "what ticket?" Ernie never *mentioned* a ticket to her. He was in no condition to talk about anything sensible. Ask Lou. Ernie was pie-eyed after a coupla drinks. He'd probably stopped somewhere else first.

Did Loretta buy a lottery ticket for the special Christmas drawing? Sure she bought some. Wanna see them? Every week when she thought of it, she'd pick up a few. Never in the same place. Maybe at the liquor store, the stationery store. You know just for luck. Always numbers she thought of off the top of her head.

Loretta scratched her right hand viciously. Damn poison ivy. She had the 1-9-4-7-5-2 winning ticket safely hidden in the sugar bowl of her best china. You had a year to claim your winnings. Just before the year was up, she'd "accidentally" come across it. Let Wilma and Ernie try to howl that it was theirs.

The bell rang. Loretta patted her bright gold hair which she'd teased into the tossed salad look, straightened the shoulder pads of her brilliantly sequined sweater, and hurried to the closet-sized foyer. As she opened the door she willed her face to become a wreath of smiles not even minding that she was trying not to smile too much. Her face was starting to wrinkle, a genetic family problem. She constantly worried about the fact that by age sixty her mother's face had looked as though it could hold nine days of rain. "Wilma, Ernie, what a delightful surprise," she gushed. "Come in. Come in."

Loretta decided to ignore the fact that neither Wilma nor Ernie answered her, that neither bothered to brush the snow from their overshoes on the foyer mat that specifically invited guests to do that very thing, that they had no friendly holiday smiles to match her greeting.

Wilma declined the invitation to sit down, to have a cup of tea or a Bloody Mary. She made her case clear. Ernie had been holding a two-million-dollar lottery ticket. He'd told Loretta about it at the Harmony Bar. Loretta had driven him home from the Harmony, gotten him into his room. Ernie had passed out and the ticket was gone.

In 1945 before she became a full-time hoofer, Loretta had studied acting at the Sonny Tufts School for Thespians. Drawing on the long-ago experience, she earnestly and sincerely performed her well-practiced scenario for Wilma and Ernie. Ernie never breathed a word to her about a winning ticket. She only drove him home as a favor to him and to Lou. Lou couldn't leave and anyhow Lou's such a runt, he couldn't fight Ernie for the car keys. "At least you agreed to let me drive," Loretta said to Ernie indignantly. "I took my life in my hands just letting you snore your way home in my car." She turned to Wilma and woman-to-woman reminded her: "You know how jealous Jimbo is of me, silly man. You'd think I was sixteen. But no way do I go into your house unless you're there, Wilma. Ernie, you got smashed real fast at the Harmony. Just ask Lou. Did you stop anywhere else first and maybe talk to someone about the ticket?"

Loretta congratulated herself as she watched the doubt and confusion on both their faces. A few minutes later they left. "I hope you find it. I'll say a prayer," she promised piously. She would not shake hands with them, explaining to Wilma about her dumb sister-in-law's greenhouse harvest of poison ivy. "Come have a Christmas drink with Jimbo and me," she urged. "He'll be home about four o'clock Christmas Eve."

At home, sitting glumly over a cup of tea, Wilma said, "She's lying. I know she's lying but who could prove it? Fifteen winners have shown up already. One missing and with a year to claim." Frustrated tears rolled unnoticed down Wilma's cheeks. "She'll let the whole world know she buys a ticket here, a ticket there. She'll do that for the next fifty-one weeks and then *bingo* she'll find the ticket she forgot she had."

Ernie watched his wife in abject silence. A weeping Wilma was an infrequent sight. Now as her face blotched and her nose began to run, he handed her his red bandana handkerchief. His sudden gesture caused a ceramic hummingbird to fall off the sideboard behind him. The beak of the hummingbird crumbled against the imitation marble tile in the breakfast nook of the kitchen and brought a fresh wail of grief from Wilma.

"My big hope was that Wee Willie could give up working nights at McDonald's and study and do her birds full-time," Wilma sobbed. "And now that dream is busted."

Just to be absolutely sure, they went to the Friendly Shamrock near the Do-Shop-Here Mall in Paramus. The evening bartender confirmed that Ernie had been there the night before just around midnight, had two maybe three drinks but never said boo to nobody. "Just sat there grinning like the cat who ate the canary."

After a dinner which neither of them touched Wilma carefully examined Ernie's undershirt which still had the safety pin in place. "She didn't even bother to unpin it," Wilma said bitterly. "Just reached in and tore it off."

"Can we sue her?" Ernie suggested tentatively. The enormity of his stupidity kept building by the minute. Getting drunk. Talking his head off to Loretta.

Too tired to even answer, Wilma opened the suitcase she had not yet unpacked and reached for her flannel nightgown. "Sure we can sue her," she said sarcastically, "for having a fast brain when she's dealing with a wet brain. Now turn off the light, go to sleep, and quit that damn scratching. You're driving me crazy."

Ernie was tearing at his chest in the area around his heart. "Something itches," he complained.

A bell sounded in Wilma's head as she closed her eyes. She was so worn out she fell asleep almost immediately but her dreams were filled with lottery tickets floating through the air like snowflakes. From time to time she was pulled awake by Ernie's restless movements. Usually Ernie slept like a hibernating bear.

Christmas Eve dawned gray and cheerless. Wilma dragged herself around the house, going through the motions of putting presents under the tree. The two boxes from Wee Willie. If they hadn't lost the winning ticket they could have phoned Wee Willie to come home for Christmas. Maybe she wouldn't have come. Wee Willie didn't like the middle-class trap of the suburban environment. In that case Ernie could have thrown up his job and they could have visited her in Arizona soon. And Wilma could have bought the forty-inch television that had so awed her in Trader Horn's last week. Just think of seeing J. R. forty inches big.

Oh well. Spilt milk. No, spilt *booze*. Ernie had told her about his plans to put the lottery ticket in her pantyhose on the mantel of the fake fireplace if he hadn't lost it. Wilma tried not to dwell on the thrill of finding the ticket there.

She was not pleasant to Ernie who was still hung over and had phoned in sick for the second day. She told him exactly where he could stuff his headache.

In mid-afternoon, Ernie went into the bedroom and closed the door. After a while, Wilma became alarmed and followed him. Ernie was sitting on the edge of the bed, his shirt off, plaintively scratching his chest. "I'm all right," he said, his face still covered with the hangdog expression that was beginning to seem permanent. "It's just I'm so damn itchy."

Only slightly relieved that Ernie had not found some way to commit suicide, Wilma asked irritably, "What are you so itchy about. It isn't time for your allergies to start. I hear enough about them all summer."

She looked closely at the inflamed skin. "For God's sake, that's poison ivy. Where did you manage to pick that up?"

Poison ivy.

They stared at each other.

Wilma grabbed Ernie's undershirt from the top of the dresser. She'd left it there, the safety pin still in it, the sliver of ticket a silent, hostile witness to his stupidity. "Put it on," she ordered.

"But . . ."

"Put it on!"

It was instantly evident that the poison ivy was centered in the exact spot where the ticket had been hidden.

"That lying hoofer." Wilma thrust out her jaw and straightened her shoulders. "She said that Big Jimbo was gonna be home around four, didn't she?"

"I think so."

"Good. Nothing like a reception committee."

At three-thirty they pulled in front of Loretta's house and parked. As they'd expected, Jimbo's sixteen-wheel rig was not yet there. "We'll sit here for a few minutes and make that crook nervous," Wilma decreed.

They watched as the vertical blinds in the front window of Loretta's house began to bob erratically. At three minutes of four, Ernie pointed a nervous hand. "There. At the light. That's Jimbo's truck."

"Let's go, " Wilma told him.

Loretta opened the door, her face again wreathed in a smile. With grim satisfaction Wilma noticed that the smile was very, very nervous.

"Ernie. Wilma. How nice. You did come for a Christmas drink."

"I'll have my Christmas drink later," Wilma told her. "And it'll be to celebrate getting our ticket back. How's your poison ivy, Loretta?"

"Oh, starting to clear up. Wilma, I don't like the tone of your voice."

"That's a crying shame." Wilma walked past the sectional which was upholstered in a red-and-black checkered pattern, went to the window, and pulled back the vertical blind. "Well, what do you know? Here's Big Jimbo. Guess you two lovebirds can't wait to get your hands on each other. Guess he'll be real mad when I tell him I'm suing you for heartburn because you've been fooling around with my husband."

"I've what?" Loretta's carefully applied purple-kisses lipstick deepened as her complexion faded to grayish white.

"You heard me. And I got proof. Ernie, take off your shirt. Show this husband-stealer your rash."

"Rash," Loretta moaned.

"Poison ivy just like yours. Started on his chest when you stuck your hand under his underwear to get the ticket. Go ahead. Deny it. Tell Jimbo you don't know nothing about a ticket, that you and Ernie were just having a go at a little hanky-panky."

"You're lying. Get out of here. Ernie, don't unbutton that shirt." Frantically Loretta grabbed Ernie's hands.

"My what a big man Jimbo is," Wilma said admiringly as he got out of the truck. She waved to him. "A real big man." She turned. "Take off your pants too, Ernie." Wilma dropped the vertical blind and hurried over to Loretta. "He's got the rash *down there*," she whispered.

"Oh, my God. I'll get it. I'll get it. Keep your pants on!" Loretta rushed to the junior-sized dining room and flung open the china closet that contained the remnants of her mother's china. With shaking fingers she reached for the sugar bowl. It dropped from her hands and smashed as she grabbed the lottery ticket. Jimbo's key was turning in the door as she jammed the ticket in Wilma's hand. "Now get out. And don't say nothing."

Wilma sat down on the red-and-black checkered couch. "It would look real funny to rush out. Ernie and I will join you and Big Jimbo in a Christmas drink."

The houses on their block were decorated with Santa Clauses on the roofs, angels on the lawn, and ropes of lights framing the outside of the windows. With a peaceful smile as they arrived home, Wilma remarked how real pretty the neighborhood was. Inside the house, she handed the lottery ticket to Ernie. "Put this in my stocking just the way you meant to."

Meekly he went into the bedroom and selected her favorite pantyhose, the white ones with rhinestones. She fished in his drawer and came out with one of his dress-up argyle socks, somewhat lumpy because Wilma wasn't much of a knitter but still his best. As they tacked the stockings to the mantel over the artificial fireplace, Ernie said, "Wilma, I don't have poison ivy," his voice sunk into a faint whisper, "down there."

"I'm sure you don't but it did the trick. Now just put the ticket in my stocking and I'll put your present in yours."

"You bought me a present? After all the trouble I caused? Oh, Wilma."

"I didn't buy it. I dug it out of the medicine cabinet and put a bow on it." Smiling happily, Wilma dropped a bottle of calamine lotion into Ernie's argyle sock.

BILL PRONZINI

HERE COMES SANTA CLAUS

*Meet Bill Pronzini's favorite character. Bill's written sev-
enteen full-length novels and a short-story collection about him,
and has collaborated with Marcia Muller on a book called
Double that features him along with Muller's private eye,
Sharon McCone.*

*Bill says he's a joy to write about, Bill knows him so well that
the stories just flow naturally and it's more fun than work. But
don't ask what this paragon's name is, because even Bill
Pronzini himself doesn't know.*

*The author was not at all sure how his fictional alter ego was
going to enjoy playing Santa Claus for a charity benefit,
though. As this one turned out, he had every reason to worry.
Even a big, jolly Nameless Detective can have serious trouble
with his "ho, ho, ho" when he finds himself with fake whiskers
on his face, a pillow stuffed under his belt, and a spectacularly
rotten little kid on his knee.*

Kerry sprang her little surprise on me the week before Christmas. And the worst thing about it was, I was no longer fat. The
forty-pound bowlful of jelly that had once hung over my belt was
long gone.

"That doesn't matter," she said. "You can wear a pillow."

"Why me?" I said.

"They made me entertainment chairperson, for one thing. And
for another, you're the biggest and jolliest man I know."

117

"Ho, ho, ho," I said sourly.

"It's for a good cause. Lots of good causes—needy children, the homeless, three other charities. Where's your Christmas spirit?"

"I don't have any. Why don't you ask Eberhardt?"

"Are you serious? *Eberhardt?*"

"Somebody else, then. Anybody else."

"You," she said.

"Uh-uh. No. I love you madly and I'll do just about anything for you, but not this. This is where I draw the line."

"Oh, come on, quit acting like a scrooge."

"I *am* a scrooge. Bah, humbug."

"You like kids, you know you do—"

"I don't like kids. Where did you get that idea?"

"I've seen you with kids, that's where."

"An act, just an act."

"So put it on again for the Benefit. Five o'clock until nine, four hours out of your life to help the less fortunate. Is that too much to ask?"

"In this case, yes."

She looked at me. Didn't say anything, just looked at me.

"*No,*" I said. "There's no way I'm going to wear a Santa Claus suit and dandle little kiddies on my knee. You hear me? Absolutely no way!"

"Ho, ho, ho," I said.

The little girl perched on my knee looked up at me out of big round eyes. It was the same sort of big round-eyed stare Kerry had given me the previous week.

"Are you *really* Santa Claus?" she asked.

"Yes indeed. And who would you be?"

"Melissa."

"That's a pretty name. How old are you, Melissa?"

"Six and a half."

"Six and a half. Well, well. Tell old Santa what it is you want for Christmas."

"A dolly."

"What sort of dolly?"

"A big one."

"Just a big one? No special kind?"

"Yes. A dolly that you put water in her mouth and she wee-wees on herself."

I sighed. "Ho, ho, ho," I said.

The Gala Family Christmas Charity Benefit was being held in the Lowell High School gymnasium, out near Golden Gate Park. Half a dozen San Francisco businesses were sponsoring it, including Bates and Carpenter, the ad agency where Kerry works as a senior copywriter, so it was a pretty elaborate affair. The decoration committee had dressed the gym up to look like a cross between Santa's Village and the Dickens Christmas Fair. There was a huge gaudy tree, lots of red-and-green bunting and seasonal decorations, big clusters of holly and mistletoe, even fake snow; and the staff members were costumed as elves and other creatures imaginary and real. Carols and traditional favorites poured out of loudspeakers. Booths positioned along the walls dispensed food— meat pies, plum pudding, gingerbread, and other sweets—and a variety of handmade toys and crafts, all donated. For the adults, there were a couple of city-sanctioned games of chance and a bar supplying wassail and other Christmassy drinks.

For the kiddies, there was me.

I sat on a thronelike chair on a raised dais at one end, encased in false whiskers and wig and paunch, red suit and cap, black boots and belt. All around me were cotton snowdrifts, a toy bag overflowing with gaily wrapped packages, a shiny papier-mâché version of Santa's sleigh with some cardboard reindeer. A couple of young women dressed as elves were there, too, to act as my helpers. Their smiles were as phony as my whiskers and paunch;

they were only slightly less miserable than I was. For snaking out to one side and halfway across the packed enclosure was a line of little children the Pied Piper of Hamlin would have envied, some with their parents, most without, and all eager to clamber up onto old St. Nick's lap and share with him their innermost desires.

Inside the Santa suit, I was sweating—and not just because it was warm in there. I imagined that every adult eye was on me, that snickers were lurking in every adult throat. This was ridiculous, of course, the more so because none of the two hundred or so adults in attendance knew Santa's true identity. I had made Kerry swear an oath that she wouldn't tell anybody, especially not my partner, Eberhardt, who would never let me hear the end of it if he knew. No more than half a dozen of those present knew me anyway, this being a somewhat ritzy crowd; and of those who did know me, three were members of the private security staff.

Still, I felt exposed and vulnerable and acutely uncomfortable. I felt the way you would if you suddenly found yourself naked on a crowded city street. And I kept thinking: What if one of the newspaper photographers recognizes me and decides to take my picture? What if Eberhardt finds out? Or Barney Rivera or Joe DeFalco or one of my other so-called friends?

Another kid was on his way toward my lap. I smiled automatically and sneaked a look at my watch. My God! It seemed as though I'd been here at least two hours, but only forty-five minutes had passed since the opening ceremonies. More than three hours left to go. Close to two hundred minutes. Nearly twelve thousand seconds . . .

The new kid climbed onto my knee. While he was doing that, one of those near the front of the line, overcome at the prospect of his own imminent audience with the Nabob of the North Pole, began to make a series of all-too-familiar sounds. Another kid said, "Oh, gross, he's gonna throw up!" Fortunately, however, the sick one's mother was with him; she managed to get him out of there in time, to the strains of "Walking in a Winter Wonderland."

I thought: What if he'd been sitting on my lap instead of standing in line?

I thought: Kerry, I'll get you for this, Kerry.

I listened to the new kid's demands, and thought about all the other little hopeful piping voices I would have to listen to, and sweated and smiled and tried not to squirm. If I squirmed, people *would* start to snicker—the kids as well as the adults. They'd think Santa had to go potty and was trying not to wee-wee on himself.

This one had cider-colored hair. He said, "You're not Santa Claus."

"Sure I am. Don't I look like Santa?"

"No. Your face isn't red and you don't have a nose like a cherry."

"What's your name, sonny?"

"Ronnie. You're not fat, either."

"Sure I'm fat. Ho, ho, ho."

"No you're not."

"What do you want for Christmas, Ronnie?"

"I won't tell you. You're a fake. I don't need you to give me toys. I can buy my own toys."

"Good for you."

"I don't believe in Santa Claus anyway," he said. He was about nine, and in addition to being belligerent, he had mean little eyes. He was probably going to grow up to be an ax murderer. Either that, or a politician.

"If you don't want to talk to Santa," I said, feigning patience, "then how about getting off Santa's lap and letting one of the other boys and girls come up—"

"No." Without warning he punched me in the stomach. Hard. "Hah!" he said. "A pillow. I *knew* your gut was just a pillow."

"Get off Santa's lap, Ronnie."

"No."

I leaned down close to him so only he could hear when I said, "Get off Santa's lap or Santa will take off his pillow and stuff it down your rotten little throat."

We locked gazes for about five seconds. Then, taking his time, Ronnie got down off my lap. And stuck his tongue out at me and said, "Asshole." And went scampering away into the crowd.

I put on yet another false smile behind my false beard. Said grimly to one of the elves, "Next."

While I was listening to an eight-year-old with braces and a homicidal gleam in his eye tell me he wanted "a tank that has this neat missile in it and you shoot the missile and it blows everything up when it lands," Kerry appeared with a cup in her hand. She motioned for me to join her at the far side of the dais, behind Santa's sleigh. I got rid of the budding warmonger, told the nearest elf I was taking a short break, stood up creakily and with as much dignity as I could muster, and made my way through the cotton snowdrifts to where Kerry stood.

She looked far better in her costume than I did in mine; in fact, she looked so innocent and fetching I forgot for the moment that I was angry with her. She was dressed as an angel—all in white, with a coat-hanger halo wrapped in tinfoil. If real angels looked like her, I couldn't wait to get to heaven.

She handed me the cup. It was full of some sort of punch with a funny-looking skinny brown thing floating on top. "I thought you could use a little Christmas cheer," she said.

"I can use a lot of Christmas cheer. Is this stuff spiked?"

"Of course not. Since when do you drink hard liquor?"

"Since I sat down on that throne over there."

"Oh, now, it can't be that bad."

"No? Let's see. A five-year-old screamed so loud in my left ear that I'm still partially deaf. A fat kid stepped on my foot and nearly broke a toe. Another kid accidentally kneed me in the crotch and nearly broke something else. Not three minutes ago, a mugger-in-training named Ronnie punched me in the stomach and called me an asshole. And those are just the lowlights."

"Poor baby."

". . . That didn't sound very sincere."

"The fact is," she said, "most of the kids love you. I overheard a couple of them telling their parents what a nice old Santa you are."

"Yeah." I tried some of the punch. It wasn't too bad, considering the suspicious brown thing floating in it. Must be a deformed clove, I decided; the only other alternative—something that had come out of the back end of a mouse—was unthinkable. "How much more of this does the nice old Santa have to endure?"

"Two and a half hours."

"God! I'll never make it."

"Don't be such a curmudgeon," she said. "It's two days before Christmas, we're taking in lots of money for the needy, and everybody's having a grand time except you. Well, you and Mrs. Simmons."

"Who's Mrs. Simmons?"

"Randolph Simmons's wife. You know, the corporate attorney. She lost her wallet somehow—all her credit cards and two hundred dollars in cash."

"That's too bad. Tell her I'll replace the two hundred if she'll agree to trade places with me right now."

Kerry gave me her sometimes-you're-exasperating look. "Just hang in there, Santa," she said and started away.

"Don't use that phrase around the kid named Ronnie," I called after her. "It's liable to give him ideas."

I had been back on the throne less than ten seconds when who should reappear but the little thug himself. Ronnie wasn't alone this time; he had a bushy-mustached, gray-suited, scowling man with him. The two of them clumped up onto the dais, shouldered past an elf with a cherubic little girl in hand, and confronted me.

The mustached guy said in a low, angry voice, "What the hell's the idea threatening my kid?"

Fine, dandy. This was all I needed—an irate father.

"Answer me, pal. What's the idea telling Ronnie you'd shove a pillow down his throat?"

"He punched me in the stomach," I said.

"So? That don't give you the right to threaten him. Hell, *I* ought to punch you in the stomach."

"Do it, Dad," Ronnie said, "punch the old fake."

Nearby, the cherub started to cry. Loudly.

We all looked at her. Ronnie's dad said, "What'd you do? Threaten her too?"

"Wanna see Santa! It's my turn, it's my turn!"

The elf said, "Don't worry, honey, you'll get your turn."

Ronnie's dad said, "Apologize to my kid and we'll let it go."

Ronnie said, "Nah, sock him one!"

I said, "Mind telling me your name?"

It was Ronnie's dad I spoke to. He looked blank for two or three seconds, after which he said, "Huh?"

"Your name. What is it?"

"What do you want to know for?"

"You look familiar. Very familiar, in fact. I think maybe we've met before."

He stiffened. Then he took a good long wary look at me, as if trying to see past my whiskers. Then he blinked, and all of a sudden his righteous indignation vanished and was replaced by a nervousness that bordered on the furtive. He wet his lips, backed off a step.

"Come on, Dad," the little thug said, "punch his lights out."

His dad told him to shut up. To me he said, "Let's just forget the whole thing, okay?" and then he turned in a hurry and dragged a protesting Ronnie down off the dais and back into the crowd.

I stared after them. And there was a little click in my mind and

I was seeing a photograph of Ronnie's dad as a younger man without the big bushy mustache—and with a name and number across his chest.

Ronnie's dad and I knew each other, all right. I had once had a hand in having him arrested and sent to San Quentin on a grand larceny rap.

Ronnie's dad was Markey Waters, a professional pickpocket and jack-of-all-thievery who in his entire life had never gone anywhere or done anything to benefit anyone except Markey Waters. So what was he doing at the Gala Family Christmas Charity Benefit?

She lost her wallet somehow—all her credit cards and two hundred dollars in cash.

Right.

Practicing his trade, of course.

I should have stayed on the dais. I should have sent one of the elves to notify Security, while I perched on the throne and continued to act as a listening post for the kiddies.

But I didn't. Like a damned fool, I decided to handle the matter myself. Like a damned fool, I went charging off into the throng with the cherub's cries of "Wanna see Santa, *my* turn to see Santa!" rising to a crescendo behind me.

The milling crush of celebrants had closed around Markey Waters and his son and I could no longer see them. But they had been heading at an angle toward the far eastside entrance, so that was the direction I took. The rubber boots I wore were a size too small and pinched my feet, forcing me to walk in a kind of mincing step; and as if that wasn't bad enough, the boots were new and made squeaking sounds like a pair of rusty hinges. I also had to do some jostling to get through and around little knots of people, and some of the looks my maneuvers elicited were not of the peace-on-earth, goodwill-to-men variety. One elegantly dressed guy said, "Watch the hands, Claus," which might have been funny if I were not in such a dark and stormy frame of mind.

I was almost to the line of food booths along the east wall when I spotted Waters again, stopped near the second-to-last booth. One of his hands was clutching Ronnie's wrist and the other was plucking at an obese woman in a red-and-green, diagonally striped dress that made her look like a gigantic candy cane. Markey had evidently collided with her in his haste and caused her to spill a cup of punch on herself; she was loudly berating him for being a clumsy oaf, and refusing to let go of a big handful of his jacket until she'd had her say.

I minced and squeaked through another cluster of adults, all of whom were singing in accompaniment to the song now playing over the loudspeakers. The song, of all damn things, was "Here Comes Santa Claus."

Waters may not have heard the song, but its message got through to him just the same. He saw me bearing down on him from thirty feet away and understood immediately what my intentions were. His expression turned panicky; he tried to tear loose from the obese woman's grip. She hung on with all the tenacity of a bulldog.

I was ten feet from getting *my* bulldog hands on him when he proceeded to transform the Gala Family Christmas Charity Benefit from fun and frolic into chaos.

He let go of Ronnie's wrist, shouted, "Run, kid!" and then with his free hand he sucker-punched the obese woman on the uppermost of her chins. She not only released his jacket, she backpedaled into a lurching swoon that upset three other merry-makers and sent all four of them to the floor in a wild tangle of arms and legs. Voices rose in sudden alarm; somebody screamed like a fire siren going off. Bodies scattered out of harm's way. And Markey Waters went racing toward freedom.

I gave chase, dodging and juking and squeaking. I wouldn't have caught him except that while he was looking back over his shoulder to see how close I was, he tripped over something—his own feet, maybe—and down he went in a sprawl. I reached him just as he scrambled up again. I laid both hands on him and growled, "This is as far as you go, Waters," whereupon he kicked me in the shin and yanked free.

I yelled, he staggered off, I limped after him. Shouts and shrieks echoed through the gym; so did the thunder of running feet and thudding bodies as more of the party animals stampeded. A woman came rushing out from inside the farthest of the food booths, got in Markey's path, and caused him to veer sideways to keep from plowing into her. That in turn allowed me to catch up to him in front of the booth. I clapped a hand on his shoulder this time, spun him around—and he smacked me in the chops with something warm and soggy that had been sitting on the booth's serving counter.

A meat pie.

He hit me in the face with a *pie*.

That was the last indignity in a night of indignities. Playing Santa Claus was bad enough; playing Lou Costello to a thief's Bud Abbott was intolerable. I roared; I pawed at my eyes and scraped off beef gravy and false whiskers and white wig; I lunged and caught Waters again before he could escape; I wrapped my arms around him. It was my intention to twist him around and get him into a crippling hammerlock, but he was stronger than he looked. So instead we performed a kind of crazy, lurching bear-hug dance for a few seconds. That came to an end—predictably—when we banged into one of the booth supports and the whole front framework collapsed in a welter of wood and bunting and pie and paper plates and plastic utensils, with us in the middle of it all.

Markey squirmed out from underneath me, feebly, and tried to crawl away through the wreckage. I disentangled myself from some of the bunting, lunged at his legs, hung on when he tried to kick loose. And then crawled on top of him, flipped him over on his back, fended off a couple of ineffectual blows, and did some effectual things to his head until he stopped struggling and decided to become unconscious.

I sat astraddle him, panting and puffing and wiping gravy out of my eyes and nose. The tumult, I realized then, had subsided somewhat behind me. I could hear the loudspeakers again—the song playing now was "Rudolph, the Red-Nosed Reindeer"—and I could hear voices lifted tentatively nearby. Just before a newspaper photographer came hurrying up and snapped a picture of me and my catch, just before a horrified Kerry and a couple of tardy security guards arrived, I heard two voices in particular speaking in awed tones.

"My God," one of them said, "what *happened*?"

"I dunno," the other one said. "But it sure looks like Santa Claus went berserk."

There were three of us in the football coach's office at the rear of the gym: Markey Waters and me and one of the security guards. It was fifteen minutes later and we were waiting for the arrival of San Francisco's finest. Waters was dejected and resigned, the guard was pretending not to be amused, and I was in a foul humor thanks to a combination of acute embarrassment, some bruises and contusions, and the fact that I had no choice but to keep on wearing the gravy-stained remnants of the Santa Claus suit. It was what I'd come here in; my own clothes were in Kerry's apartment.

On the desk between Waters and me was a diamond-and-sapphire brooch, a fancy platinum cigarette case, and a gold money clip containing three crisp fifty-dollar bills. We had found all three items nestled companionably inside Markey's jacket pocket. I prodded the brooch with a finger, which prompted the guard to say, "Nice haul. The brooch alone must be worth a couple of grand."

I didn't say anything. Neither did Markey.

The owner of the gold clip and the three fifties had reported them missing to Security just before Waters and I staged our minor riot; the owners of the brooch and cigarette case hadn't made themselves known yet, which was something of a tribute to

Markey's light-fingered talents—talents that would soon land him
back in the slammer on another grand larceny rap.

He had had his chin resting on his chest; now he raised it and
looked at me. "My kid," he said, as if he'd just remembered he had
one. "He get away?"

"No. One of the other guards nabbed him out front."

"Just as well. Where is he?"

"Being held close by. He's okay."

Markey let out a heavy breath. "I shouldn't of brought him
along," he said.

"So why did you?"

"It's Christmas and the papers said this shindig was for kids,
too. Ronnie and me don't get out together much since his mother
ran out on us two years ago."

"Uh-huh," I said. "And besides, you figured it would be easier
to make your scores if you had a kid along as camouflage."

He shrugged. "You, though—I sure didn't figure on somebody
like you being here. What in hell's a private dick doing dressed up
in a Santa Claus suit?"

"I've been asking myself that question all night."

"I mean, how can you figure a thing like that?" Markey said.
"Ronnie comes running up, he says it's not really Santa up there
and the guy pretending to be Santa threatened him, said he'd
shove a pillow down the kid's throat. What am I supposed to do?
I'd done a good night's work, I wanted to get out of here while the
getting was good, but I couldn't let some jerk get away with
threatening my kid, could I? I mean, I'm a father, too, right?" He
let out another heavy breath. "I wish I wasn't a father," he said.

I said, "What about the wallet, Markey?"

"Huh?"

"The wallet and the two hundred in cash that was in it."

"Huh?"

"This stuff here isn't all you swiped tonight. You also got a

wallet belonging to a Mrs. Randolph Simmons. It wasn't on you
and neither was the two hundred. What'd you do with them?"

"I never scored a wallet," he said. "Not tonight."

"Markey . . ."

"I swear it. The other stuff, sure, you got me on that. But I'm
telling you, I didn't score a wallet tonight."

I scowled at him. But his denial had the ring of truth; he had no
reason to lie about the wallet. Well, then? Had Mrs. Simmons lost
it after all? If that was the case, then I'd gone chasing after Waters
for no good reason except that he was a convicted felon. I felt the
embarrassment warming my face again. What if he *hadn't* dipped
anybody tonight? I'd have looked like an even bigger fool than I
did right now . . .

Something tickled my memory and set me to pursuing a
different and more productive line of thought. Oh, hell—of
course. I'd been right in the first place; Mrs. Randolph Simmons's
wallet had been stolen, not lost. And I knew now who had done
the stealing.

But the knowledge didn't make me feel any better. If anything,
it made me feel worse.

"Empty your pockets," I said.

"What for?"

"Because I told you to, that's what for."

"I don't have to do what you tell me."

"If you don't, I'll empty them for you."

"I want a lawyer," he said.

"You're too young to need a lawyer. Now empty your pockets
before I smack you one."

Ronnie glared at me. I glared back at him. "If you smack me,"
he said, "it's police brutality." Nine years old going on forty.

"I'm not the police, remember? This is your last chance, kid:
empty the pockets or else."

"Ahhh," he said, but he emptied the pockets.

He didn't have Mrs. Randolph Simmons's wallet, but he did have her two hundred dollars. Two hundred and four dollars, to be exact. *I don't need you to give me toys. I can buy my own toys.* Sure. Two hundred and four bucks can buy a lot of toys, not to mention a lot of grief.

"What'd you do with the wallet, Ronnie?"

"What wallet?"

"Dumped it somewhere nearby, right?"

"I dunno what you're talking about."

"No? Then where'd you get the money?"

"I found it."

"Uh-huh. In Mrs. Randolph Simmons's purse."

"Who's she?"

"Your old man put you up to it, or was it your own idea?"

He favored me with a cocky little grin. "I'm smart," he said. "I'm gonna be just like my dad when I grow up."

"Yeah," I said sadly. "A chip off the old block if ever there was one."

Midnight.

Kerry and I were sitting on the couch in her living room. I sat with my head tipped back and my eyes closed; I had a thundering headache and a brain clogged with gloom. It had been a long, long night, full of all sorts of humiliations; and the sight of a nine-year-old kid, even a thuggish nine-year-old kid, being carted off to the Youth Authority at the same time his father was being carted off to the Hall of Justice was a pretty unfestive one.

I hadn't seen the last of the humiliations, either. Tonight's fiasco would get plenty of tongue-in-cheek treatment in the morning papers, complete with photographs—half a dozen reporters and photographers had arrived at the gym in tandem with the police—and so there was no way Eberhardt and my other friends could help but find out. I was in for weeks of sly and merciless ribbing.

Kerry must have intuited my headache because she moved over close beside me and began to massage my temples. She's good at massage; some of the pain began to ease almost immediately. None of the gloom, though. You can't massage away gloom.

After a while she said, "I guess you blame me."

"Why should I blame you?"

"Well, if I hadn't talked you into playing Santa . . ."

"You didn't talk me into anything; I did it because I wanted to help you and the Benefit. No, I blame myself for what happened. I should have handled Markey Waters better. If I had, the Benefit wouldn't have come to such a bad end and you'd have made a lot more money for the charities."

"We made quite a bit as it is," Kerry said. "And you caught a professional thief and saved four good citizens from losing valuable personal property."

"And put a kid in the Youth Authority for Christmas."

"You're not responsible for that. His father is."

"Sure, I know. But it doesn't make me feel any better."

She was silent for a time. At the end of which she leaned down and kissed me, warmly.

I opened my eyes. "What was that for?"

"For being who and what you are. You grump and grumble and act the curmudgeon, but that's just a facade. Underneath you're a nice caring man with a big heart."

"Yeah. Me and St. Nick."

"Exactly." She looked at her watch. "It is now officially the twenty-fourth—Christmas Eve. How would you like one of your presents a little early?"

"Depends on which one."

"Oh, I think you'll like it." She stood up. "I'll go get it ready for you. Give me five minutes."

I gave her three minutes, which—miraculously enough—was

all the time it took for my pall of gloom to lift. Then I got to my feet and went down the hall.

"Ready or not," I said as I opened the bedroom door, "here comes Santa Claus!"

SHARYN MCCRUMB

A WEE DOCH AND DORIS

Large numbers of Scots emigrated to Virginia after the defeat of Bonnie Prince Charlie and the Highland clearances. Many of its inhabitants still cherish Scottish traditions, but few get more fun out of them than Sharyn McCrumb. There's Scots blood on both sides of her family; furthermore she has a Scots-born friend who learned about Hogmanay the hard way. Being tall and dark, he used to get thrust out of doors at ten minutes to midnight on December thirty-first with a lump of coal in his pocket. As the first to set foot over the neighbors' thresholds once the New Year struck, he brought them all luck for the coming year. His own luck wasn't so great, though . . . he'd be half-frozen by the time he'd done his good deed for the year and could go home to thaw out. So it's not surprising that Sharyn chose to write about Hogmanay, which is much more important to a Scot than Christmas. Who gets the luck in her story? Read it yourself, an' find oot.

He stood for a long while staring up at the house, but all was quiet. There was one light on in an upstairs window, but he saw no shadows flickering on the shades. *Not a creature was stirring, not even a mouse*, Louis smirked to himself. Christmas wasn't so hot if you were in his line of work. People tended to stay home with the family: the one night a year when everybody wishes they were *The Waltons*. But all that togetherness wore off in a week. By now everybody had cabin fever, and they were dying to get away from the in-laws and the rug rats. That's how it was in his family, anyway. By New Year's Eve his ma had recovered from the thrill of receiving candy from Anthony, bubble bath from Michael, and a bottle of perfume from Louis, and she had started nagging again. Louis always gave her a bottle of perfume. He preferred small, lightweight gifts that could be slipped easily and unobtrusively into one's pocket.

He also preferred not to have endless discussions with his nearest and dearest over whether he was going to get a job or enroll in the auto mechanics program at the community college. Neither idea appealed to Louis. He liked his schedule: sleeping until eleven, a quick burger for brunch, and a few hours of volunteer work at the animal shelter.

Nobody at the shelter thought Louis was lazy or unmotivated. He was their star helper. He didn't mind hosing down the pens and cleaning the food dishes, but what he really enjoyed was playing with the dogs and brushing down the shaggy ones. They didn't have a lot of money at the shelter, so they couldn't afford to pay him. It took all their funds to keep the animals fed and healthy; the shelter refused to put a healthy animal to sleep. Louis heartily approved of this policy, and thus he didn't mind working for free; in fact, sometimes when the shelter's funds were low, he gave them a donation from the proceeds of his night's work. Louis thought that rich people should support local charities; he saw himself as the middleman, except that his share of the take was ninety percent. Louis also believed that charity begins at home.

Christmas was good for the shelter. Lots of people high on the Christmas spirit adopted kittens and puppies, or gave them as gifts, and the shelter saw to it that they got a donation for each adoptee. So their budget was doing okay, but Louis's personal funds were running short. Christmas is not a good time of year for a burglar. Sometimes he'd find an empty house whose occupants were spending Christmas out of town, but usually the neighborhood was packed with nosy people, eyeballing every car that went by. You'd think they were looking for Santa Claus.

If Christmas was bad for business, New Year's Eve made up for it. Lots of people went out to parties that night, and did not plan on coming home until well after midnight. Being out for just the evening made them less security conscious than the Christmas people who went out of town: New Year's party-goers were less likely to hide valuables, activate alarms, or ask the police to keep an eye on the premises. Louis had had a busy evening. He'd started around nine o'clock, when even the tardiest guests would have left for the party, and he had hit four houses, passing on one because of a Doberman Pinscher in the backyard. Louis had nothing against the breed, but he found them very unreasonable, and not inclined to give strangers the benefit of the doubt.

The other four houses had been satisfactory, though. The first one was "guarded" by a haughty white Persian whose owners had forgotten to feed it. Louis put down some canned mackerel for the cat, and charged its owners one portable television, one 35mm. camera, three pairs of earrings, a C.D. player, and a collection of compact discs. The other houses had been equally rewarding. After a day's visit to various flea markets and pawn shops, his financial standing should be greatly improved. This was much better than auto mechanics. Louis realized that larceny and auto mechanics are almost never mutually exclusive, but he felt that in free-lance burglary the hours were better.

He glanced at his watch. A little after midnight. This would be his last job of the evening. Louis wanted to be home before the drunks got out on the highway. His New Year's resolution was to campaign for gun control and for tougher drunk driving laws. He turned his attention back to the small white house with the boxwood hedge and the garden gnome next to the birdbath. No danger of Louis stealing *that*. He thought people ought to have to pay to have garden gnomes stolen. A promising sideline—he would have to consider it. But now to the business at hand.

The hedge seemed high enough to prevent the neighbors from seeing into the yard. The house across the street was vacant, with a big yellow For Sale sign stuck in the yard. The brick split-level next door was dark, but they had a chain link fence, and their front yard was floodlit like the exercise yard of a penitentiary. Louis shook his head: paranoia *and* bad taste.

There was no car in the driveway, a promising sign that no one was home. He liked the look of the rectangular kitchen window. It was partly hidden by a big azalea bush, and it looked like the kind of window that opened out at the bottom, with a catch to keep it from opening too far. It was about six feet off the ground. Louis was tempted to look under the garden gnome for a spare house key, but he decided to have a look at the window instead. Using a key was unsporting; besides, the exercise would be good for him. If you are a burglar, your physique is your fortune.

He walked a lot, too. Tonight Louis had parked his old Volkswagen a couple of streets away, not so much for the exercise as for the fact that later no one would remember seeing a strange car in the vicinity. The long walk back to the car limited Louis' take to the contents of a pillowcase or two, also from the burgled home, but he felt that most worthwhile burglary items were small and lightweight, anyway. The pillowcases he gave as baby gifts to new parents of his acquaintance, explaining that they were the perfect size to use as a cover for a bassinet mattress. Even better than a fitted crib sheet, he insisted, because after the kid grows up, you can use the pillowcases yourself. Louis was nothing if not resourceful.

He stayed close to the boxwood hedge as he edged closer to the house. With a final glance to see that no one was driving past, he darted for the azalea bush, and ended up crouched behind it, just under the rectangular window. Perfect. Fortunately it wasn't too cold tonight—temperature in the mid-thirties, about average for the Virginia Christmas season. When it got colder than that, his dexterity was impaired, making it hard to jimmy locks and tamper with windows. It was an occupational hazard. Tonight would be no problem, though, unless the window had some kind of inside lock.

It didn't. He was able to chin himself on the windowsill, and pull the window outward enough to get a hand inside and slip the catch. With that accomplished, another twenty seconds of wriggling got him through the window and onto the Formica countertop next to the sink. There had been a plant on the windowsill, but he managed to ease that onto the counter, before sliding himself all the way through. The only sound he made was a slight thump as he went from countertop to floor; no problem if the house was unoccupied.

Taking out his pen-sized flashlight, Louis checked out the kitchen. It was squeaky clean. He could even smell the lemon floor cleaner. He shone the light on the gleaming white refriger-ator. Some people actually put their valuables in the freezer compartment. He always checked that last, though. In the corner next to the back door was a small washing machine and an electric dryer, with clean clothes stacked neatly on the top. Louis eased his way across the room, and inspected the laundry. Women's clothes—small sizes—towels, dishcloths . . . ah, there they were! Pillowcases. He helped himself to the two linen cases, sniffing them appreciatively. Fabric softener. *Very* nice. Now he was all set. Time to shop around.

He slipped into the dining room and flashed the light on the round oak table and the ladderback chairs. Two places laid for breakfast. Weren't they the early birds, though? The salt and pepper shakers looked silver. They were in the shape of pheas-ants. Louis slid them into his pillowcase and examined the rest of the room. The glass of the china cabinet flashed his light back at him. Bunch of flowery plates. No chance that he'd be taking those. He looked around for a silver chest, but didn't see one. He'd check on it later. He wanted to examine the living room first.

Louis flashed an exploratory light at the fireplace, the chintz couch covered in throw pillows, and the glass-fronted bookcase.

There were some candlesticks on the mantelpiece that looked promising. As he crept forward to inspect them, the room was flooded with light.

Squinting at the sudden brightness, Louis turned toward the stairs and saw that he wasn't alone. The overhead lights had been switched on by a sweet-faced old woman in a green velvet bathrobe. Louis braced himself for the scream, but the old lady was smiling. She kept coming daintily down the stairs. Smiling. Louis stared, trying to think up a plausible story. She couldn't have been more than five feet tall, and her blue eyes sparkled from a wrinkled but pleasant face. She patted her white permed hair into place. She looked delighted. Probably senile, Louis thought.

"Well, I'm that glad to see you!" the woman said brightly. "I was afraid it was going to be my daughter Doris."

Definitely senile, thought Louis. "No, it's just me," he said, deciding to play along. He held the pillowcase behind his back.

"Just after midnight, too, isn't it? That's grand, that is. Otherwise I'd have to ask you to go out and come in again, you know."

Louis noticed her accent now. It was sort of English, he thought. But she wasn't making any sense. "Come in again?"

"Ah, well, being an American you wouldn't know the custom, would you? Well, you're welcome all the same. Now, what can I get for you?"

Louis realized just in time that she meant food or drink, rather than jewelry and savings bonds. "Nothing for me, thanks," he said, giving her a little wave and trying to edge for the front door.

Her face fell. "Oh, no. Please! You must let me fix you something. Otherwise, you'll be taking the luck away with you. How about a piece of cake? I made it today. And a bit of strong drink? It's New Year's, after all."

She still didn't look in the least perturbed. And she wasn't trying to get to the telephone or to trip an alarm. Louis decided that he could definitely use a drink.

The old lady beamed happily up at him and motioned for him

to follow her into the kitchen. "I've been baking for two days," she confided. "Now, let's see, what will you have?"

She rummaged around in a cupboard, bringing out an assortment of baked goods on glass plates, which she proceeded to spread out on the kitchen table. She handed Louis a blue-flowered plate and motioned for him to sit down. When she went in the dining room to get some cloth napkins, Louis stuffed the pillowcase under his coat, making sure that the salt and pepper shakers didn't clink together. Finally, he decided that the least suspicious thing to do would be to play along. He sat.

"Now," she announced, "we have Dundee cake with dried fruit, black bun with almonds, shortbread, petticoat tails . . ."

Louis picked up a flat yellow cookie and nibbled at it as his hostess babbled on.

"When I was a girl in Dundee—"

"Where?"

"Dundee. Scotland. My mother used to bake an oat bannock— you know, a wee cake—for each one of us children. The bannocks had a hole in the middle, and they were nipped in about the edges for decorations. She flavored them with carvey—carroway seed. And we ate them on New Year's morning. They used to say that if your bannock broke while it was baking, you'd be taken ill or die in the new year. So I never baked one for my daughter Doris. Oh, but they were good!"

Louis blinked. "You're from Scotland?"

She was at the stove now, putting a large open pot on the burner and stirring it with a wooden spoon. "Yes, that's right," she said. "We've been in this country since Doris was five, though. My husband wanted to come over, and so we did. I've often thought of going home, now that he's passed on, but Doris won't hear of it."

"Doris is your daughter," said Louis. He wondered if he ought to bolt before she showed up, in case she turned out to be sane.

"Yes. She's all grown up now. She works very hard, does Doris. Can you imagine having to work on Hogmanay?"

"On what?"

"*Hogmanay*. New Year's Eve. She's out right now, poor dear, finishing up her shift. That's why I was so glad to see you tonight. We could use a bit of luck this year, starting with a promotion for Doris. Try a bit of the Dundee cake. It's awfully rich, but you can stand the calories, from the look of you."

Louis reached for another pastry, still trying to grasp a thread of sense in the conversation. He wanted to know why he was so welcome. Apparently she hadn't mistaken him for anyone else. And she didn't seem to wonder what he was doing in her house in the middle of the night. He kept trying to think of a way to frame the question without incriminating himself.

Steam was rising in white spirals from the pot on the stove. The old lady took a deep breath over the fumes and nodded briskly. "Right. That should be done now. Tell me, lad, are you old enough to take spirits?"

After a moment's hesitation, Louis realized that he was being offered a drink and not a seance. "I'm twenty-two," he mumbled.

"Right enough, then." She ladled the steaming liquid into two cups and set one in front of him.

Louis sniffed it and frowned.

"It's called a het pint," said the old lady, without waiting for him to ask. "It's an old drink given to first footers. Spirits, sugar, beer, and eggs. When I was a girl, they used to carry it round door to door in a kettle. Back in Dundee. Not that I drink much myself, of course. Doris is always on about my blood pressure. But tonight *is* Hogmanay, and I said to myself: Flora, why don't you stir up the het pint. You never know who may drop in. And, you see, I was right. Here you are!"

"Here I am," Louis agreed, taking a swig of his drink. It tasted a little like eggnog. Not bad. At least it was alcoholic. He wouldn't have more than a cup, though. He still had to drive home.

The old lady—Flora—sat down beside Louis and lifted her cup. "Well, here's to us, then. What's your name, lad?"

"Louis," he said, before he thought better of it.

"Well, Louis, here's to us! And not forgetting a promotion for Doris!" They clinked their cups together and drank to the new year.

Flora dabbed at the corners of her mouth with a linen napkin and reached for a piece of shortbread. "I must resolve to eat fewer of these during the coming year," she remarked. "Else Doris will have me out jogging."

Louis took another piece to keep her company. It tasted pretty good. Sort of like a sugar cookie with delusions of grandeur. "Did you have a nice Christmas?" he asked politely.

Flora smiled. "Perhaps not by American standards. Doris had the day off, and we went to church in the morning, and then had our roast beef for dinner. She gave me bath powder, and I gave her a new umbrella. She's always losing umbrellas. I suppose that's a rather subdued holiday by your lights, but when I was a girl, Christmas wasn't such a big festival in Scotland. The shops didn't even close for it. We considered it a religious occasion for most folk, and a lark for the children. The holiday for grown people was New Year's."

"Good idea," grunted Louis. "Over here, we get used to high expectations when we're kids, and then as adults, we get depressed every year because Christmas is just neckties and boredom."

Flora nodded. "Oh, but you should have seen Hogmanay when I was a girl! No matter what the weather, people in Dundee would gather in the City Square to wait out the old year's end. And there'd be a great time of singing all the old songs . . ."

"'Auld Lang Syne'?" asked Louis.

"That's a Scottish song, of course," nodded Flora. "But we sang a lot of the other old tunes as well. And there was country dancing. And then just when the new year was minutes away, everyone would lapse into silence. Waiting. There you'd be in the dark square, with your breath frosting the air, and the stars shining down on the world like snowflakes on velvet. And it was so quiet you could hear the ticking of the gentlemen's pocket watches."

"Sounds like Times Square," said Louis, inspecting the bottom of his cup.

Flora took the cup and ladled another het pint for each of them. "After the carrying on to welcome in the new year, everyone would go about visiting and first footing their neighbors. My father was always in great demand for that, being tall and dark as he was. And he used to carry lumps of coal in his overcoat to be sure of his welcome."

"What," said Louis, "is *first footing*?"

"Well, it's an old superstition," said Flora thoughtfully. "Quite pagan, I expect, if the truth were told, but then, you never can be sure, can you? You don't have a lump of coal about you, by any chance?"

Louis shook his head.

"Ah, well. First footing, you asked." She took a deep breath, as if to warn him that there was a long explanation to follow. "In Scotland the tradition is that the first person to cross your threshold after midnight on Hogmanay symbolizes your luck in the year to come. The *first foot* to enter your house, you see."

Louis nodded. *It's lucky to be burgled?* he was thinking.

"The best luck of all comes if you're first footed by a tall, dark stranger carrying a lump of coal. Sometimes family friends would send round a tall, dark houseguest that our family had not met, so that we could be first footed by a stranger. The rest of the party would catch up with him a few minutes later."

"I guess I fit the bill all right," Louis remarked. He was just over six feet and looked more Italian than Tony Bennett. His uncles called him *Luigi*.

"So you do," smiled Flora. "Now the worst luck for the new

year is to be first footed by a short blond woman who comes in empty-handed."

Louis remembered the first thing the old woman had said to him. "So Doris is a short blond?"

"She is that. Gets her height from me. Or the lack of it. And she can never remember to hunt up a lump of coal or bring some wee gift home with her to help the luck. Ever since Colin passed away, Doris has been first foot in this house, and where has it got us? Her with long hours and precious little time off, and me with rheumatism and a fixed income—while prices go up every year. We could use a change of luck. Maybe a sweepstakes win."

Louis leaned back in his chair, struggling between courtesy and common sense. "You really believe in all this stuff?" he asked her.

A sad smile. "Where's the harm? When you get older, it's hard to let go of the customs you knew when you were young. You'll see."

Louis couldn't think of any family customs, except eating in front of the TV set and never taking the last ice cube—so you wouldn't have to refill the tray. Other than that, he didn't think he had much in common with the people he lived with. He thought about telling Flora about his work at the animal shelter, but he decided that it would be a dangerous thing to do. She already knew his name. Any further information would enable her and the police to locate him in a matter of hours. If she ever cottoned on to the fact that she had been robbed, that is.

"Do you have any pets?" he asked.

Flora shook her head. "We used to have a wee dog, but he got old and died a few years back. I haven't wanted to get another one, and Doris is too busy with her work to help in taking care of one."

"I could get you a nice puppy, from—" He stopped himself just in time. "Well, never mind. You're right. Dogs are more work than most people think. Or they *ought* to be."

Flora beamed. "What a nice young man you are!"

He smiled back nervously.

Louis nibbled another piece of shortbread while he considered his dilemma. He had been caught breaking into a house, and the evidence from the rest of the evening's burglaries was in the trunk of his Volkswagen. The logical thing to do would be to kill the old dear, so that he wouldn't have to worry about getting caught. Logical, yes, but distasteful. Louis was not a killer. The old lady reminded him of one of the sad-eyed cocker spaniels down at the shelter. Sometimes people brought in pets because they didn't want them anymore or were moving. Or because the kid was allergic to them. Often these people asked that the animal be destroyed, which annoyed Louis no end. Did they think that if they didn't want the pet, no one else should have it? Suppose divorce worked like that? Louis could see putting an old dog to sleep if it was feeble and suffering, but not just because the owners found it inconvenient to have it around. He supposed that his philosophy would have to apply to his hostess as well, even if she were a danger to his career. After all, Flora was old, but she was not weak or in pain. She seemed quite spry and happy, in fact, and Louis couldn't see doing away with her just for expedience. After all, people had rights, too, just like animals.

He wondered what he ought to do about her. It seemed to boil down to two choices: He could tie her up, finish robbing the house, and make his getaway, or he could finish his tea and leave, just as if he had been an ordinary—what was it?—*first footer*.

He leaned back in his chair, considering the situation, and felt a sharp jab in his side. A moment's reflection told him what it had been: the tail of the pheasant salt shaker. He had stashed the pair in the pillowcase, now concealed under his coat. He couldn't think of any way to get rid of his loot without attracting suspicion. *Then* she might realize that he was a burglar; *then* she might panic and try to call the police; *then* he would have to hit her to keep himself from being captured. It was not an appealing scenario. Louis decided that the kindest thing to do would be to tie her up, finish his job, and leave.

Flora was prattling on about Scottish cakes and homemade icing, but he hadn't been listening. He thought it would be rather rude to begin threatening his hostess while he still had a mouthful of cake, but he told himself that she had been rather rude, too. After all, she hadn't asked him anything about himself. That was thoughtless of her. A good hostess ought to express a polite interest in her guests.

Flora's interminable story seemed to have wound down at last. She looked up at the kitchen clock. It was after one. "Well," she said, beaming happily at Louis. "It's getting late. Can I get you a *wee doch and dorris*?"

Louis blinked. "A what?"

"A drink, lad. *Wee doch and dorris* is a Scottish expression for the last drink of the evening. One for the road, as you say over here. Scotch, perhaps?"

He shook his head. "I'm afraid not," he said. "I do have to be going, but I'm afraid I will have to tie you up now."

He braced himself for tears, or, even worse, a scream, but the old lady simply took another sip of her drink and waited. She wasn't smiling anymore, but she didn't look terrified, either. Louis felt his cheeks grow hot, wishing he could just get out of there. Burglars weren't supposed to have to interact with people; it wasn't part of the job description. If you liked emotional scenes, you became an armed robber. Louis hated confrontations.

"I hope this won't change your luck for the New Year or anything," he mumbled, "but the reason I came in here tonight was to rob the house. You see, I'm a burglar."

Flora nodded, still watching him closely. Not a flicker of surprise had registered on her face.

"I really enjoyed the cakes and all, but after all, business is business."

"In Scotland, it's considered unlucky to do evil after you've accepted the hospitality of the house," the old lady said calmly.

Louis shrugged. "In America it's unlucky to miss car payments."

She made no reply to this remark, but continued to gaze up at him impassively. At least she wasn't being hysterical. He almost wished that he had given up the whole idea.

Louis cleared his throat and continued. "The reason I have to tie you up is that I have to finish getting the stuff, and I have to make sure you can't call for help until I'm long gone. But I won't beat you up or anything."

"Kind of you," she said dryly. "There is some spare clothesline in the bottom drawer of the left-hand cabinet."

He looked at her suspiciously. "Don't *try* anything, okay? I don't want to have to do anything rough." He didn't carry a gun (nobody was *supposed* to be home), but they both knew that a strong young man like Louis could do considerable damage to a frail old lady like Flora with his fists—a candlestick—almost anything could be a weapon.

Keeping his eyes on her, he edged toward the cabinet, squatting down to pull out the drawer. She watched him steadily, making no move to leave her seat. As he eased the drawer open, he saw the white rope clothesline neatly bundled above a stack of paper bags. With considerable relief at the ease of it all, he picked up the rope and turned back to the old lady.

"Okay," he said, a little nervously. "I'm going to tie you up. Just relax. I don't want to make it so tight it cuts off circulation, but I'm not, like, experienced, you know? Just sit in the chair with your feet flat on the floor in front of you."

She did as she was told, and he knelt and began winding the clothesline around her feet, anchoring it to the legs of the chair. He hoped it wasn't going to be too painful, but he couldn't risk her being able to escape. To cover his uneasiness at the silent reproach from his hostess, Louis began to whistle nervously as he worked. That was probably why he didn't hear anything suspicious.

His first inkling that anything was wrong was that Flora

suddenly relaxed in her chair. He looked up quickly, thinking, *"Oh, God! The old girl's had a heart attack!"* But her eyes were open, and she was smiling. She seemed to be gazing at something just behind him.

Slowly Louis turned his head in the direction of the back door. There was a short blond woman of about thirty standing just inside the door. She was wearing a dark blue uniform and a positively menacing expression. But what bothered Louis the most about the intruder was the fact that her knees were bent, and she was holding a service revolver in both hands, its barrel aimed precisely at Louis's head.

Louis looked from the blond woman to Flora and back again, just beginning to make the connection. A jerk of the gun barrel made him move slowly away from the chair and put his hands up.

"This is my daughter Doris," said Flora calmly. "She's a policewoman. You see, you were lucky for us, Louis. I'm sure she'll get her promotion after this!"

HENRY SLESAR

THE MAN WHO LOVED CHRISTMAS

Henry Slesar is one of the busiest authors in the field. He's written an incredible number of short stories, along with many motion picture and television scripts for Alfred Hitchcock and others. He's even been head scriptwriter for a long-running daytime serial show. So it's hardly surprising that when Henry sat down to write a Christmas story, he chose as his principle character an overachiever who carried his holiday celebrating to the ultimate extreme . . . and one step beyond.

When Lev Walters felt the waking touch of his wife's hand on his shoulder he was sure it was about the baby. Wow! he thought, his kid might be born on Christmas after all! They had discussed that possibility for weeks, wondering if John Alexander Walters would resent sharing his day with a better-known Birthday Boy. (They knew the baby's sex because of Elly's amniocentesis. She was thirty-two and it was her first kid, so why take chances?) But as soon as Lev was fully awake, a process which took longer than usual since he had been wrapping packages until two A.M., he knew that contractions weren't the reason for the wake-up call. Elly was holding a telephone in her left hand. That always meant the same thing. Lev Walters was a cop.

Captain Ab Peterson answered his first question before he asked it. "No, Sam isn't here. There was a three-car accident on the Interstate, too many eggnogs I guess. I've only got Lutz and the Kid, and neither one of them has the brains for it."

"For what?" Lev asked.

"A vanishing act," Ab said. "A man named Barry Methune, lives on Holly Road, disappeared last night."

"You're kidding me," Lev said. "Nobody qualifies as a Missing Person in less than forty-eight hours."

"This guy vanished out of his own *bed*, and his wife is pretty hysterical. He's got two kids, they haven't even opened their presents yet, and Daddy is just plain gone . . . At least talk to the woman, okay? She's ten minutes from your house."

Lev knew he would, despite the pout he saw on Elly's face. There were only six officers serving the town of Lewisfield, and holidays were always a headache, logistically and emotionally, and none worse than Christmas. Lev had traded off two days for the privilege of staying home on December twenty-fifth, but here he was, yanking up his socks and stumbling into his pants, preparing to hold the hand of some housewife whose husband had probably gotten too full of Christmas spirits to remember where he lived.

"Don't be gone long," Elly told him. "I don't want to have this baby without you."

"You couldn't have done it without me," Lev said.

He got as close to her as he could to kiss her.

Lev Walters had lived in Lewisfield for all of his thirty-four years, and watched his town spread out like a stain to become the suburb of a neighboring city. Growth had made the town prosperous, but less of a community. It had also created new neighborhoods, and Holly Road was one of them, a stretch of cookie-cutter houses with lawns like green stamps.

Christmas had imposed another kind of conformity on Holly Road. There were wreaths on almost every door, and Christmas trees glowed or blinked in almost every window. But when his station wagon turned into the driveway of the Methune house, Lev started to blink himself. If there had been a contest for the most Christmas-decorated house in Lewisfield, the Methunes would have taken first prize. There was a life-size sleigh on the front lawn, with a plastic Santa holding the reins of four plastic reindeer, one of which boasted a tiny red light bulb in its nose. There was an almost life-size creche on the patio, strung with colored lights that made baby Jesus look jaundiced and his admirers green, orange, and blue. Lights bordered all the gutters and downspouts, the windows, the front door. There were two light-festooned trees on the lawn, but neither rivaled the one inside, a seven-footer draped with every conceivable decoration, rising out of a jumble of brightly wrapped packages, all of them still unopened.

"Somebody likes Christmas," he mumbled when Mrs. Methune let him in.

"My husband," the woman said, catching a sob. "That's what makes it so terrible. That this could happen *today!*"

"That what could happen?" Lev said.

She was a thin, pretty woman with pulled-back hair and slightly protruding teeth that gave her an endearing, rabbity look. Fortunately, her eyes were dark and her mouth strong, although the former was tearstained and the latter quivery.

"We went to bed after midnight, Barry and me. The kids usually go to sleep around nine, but they were so excited we let them stay up until ten. That gave us a couple of hours to put out all the presents. We were both exhausted, naturally, but Barry was happy, happy the way he always is this time of year. That man loved Christmas so much, I swear he'd start planning next year's Christmas on December twenty-sixth."

"What time did you wake up?"

"Seven o'clock. I set the alarm because I didn't want to sleep too late; I knew Dodie and Amanda—those are my little girls—would be up at the crack of dawn, dying to open their presents. I wasn't surprised when I saw my husband was already out of bed. Barry is usually a heavy sleeper, but this was his favorite morning of the whole year . . ."

"Your bedroom is upstairs?"

"Yes. I threw on a robe and came down here, and sure enough, there were the kids, shaking and rattling all the packages, trying to guess what Santa had brought them. I mean that literally, by the way, Dodie is five and Amanda is not quite seven, and they still believe in Santa, or at least do a good job of faking it . . . That's the way Barry wanted it, for them to *believe*." She gulped down a sob. "Oh, my God, I'm talking about him in the past tense! Tell me I don't have to do that, please!"

"You don't have to do that," Lev said with firm conviction. "There are dozens of possible explanations for your husband's disappearance, Mrs. Methune, and the odds are terrific that he'll walk through that door in the next couple of hours."

"I've been trying to think of *one* explanation," she said. "Just *one* that I can hang on to. But I can't. I can't!"

"All right, I'll take a crack at it. He woke up and realized he had left one of his presents at his office. He figured he could hop into his car—"

"No," the woman said sharply. "That's one thing he didn't do. We have two cars, his Ford, my little Mazda. They're both in the garage. He didn't *walk* to his office, it's in the city, in Dayton. He runs a small surgical supply house. He does own a motor bike, but that's here, too."

"He may have called for a taxi. That's not impossible, is it?"

"In the middle of the night? Why would he do that?"

Lev didn't know. But he kept on speculating.

"Maybe somebody picked him up. If a car drove up you might not have heard it, being so tired, sleeping deeply, you know?"

"That's even worse. A car picking him up! Who was driving? Where were they going?" He started to reply, but she stopped him. "You're thinking about another woman, aren't you? That he picked *Christmas Eve* to run off with another woman! God, what a thing to say!"

Lev didn't point out the fact that he hadn't said it, especially since the thought had been hovering in his mind.

"All right," he said. "Let's stop speculating and stick to the facts. His clothes, for instance."

"They're all here," Mrs. Methune said. "At least I think they are. I don't keep an inventory of Barry's clothes any more than he does mine. But I know he has five suits, and they're still in the closet. He owns three suitcases, it's a set, and all three are where they always were. Would he run off with someone without even packing his toothbrush? That's here, too."

Lev cleared his throat, wanting to make sure he wasn't misunderstood.

"I've worked on a couple of runaway husband cases, Mrs. Methune. They can get pretty ingenious. One guy I know, he sent all his clothes to the laundry over a period of months and gave them a new address for delivery. Before his wife realized what was happening, practically all his stuff was out of the house."

"But I just told you—"

"I know, I know. All his stuff is here. But some men are willing to buy whole new wardrobes when they start a new life . . ." He felt rotten as soon as the sentence was out.

"Maybe Barry wanted to leave me," the woman said, her eyes misting over. "I don't know. He never acted like he did. But his kids? His darling little girls? And on *Christmas*, the biggest day of their lives?" She shook her head so hard she undid the elastic ribbon holding her hair in place. It shook loose and her soft brown hair tumbled in all directions; she looked even younger and prettier, and Lev began to feel chilled with a doubt that was downright eerie. Where *was* Barry Methune? What Christmas ghost whisked him away from a family like this?

Lev didn't leave the area until three o'clock that afternoon, and was stricken with the guilty realization that he hadn't even called Elly to see if her contractions had started. He violated the local speed law on the way back, trusting to his badge to get him out of trouble. Luckily, he wasn't stopped. Even luckier, Elly wasn't home. She had been visiting her sister. She apologized to *him*. Lev accepted it gracefully.

When he told her about the Methune case, Elly identified just as she always did.

"You ever do something like that to *me*, copper, I'll scratch your eyes out."

"But we don't know what Methune did. His wife doesn't know. Neither do his neighbors."

"You talked to them?"

"I covered half the road. Nobody saw Methune leave the house, nobody heard a vehicle in the middle of the night. I even talked to his kids, two little girls, faces like sunshine. You make me one of those, I wouldn't mind a bit."

"You're getting a boy, remember?"

"You keep saying that, only when?"

Elly's reply was wistful. "Not on Christmas Day, the way it looks . . . What was that you said about this man not being home every Christmas?"

"That's what his wife told me. He employs only one salesman at this surgical supply company he owns, so they take turns covering their out-of-town territory during the holidays. But he makes up for the Christmases he misses by going all out every other year. He spends a fortune on Christmas decorations, spends days getting them up. He buys tons of presents and wraps each one himself. He doesn't just rent a Santa Claus costume, he had one tailored for him. He sends out Christmas cards to everybody he ever knew, and some people he barely knows . . . It's the happiest day of his year, and he's not here to enjoy it."

The phone rang at six. Elly picked it up in the kitchen, where she was preparing a lamb roast. She came out to give her husband a mock-suspicious look and said: "And exactly who is Pola Methune?"

"Is that her first name?" Lev said. "I never did ask."

He took the phone, hoping to hear that Pola's wandering husband had returned, that it was Christmas as usual at the Methune homestead. But her first words were wrapped in a sob, and Lev knew that his Christmas dinner would have to wait.

He grumbled to himself throughout the return trip to the Methune house. He never should have given Pola Methune his home number; he should have referred her back to headquarters, let Sam Reddy take the problem. He felt victimized by sentiment. If this was the result of being a "family" man, he wasn't sure he liked it.

The daylight was gone by the time he reached Holly Road. He was conscious of an added poignancy to the lights ornamenting its houses. By tomorrow they would be dimmed. Christmas was almost over. Barry Methune would have to wait 364 days to express his seasonal joy. Or would he ever express it again?

Pola greeted him with hollowed eyes and a hushed voice. In counterpoint, Dodie and Amanda were shrieking with laughter on the living room carpet, wallowing in a litter of boxes and wrapping paper. Obviously, Pola had decided not to deny them their Christmas presents, even if her own remained unopened.

"I know what you told me," she said. "About that Missing Persons regulation, about having to wait . . . But isn't there anything you can do?"

"I've already done some things," Lev told her. "I canvassed the neighborhood after I left you this morning. I also checked the accident reports, the local hospitals, the morgue. You'll be glad to know it was all negative. Now, did you do what I asked you to do?"

She looked even more miserable. "Yes," she said. "I went through Barry's papers. I even looked in all his pockets. I hated doing that. It was so—distrustful."

"Did you find anything?"

"No. At least, nothing that meant anything to me."

"Would you be willing to let me have a look?"

"I suppose so . . . I put everything into a box. Including his address book. Except for a few business numbers, it's just like mine."

"Let me see it anyway," Lev said. "And if you have any photos of your husband, let me have them, too."

She turned and went upstairs, with the trudging steps of a woman twenty years older.

He watched the little girls while he waited. They had stopped playing and were absorbed in their own Christmas prizes. The older one—Amanda?—appeared frustrated by one of her toys and decided that he was a passable father-substitute. She brought it to him and thrust it into his hands.

"How do you play this?" she asked. "Can you show me?"

Lev looked it over. It was some kind of electronic game, a football simulation. There was a liquid display screen depicting the playing field, and dual buttons on both sides, one controlling offense, the other defense. But when he pressed the buttons, nothing happened.

"Maybe the batteries are dead," he said.

Relieved at having an easier problem to solve, he searched among the scattered gifts and saw a small silver flashlight. Sure enough, it operated on the same size batteries, and they were in working order. The younger child, Dodie, didn't object to his tampering with her present; she didn't seem very interested in it. Lev himself couldn't help wondering why anyone would give a flashlight to a little girl. Or, for that matter, an electronic football game.

Unfortunately, the toy didn't respond to its new source of power. When Pola Methune came downstairs, holding a white cardboard box, she saw Amanda's disappointed face and asked what was going on. Lev told her and said:

"Do you remember where you bought this?"

"I didn't buy it, Barry did. Some toy shop near his office, on Broad Street, 900 Broad, the Wyatt Building."

"I can probably find the place," Lev said. "I'll take it in for exchange, if you like."

"You're so kind. That's just what Barry would have done."

New tears threatened, and Lev became anxious to conclude his inquiry. He went through Barry Methune's papers and had to agree with his wife that they were innocuous and unrevealing. Methune also proved to be camera-shy. There was only one photograph, probably taken too long ago to be useful. It was a candid shot of a plumpish young man with dark curly hair already receding at the temples. He had crinkly eyes, a broad nose, a smile that had the appearance of being permanently affixed.

That night, Lev lay awake beside what he called Mt. Eleanor and studied the ceiling. His wife, citing inflation, offered him a nickel for his thoughts.

"I was thinking about their presents," he said.

"Whose presence?"

"Not presence, presents. As in gifts. What the little girls got for Christmas."

"The football game, you mean?"

"And a flashlight."

"So?"

"It just seemed a little odd, that's all."

"Odd how?" There was the hint of bristle in Elly's voice. "Because there weren't any dolls or cooking sets or sewing kits?"

"Well, there might have been dolls and cooking sets. I didn't see all the gifts."

"But the football game bothered you, because it's a *man's* sport, is that it?"

"It's too late at night for feminist polemics."

"I'll tell you one thing," Elly said. "When John Alexander is old enough, I'm getting him a baby doll."

"Have a baby first," Lev said, turning over on his side.

Half an hour later he was still awake, wondering where the man who loved Christmas had gone.

He filed his report the next morning, and Ab Peterson read it with narrowed eyes. "*Churches la femme,*" he said. "Did you ever think of that?"

"I thought of it," Lev said wearily.

At noontime, he lunched at the Lewisfield Diner with Sam Reddy and told him about the case Sam should have been handling. Like Ab Peterson, Sam had a theory.

"Suicide," he said succinctly. "These bouncy types are always hiding something. Maybe he didn't really *love* Christmas. Maybe it depressed him."

"Then where's the body?"

Sam shrugged. "How about the reservoir? He could have walked there from Holly Road, it's less than a mile away. Maybe people downstate are drinking Methune-flavored water right now."

He chuckled into his coffee, untroubled by Lev's look of disgust.

Instead of riding back to headquarters with Sam, he asked to be dropped off in downtown Dayton, at McReady's Toyshop. He had brought Amanda's inoperative toy with him and presented it to the man at the counter.

"What's wrong with it?"

"Other than the fact that it doesn't work, nothing."

The man had a demeanor like a burnt-out pawnbroker.

"You got a sales slip?"

"No," Lev said. "It was bought by someone else."

"How do I know it was bought here?"

"Take my word for it," Lev said. To his credit, he didn't use his badge as a voucher.

"I don't know," the man said. "This is a $49.50 item. I been stiffed before. You give me proof, I'll exchange it."

The heck with this, Lev said, reaching for his wallet. Then he changed his mind and said: "Maybe it was paid for with a credit card. Could you check your records? The name was Methune, Barry Methune."

"Can you describe him?"

Lev did the best he could. He was gratified when the proprietor started nodding his head.

"Yeah, yeah. I think I know the guy. I think he was in here last week. Let me have a look at my slips."

Five minutes later, he came up with a receipt for one electronic football game, one mini flashlight, and two Captain Wango ray guns.

"I'm sure this is the guy who bought this stuff. The only thing is, his name isn't what you said. It's Munsey. Benjamin Munsey. See?"

He handed Lev the receipt, and despite the pale carbon, the name and signature were clear enough. Munsey, Benjamin Munsey. Lev shook his head. Wrong guy, he said. Mistake. But that didn't alter his conviction that the faulty game was purchased here. He wanted a replacement, and he was impatient. He had more important things to do, he said. And if you must know, I'm a cop. He sighed when he said it; a principle had been violated. But it did the trick. The toyshop owner shrugged and gave him a working copy of the electronic football game.

"But I still say that's the guy," he grunted. "He's in here, three, four times around the holidays, asking questions, trying things out. The guy's a real nut about Christmas."

Lev's hand froze on the door handle.

"Can I see that credit card slip again?"

There was no mistaking the signature. *Benjamin Munsey*. The address was 18 Skyblue Lane, Sycamore Village, a suburban enclave some thirty miles north of Dayton.

"Thanks," he said.

He stood on the sidewalk, reflecting on what was only a mild coincidence. Two men who looked alike and loved Christmas.

Well, why not? Two men who looked alike, loved Christmas, and bought almost the same toys. More than possible.

Two men who looked alike, loved Christmas, bought the same toys, and had the same initials.

He found a phone booth and called Pola Methune.

"Did the kids get *what*?" she said.

"Ray guns," Lev said. "Captain Wango's ray guns, whatever they are."

"I could kill Captain Wango," Pola said fiercely. "That buzzing noise is driving me crazy. If you ask me, they shouldn't make *any* kind of guns for kids!"

Lev started to leave the booth, but then changed his mind. He asked directory assistance for a number in Sycamore Village and dialed it. A woman answered in a depressed voice that turned anxious when he identified himself.

"No, there's nothing wrong," he said quickly. "I just had a couple of questions to ask you. Just routine," he said, wondering how many times a week he used that word.

He didn't give her an opportunity to protest. He hung up and made three more calls in rapid succession: one to headquarters, one to home quarters, and one to the Dayton Cab Company.

Forty-five minutes later, the driver managed to find Skyblue Lane, a dirt road that tried to hide itself from the proliferating traffic in the area. Number 18 was the third house on the left, two stories of brick and stucco, twice the age and size of the Methune residence in Lewisfield.

But there was at least one similarity. Strings of Christmas bulbs traced the contours of the house from its wide chimney to its sloping roof, running down all four corners and framing every door and window. At night, it would look like the skeleton of a house outlined in multicolored lights. There was no plastic sleigh on the lawn, but there *was* a gigantic Santa, waving his mittened hand at passersby.

Lev made still another comparison when Mrs. Benjamin Munsey answered the door. She was taller and heavier than Pola Methune, but there was still a superficial resemblance around the eyes. Later he realized it was effect more than physiognomy. Both women had been shedding tears, in copious amounts.

"It's about my husband, isn't it?" she said, even before the door closed behind him. "Something's happened to him! You just didn't want to tell me on the phone!"

"No," Lev said. "That's not why I'm here, really."

"I thought of calling the police," she said. "But I keep thinking he'll walk in any minute, or the phone will ring and he'll say he's stuck someplace. There's a blizzard in Illinois, you know, he has customers in Chicago . . ."

"Mrs. Munsey, are you saying your husband is missing?" He almost added the word "too."

"He said he would be home the day before Christmas, but he never showed up! I called his office, but the man who works for him was away, on a sales trip his secretary said. And she was only a temp, so she knew nothing, nothing at all . . ."

Then it wasn't a disappearance, Lev thought. It was a nonappearance.

"Maybe you should have called the police. Your husband might have been in an accident, for instance."

"I just didn't want to think that!" she said, clamping a hand over her mouth. "Not the day before Christmas. That would be just too awful. Ben loved Christmas so much!"

"May I please come in?" Lev said gravely.

She let him into the house, and his eyes were drawn to the Christmas accents all over the interior. There was an oversize wreath in the hallway, holly and mistletoe on every wall, a spray of white branches in the baronial fireplace, and a tree that towered at least twelve feet in the high-ceilinged living room. There was another jumble of opened gift boxes, although someone had already cleared away the wrapping paper.

There was a different kind of debris at the base of the tree, and

Lev had to look twice to make sure his eyes weren't deceived. It appeared to be the scene of a Toyland massacre. There were dismembered arms and legs, a doll's head with gouged-out eyes, another with its eyes intact looking even more grotesque as it stared at its own torn and mangled torso. The woman must have seen his expression, because she said:

"That was Michael's doing." Her voice was sad. "He's been out of control these past couple of days, and I'm sure it's because his father isn't here."

"Is Michael your son?"

"Yes. He's only six, but he's got a temper. God knows where he got it from. Not from me, certainly, or Ben, although my own father used to throw things when he got angry . . ."

"Are you saying your little boy—did this?" He nodded at the carnage.

"Yes. It was sort of like the last straw, Santa Claus not showing up, his daddy not here, and then those presents he opened. It must have been a mistake, of course. Ben must have ordered toys by phone and the store got the delivery mixed up. I mean, twin dolls, *girl* dolls! Michael went berserk when he saw them. Honestly, it's amazing; it must be television the way these kids know about *macho*."

"What *was* he expecting for Christmas?" Lev asked carefully. "A football game, maybe? Ray guns?"

"I don't know," the woman said. "He was in such a bad mood after the argument he had with his father, when he announced that there was no such person as Santa Claus . . . I told Ben not to take it so seriously, that sooner or later, kids find out the truth. They learn it on the street, don't they?"

"I suppose they do."

"Only last year, Michael put out milk and cookies for Santa. This year he refused. I mean, he wouldn't even try to *humor* us, the way some kids do. Ben got so upset, he couldn't sleep that night. Like I said, that man really *loved* Christmas."

"Mrs. Munsey," Lev said, "would you happen to have a picture of your husband?"

"It's funny you ask that," she said. "That's one thing I put on my Christmas list every year, a camera, but I never get one. I mean, we just don't have any family pictures. Ben hates to have his picture taken . . ."

"Then maybe you can describe him for me."

Mrs. Munsey described him.

Ten minutes later, Lev was at the front door, and the woman remembered to ask him the purpose of his visit.

"Just routine," Lev said.

He promised to be in touch and asked her to call him either at headquarters or at home if there was any word from her errant spouse.

He didn't expect to hear from her.

Lev could have returned to headquarters to make his report. Ab Peterson, who liked gossip, would have enjoyed it. Sam Reddy would have been disappointed at missing out on a juicy case. Both reactions might have been satisfying, but Lev needed to talk to Elly first.

At home, he found her on the kitchen telephone, saying:

"Oh, about every fifteen or twenty minutes."

"What every fifteen minutes?" he asked anxiously.

"I'm telling Fawn Cohen how to baste a turkey."

"Oh."

Then he told her about his day. Her eyes and mouth described three perfect *O*s when she realized his implication.

"Are you really *sure*, Lev?"

"The physical descriptions fit. The character descriptions fit. Even the job descriptions matched. Barry Methune owned a small surgical supply company in Dayton. Ben Munsey owned an entirely different surgical supply company, also in Dayton. Both served the same customers with different products."

"You mean he just . . . split his life in two?"

"He had to, in order to maintain two households. He never worked Christmas; he let somebody else service the accounts. He went through all the holiday preliminaries in *both* houses, but he actually spent one Christmas Day on Holly Road, one Christmas Day on Skyblue Lane . . . The man loved Christmas so much, he had to celebrate *two* of them every year."

"But what happened this year? Why did he disappear?"

"He was obviously strained to the breaking point. He was getting absentminded. He was mixing up his addresses, his kids, his Christmas gifts. He sent the girls' gifts to his son, his son's gifts to the girls. He just couldn't handle it anymore."

"So he ran away from *both* of his lives."

"And now we have a stronger reason to look for the guy. He's committed a crime. Bigamy."

"Lev Walters," Elly said, "you're a good detective."

"Thanks," he said smugly.

"However," Elly said, "you didn't detect that I was lying. Fawn Cohen never cooked a turkey in her life. I was talking to Dr. Ramirez."

Lev didn't remember the next half hour. But somehow, he got Elly's bag together, got her into his car, and managed to get her to the hospital just one hour before he became the father of John Alexander Walters.

When he saw his wife again she was sweaty but beautiful, looking like she had just run the marathon and won.

"I'm glad about one thing," he said. "I'm glad Alex wasn't born on New Year's Eve. He would have grown up thinking every party was for him."

"Have you seen him yet?"

"Yes," Lev said. "He's gorgeous."

"Liar. He looks like a hundred-year-old Pueblo Indian. I was thinking of complaining to the stork." When Lev didn't answer, his gaze wandering off to the middle distance, she tugged at his wrist. "Hey, did you hear what I said?"

"Yes, sure."

"I lost you for a minute. What were you thinking about?"

"The stork," Lev said. "The way the stork delivers babies. And now I'm thinking of something else."

It was late in the day when he returned to the Methune house. He dreaded this visit more than he had dreaded the phone calls he had made earlier.

"Have you found him yet?" Pola Methune said icily.

"No," Lev said. "We haven't found your husband, Mrs. Methune. But I have an idea about where he is."

"Tell me! Just give me time to buy a shotgun!"

"Remember what you said about his disappearance? That he just seemed to vanish in the middle of the night?"

"He probably went to see his other wife."

"No," Lev said. "He was confused. About *which* wife he meant to be with, about which gifts to give which children. And he may have been confused about something else. About where he intended to play Santa, convincingly enough to restore the faith of a cynical six-year-old . . ."

"Neither of my kids are six years old."

"No," Lev said soberly. "But Michael Munsey is. And maybe your husband decided to put on a convincing performance for him. The only thing is, he may have attempted that performance in *the wrong house.*"

He went to the Methune fireplace and pulled aside the fire-screen and andirons. He ducked his head and stepped into the inner hearth. He was hoping he was wrong, but he wasn't. When he reached his hand upward, into the hollow of a too-narrow chimney, he felt the soles of two rubber boots.

EDWARD D. HOCH

THE TOUCH OF KOLYADA

Since we're in a holiday mood, we might say that Edward D. Hoch has much the same relationship with the mystery short story as Guy Lombardo had with New Year's Eve. He's written something like 800 of them; ever since the late 1950s they've been appearing in all the American crime magazines, in collections, and in television productions. Edward D. Hoch also has a big following in many foreign countries, so it's not surprising that we find an exotic note even in this Christmas story. And since the festive season is a time for nostalgia, he's brought back the first character he ever created to play Lord of Misrule. Simon Ark has by now been involved in many a strange adventure, but this is the first time he's ever had to deal with the Russian equivalent of Santa Claus.

My old friend Simon Ark had been living at a university near the northern tip of Manhattan, not far from the Cloisters, pursuing his study of medieval legends. I had seen him occasionally through the year, and in a burst of preholiday goodwill my wife Shelly suggested I invite him to our suburban home for Christmas dinner. When I phoned him with the invitation three days before the holiday, he thanked me but hesitated about accepting it.

"My friend, an unusual situation has developed up here among some of my academic friends. I am attempting to resolve it, and I trust I can do so by Christmas Day."

Something in his tone of voice make me ask, "Have you gotten yourself involved in another mystery, Simon?"

"I suppose you might call it a mystery of sorts, though the events thus far suggest a mystery of good rather than evil."

"Now you've sparked my curiosity."

"Do you have time to journey up here?"

"Not today. I have a meeting with one of our authors this afternoon. But tomorrow is only the office Christmas party, and I'd like an excuse to miss that."

"Then come, by all means! I will meet you at the university library at noon."

And so on the following day, the eve of Christmas Eve, I took the subway up the West Side of Manhattan to the end of the line at 207th Street. The university was across the street from Inwood Hill Park, and as I walked briskly across campus in the thirty-degree weather I wondered if the city might have its first white Christmas in years. Up here the ground was barely covered with a half inch of snow, but more was predicted for Christmas Eve.

Simon Ark was waiting for me just inside the big brass doors of the library building. He seemed a bit thinner than the last time I'd seen him, and his dark clothes gave him an almost gaunt appearance. I could remember a huskier Simon, back when I'd first known him more than thirty years ago. Yet the tiny lines of age on his face had not deepened with the passing years. One might easily have taken his age for a vigorous seventy at most. It was only in rare moments, among those who knew him best, that he was likely to repeat his claim of being some two thousand years old. No one really believed it, of course. Nor did we believe he'd been a Coptic priest in Egypt shortly after the time of Christ. Still, there were times when I imagined I could detect all the knowledge of the world behind those glistening dark eyes.

"It is good to see you again," Simon said, greeting me with an unaccustomed handshake. "I have just been studying up on Russian folklore."

"Oh? Are you planning a journey there?"

"No. There is a program of Russian Studies here at the

university. Many of the faculty members are Russian emigrés who came here with their families during the past twenty years. I have become friendly with a number of them. The little mystery I mentioned on the telephone concerns them."

"Tell me about it."

The library was built on a hill, with a cafeteria on the lower level. We went down there, bought coffee and sandwiches, and found a table by a sunny window looking out on the running track at the bottom of the hill. There were a number of noonday joggers on it, unfazed by the cold.

"Have you ever heard of the elf maiden Kolyada?" Simon asked when we'd unwrapped our sandwiches.

"Is this more Russian folklore?"

"In a way. Russian children sing songs of Kolyada each Christmas Eve, and she is said to ride a sleigh from house to house, delivering gifts much as Santa Claus does in Western countries. She is very beautiful and always wears a luxurious white robe and hood. During the past week some of the children here have reported seeing Kolyada. She has even entered their homes."

"A pleasant tale. The newspapers would probably like a female version of Santa, especially a beautiful one."

"She has been leaving gifts for the children."

"How nice," I murmured.

"Why? Why is she doing it?"

"You're not supposed to look a gift horse in the mouth, Simon. That's some sort of folk saying too, I think."

"There was another visit last evening. Will you come with me while I speak to the children?"

"Of course, if you want me to. I came all the way up here, after all."

We finished our sandwiches and coffee, and I accompanied Simon past the administration buildings to a street on the other end of the campus. There a row of large old houses lined the street, each of them tastefully painted and landscaped. "These are faculty homes," Simon explained. "Down there farther are some fraternity houses."

"It becomes quite a closed community with the faculty living on campus," I commented.

"The houses were made available to emigré families who arrived here without a place to live. Some have moved on to other homes, but six of the houses are still occupied by Russian scholars on the faculty here. These are the ones that have received visits from Kolyada."

"How many?"

"The first four when I spoke to you yesterday. The fifth house last evening. Jeff and Lenore Rodgers live there."

It was at the fifth house that we turned in, and were met at the front door by a pretty young woman with brown hair worn in a long braid. "Simon Ark—it was good of you to call. Come in, please."

Simon introduced me and we entered the big old house. I was surprised by the bright colors and modern decor inside, so different from the outward appearance of the place. "The university is trying to get this declared a landmark district," Lenore Rodgers explained. "They won't allow us to change the exterior, so we compensate inside. These houses used to be dorms and it took a lot of work to make them livable for one family again. Of course we've still got two shower rooms upstairs, and a restaurant-size refrigerator and freezer in the kitchen, but at least it's a bit more homey in the family room and bedrooms. Our two daughters like it, and that's important."

"You're not Russian," I said, stating the obvious. "I thought—"

She laughed. "We're the exceptions on the street. Jeff is an assistant professor in Russian Studies, and this house was available so they offered it to us. His starting salary wasn't all that great and we jumped at the chance."

"Are your daughters here?" Simon asked.

"I'll call them. They're dying to talk about Kolyada to anyone who'll listen."

Cynthia and Clarice proved to be two lovely little girls, aged four and five, who captured my heart immediately. "We saw Kolyada," the five-year-old Cynthia told me. "She was a beautiful lady in a long white cape and she touched me on the cheek."

"And she gave us gifts!" Clarice chimed in. "Candy and dolls!"

"Did you see her, too?" Simon Ark asked their mother.

"No, but I heard the excitement. They were down here playing and I'd gone up to make the beds. I work in the administration office during the day and a couple of students take turns sitting with them. So the housework gets done in the evenings. I heard this uproar, but it didn't seem too unusual for this pair. When I heard them calling to me I came down right away, but by that time she was gone. They were each clutching a doll and a little box of Christmas candy."

Simon patted the children on the head as he examined the dolls. "Made in Taiwan, but that's not too unusual these days. And the candy is a popular brand. Tell me, Cynthia, did Kolyada ring the doorbell?"

The older girl nodded. "At the back. I answered it. She came in the kitchen in her white robe. Her sleigh must have been parked out back but I didn't see it."

Simon Ark smiled benevolently. "Suppose we have a look now, during the daytime." We followed him out through the spacious kitchen to the back door. The thin layer of snow had melted in spots and the rest was trampled by the footprints of running children, but we could see no sign of sleigh runners.

"I have to be getting back to work," Lenore Rodgers said with a touch of regret. "The administration office is closed tomorrow for Christmas Eve, but we work a full day today. I just came home to get lunch for the girls. Their afternoon sitter will be here any minute."

"It must be expensive for you," I said.

"They keep promising day care for the staff's children, but I haven't seen it yet."

We said good-bye to the girls and walked around the house to the street. The man next door was just coming home and Simon hailed him. "Mr. Trevitz, do you have a moment?"

Trevitz was a small man in his sixties with thick glasses and a little beard that strengthened the foreign appearance of his features. "Simon Ark! It is good to see you again! How is your research going?"

"As well as could be expected."

Trevitz turned to me and I caught the little glint of humor in his eyes. "Mr. Ark is the only one I know presently conducting research into the hoof structure of unicorns."

"Really?"

Simon was more interested in the matter at hand. "Did you know your neighbor was visited by Kolyada last evening?"

Professor Trevitz wagged his head. "Mrs. Rodgers told me about it this morning. I am the last house in line, though I doubt if she will visit here. My daughter is married and long gone from home."

"The Vladimers have no children at home, but they were visited on the second night. Kolyada left a basket of fruit and candy on their back porch."

The balding professor snorted. "No doubt it's all a publicity stunt for some new shop in the area. I'm too busy to concern myself with such things. If she comes, she comes."

As we walked out to the street I asked, "Does he live there alone?"

Simon Ark nodded. "His wife died in an auto accident last year, on Christmas morning. He was driving the car and the accident severely depressed him for several months. He's getting back to his old self now, though—crusty and cynical as ever!"

"I gather these visits by the white-robed woman have occurred on each of the last five nights."

"That is correct. Navogard, Vladimer, Batovrin, Tolstoy, and Rodgers. It stands to reason she will visit the Trevitz home tonight. I would like your help in intercepting her."

"But she's committed no crime!" I insisted.

"Not yet."

I explained to Shelly on the telephone that Simon had tentatively accepted our invitation to Christmas dinner, but it was necessary for me to help him finish some research work first. That was more or less true, and it explained my absence from home that evening as I huddled in the cold with Simon at the rear of Professor Trevitz's house, awaiting the arrival of the elf maiden Kolyada.

"What am I supposed to do if she tries to get away?" I asked.

"I just want to know who she is and why she's doing this. I suspect—" He broke off and gripped my arm. "There!"

I saw her in the same instant. She'd emerged from the shadows and moved into the light from Trevitz's windows. She was short, dressed in a white-hooded robe that all but hid her features. In one gloved hand she carried a basket that appeared to contain candy and fruit. Before we could act she was on the back porch. The kitchen door was unlocked and she entered without hesitation. We waited a few moments but she didn't emerge.

Simon and I followed her through the back door. Trevitz's kitchen was identical to the one next door, except for its disarray. There were cartons of melting ice cream in the sink and a pile of metal racks on the counter next to Kolyada's basket. We could see her through the doorway into the living room, standing on the scuff-marked carpet as she bent over the hunched-up figure of Professor Trevitz in his chair.

Her outstretched fingers were touching the skin of his cheek when Simon Ark spoke her name. "Kolyada."

She stiffened and turned toward us, revealing a rosy-cheeked face with slightly Oriental features. Then she hurried toward the front door. I was after her in an instant, but she was too fast for me. She was out the door and down the steps before I could catch hold of her flowing white robe. In the front yard I caught a glimpse of firm white legs as the robe came open and she broke into a run. At my age I knew there was no chance of catching her.

I went back inside and was surprised to find Simon crouched over Professor Trevitz. "She got away. Is the professor still asleep?"

"He's dead," Simon informed me quietly.

"Dead! A heart attack?"

"Feel his skin."

I did so and immediately pulled my fingers away. "It's ice-cold, Simon!"

He nodded. "It almost appears that Professor Trevitz has frozen to death."

We called the police, of course, and told them what little we knew. The man from the Medical Examiner's office agreed that rigor mortis could not have set in that quickly under normal circumstances, but he declined further comment until the autopsy.

The detective in charge of the investigation, a big Irishman named O'Connor, wanted to know if this Kolyada person could have killed him. Simon Ark thought about it and replied, "Not unless she froze him with a touch of her fingers."

O'Conner wasn't too satisfied with that response, but promised to put out an alarm for the mysterious Kolyada. "You say she's been bringing gifts to the children? I feel like I'm ordering the arrest of Santa Claus."

"In a sense that's exactly what you're doing," Simon agreed.

I left for home, promising to phone Simon in the morning. The version of the night's events that I presented to Shelly was laundered a bit, but she still saw through it to the core of the matter. "You're involved in another one of those bizarre murders Simon Ark loves so much, aren't you?"

"I'd hardly say that. The autopsy may show he died a completely natural death."

"I wouldn't bet on it!"

Christmas Eve morning dawned with a few flurries in the air as predicted. The office was closed and I wasn't surprised when Simon urged me to come up to the university once again. An hour later, after my subway ride, I found him in his room with a middle-aged Russian whom he introduced as Ivan Tolstoy.

I shook hands and made the obvious comment. "Any relation to Leo?"

He chuckled as if he'd never heard it before. "No, although when we read *War and Peace* at school I used to tell my classmates he was my great-uncle. They never believed me."

"Professor Tolstoy and his family reside in the fourth house along the street," Simon pointed out. He'd drawn six squares on a sheet of paper and labeled the fourth one with the Tolstoy name. "His children were visited three nights ago by Kolyada."

"I came here when I heard the news of Professor Trevitz's death," Tolstoy explained. "I couldn't believe it—especially the part about Simon seeing Kolyada touch the body. It's as if—" He hesitated.

"As if she killed him with a touch," Simon completed the sentence for him. "That's like something out of a Russian folktale, isn't it, Professor?"

Tolstoy was a handsome, dark-haired man in his mid-forties, who obviously kept in shape. I imagined the women students were especially pleased with his classes. "Well," he began in answer to Simon's question, "it's true that our legends of Frost—or King Frost as he's sometimes called—do contain instances of people frozen to death by the touch of his fingers, but there's no connection between the vengeful Frost and the kindly gift-giving Kolyada."

"There may not be any connection between Professor Trevitz's death and our Kolyada either, but we don't know that yet."

"I must be getting on. We'll keep you advised of any developments, Simon."

"Will you be attending the party at the Rodgers home tonight?"

"I expect so, if they don't cancel it because of this unfortunate event."

When he'd gone I asked Simon about the party. "Apparently it's an annual custom," he told me. "The faculty of the Russian Studies program all dress up in their fancy clothes and attend a Christmas Eve party at one of their homes. This year it will be Jeff and Lenore Rodgers's turn. Last year I believe the Navogards had it at their old house, some distance away." He moved to the telephone. "I want to call Detective O'Connor about the autopsy report while I'm thinking of it."

He waited for several minutes before O'Connor came on the phone. "No reason for not telling you," the detective said. "The papers'll have it for their noon editions. There was a blow to the head, but not enough to kill him. Death was due to suffocation."

"Suffocation!"

"It's impossible to place the time of death accurately because of the temperature of the body. He hadn't eaten dinner, so the blow on the head probably occurred during the afternoon."

"I know he had a class just after lunch."

"I'll want to speak with you again, Mr. Ark. Perhaps as soon as this afternoon. I'll see how the investigation goes."

I'd been listening with my ear close to the phone, and when Simon hung up I asked, "How could he have been suffocated?"

"There are numerous ways, my friend. A pillow, a plastic bag over his head, even a soft towel around the neck that wouldn't leave marks. The important thing is that it's murder, and Kolyada's touch of ice didn't kill him."

"Did you think it had?"

"One never knows. Let us go and speak with some of the others. There are no classes today and everyone should be at home."

On the way across campus he explained that the brief Christmas break helped undergraduates prepare for examinations at the end of the semester in early January. Then there was a two-week recess before the beginning of the second semester.

We went to the first house on the campus street, where the Navogard family was preparing for Christmas. Here the wife was the scholar, and I was pleasantly surprised to find Professor Lara Navogard to be a charming woman with a quick wit and ready smile. The man drinking coffee with her was not her husband, who worked downtown, but Jeff Rodgers from the house we'd visited the previous day.

"Kolyada, Kolyada," Lara Navogard marveled. "That's all my son has talked about since the first night."

"It's the same with my girls," Rodgers confirmed.

But Lara's son was older, around eight, and this immediately interested Simon. He called the boy over and placed a friendly hand on his shoulder. "You're Mark? You look like a fine growing lad. You'll be playing football in a few years."

"Yeah," the boy agreed. "I guess so." He seemed to be completely Americanized, and I guessed he'd been born in this country.

"Did you talk to the nice lady with the gifts?"

"Sure, but I don't believe in that stuff anymore. Kolyada is like Santa Claus. She's not for real."

"But she seemed real when she spoke to you, didn't she?"

"Naw. Her lips didn't even move."

"What's that?" Simon asked. "If she spoke her lips must have moved."

"She was wearing a mask," the boy said, "like on Halloween."

I tried to remember the face I'd seen so briefly, shrouded by that white hood. Yes, it could have been a mask of rubber or plastic. "I can't understand you, Mark," his mother said. "Why have you been talking about her all week if you didn't even believe in her?"

"Because she came to see me first," he announced with some sort of childish pride. "Before all the others."

Simon Ark had one more question. "Did she touch you, lad?"

"Yeah, just once."

"And was her touch cold or warm?"

"I don't know. It was like Mom's."

Simon nodded. "We'll be going on, Lara. Thank you for your help."

Jeff Rodgers left with us, turning up his jacket collar against the thickening snow flurries. "We might be in for a white Christmas," he decided.

"That's what they say." Simon turned his face skyward, the fat flakes turning his lashes white almost immediately.

"I'll see you at our party tonight, Simon?"

"I'd be please to attend."

"Your friend is welcome too."

"Thanks," I said, "but I really should be at home."

Simon Ark peered through the snowfall. "Who's that entering the Trevitz house?" A woman had emerged from a car at the curb.

"It could be his daughter," Rodgers speculated. "She's come for the funeral, and to start clearing out the house."

"Come from where?"

"North of the city. White Plains, I think."

We hurried along and intercepted the young woman. She had a plain appearance, with pulled-back hair and no makeup, of average height though she wore boots with quite high heels. Her married name was Marta Frazier, and Rodgers made the introductions. "Let me express my deep regrets," Simon told her. "I knew your father well."

She picked up on the name. "You're the one who found the body, aren't you?"

"That is correct."

"The police think he was murdered."

"That seems to be the case," Simon agreed.

The snow was coming harder now, and we sought shelter on the front porch of the Trevitz house. "Tell me about finding him. That Detective O'Connor says there was a woman with him."

"It may have been a woman," Simon told her. "The person was wearing a mask and we can't be certain."

For the first time I realized the truth of his words. Although Kolyada had spoken to the children, she'd uttered not a sound when we came upon her with the body of Professor Trevitz. If the face was a mask, the person behind it could have been male or female. I stared out at our footprints in the snow, and Marta Frazier must have been looking at them too. "There wasn't enough snow for footprints, but couldn't this Kolyada have left fingerprints on the knob of the back door?"

"She was wearing mittens," I said.

"Did she flee in a car or on foot?"

"On foot, but there might have been a car waiting in the next block," I told her. "There might have been a sleigh, for all I know."

"The Christmas Eve party's at our house this year," Jeff Rodgers volunteered. "We decided your father would have wanted it to go on as planned."

"You can be sure of that," Marta answered.

"Naturally you're invited. And your husband too, if he can make it."

"My husband's moved out."

"I'm sorry to hear that."

"How soon does the university want Dad's things out of here?"

"Take all the time you need."

She nodded. "Thank you."

"Will we see you tonight?"

"I doubt it. I still have arrangements to make with the funeral director. The holiday tomorrow makes everything so difficult."

We left her on the porch and Rodgers headed for his own house. "Remember—anytime after eight. We've got a sitter coming then to take care of all the kids over at Tolstoy's house."

Simon and I walked back through the snow to his room. I looked back at that row of six nearly identical old houses and I said, "You know something, Simon? After thirty years of associating with you, sometimes I can figure these things out too. There's a very important point that you've completely overlooked."

"What would that be, my friend?"

"I think these people are all lying about Kolyada, every last one of them! Kolyada comes with gifts for Russian children just before Christmas, right?"

"That is correct."

"But don't Russians exchange gifts on the Epiphany, January sixth, rather than Christmas Day? Isn't that when Kolyada would come?"

"Very good, my friend, and quite true of some Russians. But you'll remember I told you earlier the university has a brief recess at Christmas because the semester's final examinations are given in early January. So the Russian community here has adapted to Western ways and celebrates on December twenty-fifth. Obviously our Kolyada does, too."

"All right, you've got me again. Do you have any better theories?"

"Only the beginning of one, my friend. But I think it's important that we attend the Christmas Eve party at the Rodgers house tonight."

When we arrived that evening the other guests were already there. It was a smaller gathering than usual, because the Vladimers were spending Christmas with their married son in Philadelphia and the Batovrins were laid low with the flu. But

Lara Navogard and her husband were there, along with Ivan Tolstoy and his wife and our hosts Jeff and Lenore Rodgers.

"I think we all miss Professor Trevitz," Ivan Tolstoy said, balancing a cup of eggnog with one hand while he helped himself to some of the food. "He really knew how to celebrate at parties. Were you here for last year's party, Simon?"

"I was doing some research at the university but I hadn't gotten to know all of you quite so well at that point. This is my first holiday gathering."

Tolstoy turned to their host and began a discussion of the latest developments in Russia, where new leadership was already bringing changes none of them could have imagined a short time ago. "It's certainly given a whole new lift to Russian Studies," Jeff Rodgers agreed.

I made my way over to Lara Navogard, who seemed the most interesting of those present. "You look a bit bored," I observed.

She laughed and nodded impishly. "I have to come because it's the Department Christmas party, but I'd much rather be spending Christmas Eve at home." Her husband was a hearty Russian who spoke English with a thick accent and seemed to ignore her.

I tried not to think of Shelly at home alone as I chatted with her, keeping an eye on Simon across the room, deep in conversation now with Ivan Tolstoy and his wife. That was the position we were in when the doorbell rang and Lenore Rodgers went off to answer it. All conversation ceased as we turned to greet the newest arrival.

"Perhaps the Batovrins are feeling better and came after all," Lara speculated.

But it was not the Batovrins. It was the short, white-caped figure of the elf maiden Kolyada.

In that instant she was not a figure of Christmas joy or giving, even though she carried a basket full of gifts. In my mind, and perhaps others as well, she was a figure of dread, bending over the body of Professor Trevitz to touch his cheek.

For an instant no one spoke. Then Jeff Rodgers took a step forward, staring into the mask that hid her true features. "Who are you?" he asked, his voice tense.

But it was Simon Ark who answered the question. "It's Marta Frazier, Professor Trevitz's daughter, of course. Take off your mask, Marta, and join the festivities."

It was indeed Marta Frazier, though how Simon had known it was beyond me at that moment. She slipped off the rosy-cheeked, slightly Oriental face and became the woman we'd met earlier that day. "I owe you all an explanation," she said with a smile.

Ivan Tolstoy snorted. "I guess you do!"

Lenore hurried forward with a mug of eggnog. "Have a little Christmas cheer first, Marta. I can tell you my children certainly loved your visit the other evening."

"It was all my father's idea," Marta Frazier told them. "I was going to be with him here tonight, but now he's gone. I decided I should come anyway, so you wouldn't have to keep on wondering."

"How did you know, Simon?" Lara Navogard asked.

"She was the right height, for one thing. When we saw Kolyada fleeing yesterday she was short—shorter than Marta, it seemed, until I noticed the high-heeled boots Marta was wearing. Marta mentioned knowing there wasn't enough snow for footprints to show, and she even mentioned Kolyada entering her father's house by the back door. These were all things she wasn't likely to know unless she was playing the part of Kolyada."

"But why did you flee when you found your father dead?" Jeff Rodgers asked.

"I panicked, I guess. It was such a shock. I hadn't been on the best of terms with my father and I suppose I was afraid someone might think I really did kill him with a touch."

"You knew he was dead immediately?"

A little shudder went through her. "His cheek was so cold—"

Jeff helped her out of her white cape and she joined them in reminiscing about her father. I listened for a time, as did Simon, but I noticed that his eyes kept returning to Kolyada's white cape, hanging from a clothes tree in the front hall.

"I was a great friend of your father's," Lara was saying. "We even knew each other in Moscow, years ago. He was much older than me, of course, but we formed a friendship that rekindled when we met each other again on this campus."

Through all of this Ivan Tolstoy merely shook his head sadly. "Trevitz was in the prime of his life. Whatever happened to him in his home last night, it was not deserved."

I glanced at my watch and finally decided I had to head for home. "Simon—"

"I know, my friend. Thank you for coming and staying this long."

"Well, the mystery of Kolyada is cleared up, at least."

"But not the mystery of what happened to her father. Perhaps it was the touch of her fingers that killed him."

"Do you really believe that, Simon? Like King Frost in the Russian folktales?"

He'd slipped into his coat and walked out with me to the car, after we'd said good-bye to the others. "I must be going, too," he said. But then, as we stood by the car, I saw his body suddenly tense. Someone else was leaving the Rodgers house.

"One of the women," I observed.

"Lara Navogard, going home without her husband."

"But first stopping at the Tolstoys' house for her son."

Simon shook his head. "She's going right home. The children must be having their own party."

"Why were you looking at Kolyada's white cape so intently?"

"I was thinking that anyone could wear it, even a large child. A cape is a garment of complete concealment."

"You sleep on it, Simon," I told him, sliding behind the wheel of my car. "Will we be seeing you for dinner tomorrow?"

Suddenly he was pulling me out of the car. "Of course—they're all alike!"

"What? What are you talking about?"

"Hurry, my friend! We have not a moment to lose."

"What're all alike, Simon?" I asked, hurrying after him through the snow. "White capes?"

"No—the houses!"

"What?"

But he kept on going in silence, as fast as I'd ever seen him move. We must have reached the Navogard house not three minutes after Lara had entered it. Simon tried the front door and it was unlocked, probably in anticipation of her son's or husband's return. But the downstairs was dark.

"She must have gone up," I suggested.

"No," Simon said at once. "The kitchen—"

I was right behind him going in. We saw the figure in white, outlined against the glow from the outside snow. "Kolyada again," Simon murmured. "And this time is the last."

She moved, and so did he, fastening his arms around her. Then he called over his shoulder to me. "The freezer—quickly!"

I switched on the ceiling light and found the big freezer door and yanked it open. Lara Navogard was inside, unconscious, her body folded to fit the space where the shelves had been removed.

"She's alive!" I told Simon.

He pulled the mask from Kolyada's face and it was Marta Frazier again, only this time her face was twisted into a murderous rage.

Shelly had cooked a traditional Christmas dinner for the following day, and while we sat around the table I filled her in on the Kolyada affair. "The whole thing sounds weird!" she said, scooping mashed potatoes from the bowl. "Are you telling me she killed her own father the same way, by stuffing his body into the kitchen freezer?"

"I'm afraid so," Simon Ark told her. "The date should have told me her motive from the beginning. We knew her mother had been killed in an auto accident last Christmas morning, and that her father had been driving. There were certainly hints that Professor Trevitz drank a great deal at parties, and we know last year's faculty party was at the Navogard home, when they were still in their old house some distance away. It's reasonable to assume that Mrs. Trevitz—Marta's mother—died in an auto accident on the way home from the Christmas Eve party last year, and that the professor was driving the car while drunk or at least impaired."

"She killed her father because he had caused her mother's death a year ago."

"Exactly! And she tried to kill Lara Navogard because she'd given the party. After hearing Lara speak tonight about her rekindled friendship with Trevitz, Marta might even have imagined she had an additional motive."

"But what was all this business with the elf maiden Kolyada?" Shelly asked.

Simon Ark sighed. "First we must realize that the woman has serious mental problems. Perhaps she imagined herself to be Kolyada. Certainly by delivering those gifts each evening in the week before Christmas she accomplished two things. She learned the layout of the other houses, while managing to steal a spare key to the Navogard back door, and established Kolyada as a familiar neighborhood figure. If she was seen cutting through the backyards or entering her father's house, no one would call the police. The houses, all originally dormitories, were the same on the outside, and the kitchens were identical. All had the restaurant-size refrigerator and freezer that Lenore Rodgers mentioned to us."

"She got her father in there and then out again after he was dead?"

"He was a small man, remember, and though she was small too, the impetus of her rage must have given her strength. She hit him with something that afternoon, knocking him out, and then put him in the freezer. When she returned in the evening she dragged the body into the living room and seated him in his chair. The rigor mortis of the body caused it to be bent over as we found it. Of course he died of suffocation in the airtight freezer before the cold killed him. Lara Navogard would have died the same way."

"How did you know all this?"

"I didn't, until it was almost too late. But then I remembered the Trevitz kitchen when we entered it, with ice cream melting in the sink and metal racks on the counter. They'd been removed from the freezer, of course, to make room for the professor's body. Last night she made these arrangements at Lara's home before coming to the party. Then when Lara left, Marta went out the back door and across the yards. She was already waiting in the kitchen when Lara entered it. If you think back to that moment we entered the Trevitz house, my friend, there were scuff marks on the living room carpet from dragging the body, and what we took to be a touch to the cheek was Marta arranging the body in the chair as best she could. No wonder she ran out in a panic, not knowing how much we'd witnessed."

"She still might have found the body after someone else killed him," I suggested.

But Simon shook his head. "We had heard that Kolyada rang the doorbell at each house, yet she rang no bell at her father's house. We saw her walk right in. She didn't ring first because she knew there was no one alive to answer the door. Even more important, Kolyada's basket of gifts was left on the kitchen counter. Why, if she was taking it to her father? Because she needed both hands to drag his body out of the freezer and across the floor to the chair."

"Why did she go through all that trouble to freeze the body?" Shelly asked.

"The human mind is always a strange thing," Simon admitted.

"Somehow, for her, it must have been a return to the past, to Russia in the days when her mother was still alive."

But we talked no more about the touch of Kolyada. It was Christmas, after all.

AARON ELKINS

DUTCH TREAT

When it comes to writing mystery novels, 1987 Edgar Award winner Aaron Elkins manages just fine. Where short stories are concerned, though, he suggests the reader may wish to think of this as a collector's item. Aaron has never tried one before and found out as many other writers had that they're by no means so easy as the reader might think. This one gave him such a tussle that he says it may well be his last. The idea came to this Washington State writer while he was crossing Puget Sound on a ferryboat. Evidently ferryboats in fog can be risky in ways that a person might not expect.

"I believe it's closed, Frank. Were it open, surely there'd be some sign of activity. It's Christmas Eve, after all, and you can't expect—"

He was cut short by Fundy's snort of laughter. "Were it open," he mimicked with his execrable version of an English accent. "Oh, I say, old chap. Cheerio. Indubitably."

Claude Fleming clenched his teeth and smiled politely. As a senior attorney with Whatcom, Bennis, Fistule and Sissey, he had long ago learned to bear fools (i.e., clients) gladly, or at least courteously. This restraint had been put to its most severe test in the seven months since Franklin J. Fundy had retained the firm to represent him in the endless disputes in which he was involved. Claude had been flattered when Ian Whatcom had assigned him to Fundy's affairs and had approached the responsibility with enthusiasm.

Who, after all, had not seen "Funnie Frankie Fundy" on television hawking his own chain of major-appliance discount stores? Who could *avoid* seeing him? Funnie Frankie was an inspiring example of entrepreneurial daring and success, a man who had built a hole-in-the-wall household appliance store in Tacoma into a chain of sixty-six giant, warehouselike retail outlets in forty-nine cities across the country.

His commercials were rightly regarded by students of the genre as classics of boorish vulgarity, skillfully geared to the lowest taste level of the American buying public. Why this level should be disproportionately represented among purchasers of large appliances (and exceeded only by purchasers of used cars) was a phenomenon not yet fully understood as far as Claude could make out. In any event, Funnie Frankie's ads had everything: pies in the face; pratfalls; washing machines done in with sledge hammers, automobile crushers, and, in one memorable but quickly yanked instance, an AK-47 assault rifle.

Claude had looked forward to his first meeting with the creator of this empire and the shrewd originator of the Funnie Frankie persona. To his surprise, however, there was no persona. There was just Funnie Frankie Fundy, the same offscreen as on: coarse, ignorant, and unremittingly offensive.

"Beards give me the creeps" had been his first words when Mr. Whatcom had introduced them. "I'm not working with any beards."

"I've had it a long time, Mr. Fundy," Claude had replied with the first of many stiff smiles that were to come. "I'd hate to take it off."

"Hey, I'm broad-minded," Fundy had said. "You don't have to cut it off. Just don't wear it when you're around me, that's all."

"Of course he won't, Mr. Fundy," Mr. Whatcom had simpered with a meaningful glance at Claude.

And so the lovely, beautifully trimmed ginger beard had had to go. Ah, well, that was business; he no longer minded it so much.

What he *did* mind was Fundy's blithe assumption that he could intrude on Claude's personal time whenever he chose. That he resented. Right now, for example—a dreary four P.M. on the day before Christmas—Claude would much rather have been comfortably at home than standing across the street from a brightly lit but obviously closed art gallery in Seattle's rainy, windswept Pioneer Square.

But Fundy had telephoned Mr. Whatcom at home to demand help with an urgent personal problem: He'd meant to get his wife a new painting for Christmas, but he'd forgotten all about it. Now, at the last minute, he wanted to go looking for one at the downtown art galleries, but he needed someone along who was a lawyer and who knew something about art besides. Otherwise he was sure those Jews and Armenians or Iranians or whatever the hell they were would rob him blind. So how about shaking out that English guy that sounds like Ronald Colman—Claude Whatshisname; he likes art—and telling him to get his ass down to Pioneer Square.

This English business was getting under Claude's skin, too. He was as American as Fundy. He did not sound like Ronald Colman. He spoke correctly and literately, that was all; the welcome product of a decent education at Andover, Dartmouth, and Harvard. This he had discreetly explained, but it had made no impression. As far as Funnie Frankie was concerned, if you used three-syllable words and threw in an occasional subjunctive, then you had to be English.

"Let's check the place out anyway," Fundy said, and they crossed First Avenue to the apparently deserted Suffield Gallery. "Clarice'll kill me if I don't get her something. And I'm not talking some lousy box of candy."

The gallery was open. That was another irritating thing about Fundy; the number of times he was right about little things he had no business being right about. When they stepped in a man in his sixties stuck his head around a partition at the back, looking surprised. "Well, hello." He emerged, in his shirtsleeves and suspenders, holding a cordless screwdriver in his hand; a slight man with a dewlapped throat and a small, cigar-shaped mustache that seemed to be tickling his nose. "I wasn't expecting . . . I was just . . . that is, may I help you?"

"That's okay, we're just looking," Fundy said with a salesman's hard-eyed suspicion of other salesmen.

"Well, that's fine," the man said amiably, with something like relief. "Then I'll just get back to my uncrating." He disappeared around the partition, twitching his upper lip like a rabbit. Once more his face popped back. "Oh, I'm Theodore Suffield. Just call if you have any questions."

"Yeah, you bet," Fundy said, and took his first good look at what was hanging on the gallery walls.

"Jesus Christ," he said, "what kind of crap is this?"

Claude put his finger to his lips. "He's right on the other side of the partition," he mouthed. Not that he didn't agree with Fundy, which was probably a first. The Suffield Gallery's collection tended toward the very abstract, the very bright, and the very improvisational: spatters of yellow, streaks of brilliant white, splots of blue, globby crimson footprints (*footprints?*).

Fundy bent to look at the printed card on the wall next to a big canvas with four tarry blobs of purple on a field of blinding white. "Chows Number Nine?" he said, scowling.

Claude looked too. *CHAOS #9*, it said. He sighed and held his tongue. *Chows*. If it weren't so pathetic it would be funny.

Underneath the painting was a tiny white cardboard rectangle. Fundy bent to that too. "They want 9,200 bucks for *this*?"

"It looks like it," Claude said, more quietly, but only slightly less incredulously.

"I wouldn't pay 9,200 cents for this crap," Fundy said.

When Claude winced and raised his finger to his mouth again, Fundy shrugged his irritation. "Hey, what do I care if he hears me?"

He walked around the partition at the back of the room. Claude followed. Suffield was on his knees, surrounded by a litter of cartons, packing materials, and crates. Three small paintings stood on the floor, tipped against the burlap-covered walls. At their approach, Suffield, who was unscrewing the bracing at the corner of a crate, looked up and smiled pleasantly at Fundy. "Find anything you like?"

"No. You got any pictures with people in them? Clarice likes people. You know, kids, clowns? Dogs, even. Puppies."

"Puppies?" Suffield's pale blue eyes were perplexed. "Well, as you see, we do specialize in mainstream Abstract Expressionism, although we're beginning to get into the Russian Constructivists as well." He smiled wanly. "Not too much in the way of recognizable people, I'm afraid. If you're interested in something more representational, you might try Frieda Weitzmann just down the street, near Yesler."

"Everybody else is closed. That's why we came in here," Fundy said with his usual tact.

"Well, then," Suffield said without visible offense, "you might—"

"What about that one?" Fundy pointed at one of the three paintings leaning against the wall, an age-darkened portrait of a scraggly bearded man in a wide-brimmed cavalier's hat, firmly clutching a pewter mug of red wine. Not his first mugful of the day either, from the loose-lipped, devil-may-care grin on his face.

"I'm sorry," Suffield said without looking at it. "You see, these are all from an estate sale in Denver. Nineteenth-century English watercolorists, mostly. I have a client who collects them, and I was acting for her on a contingency basis."

"How much?" Fundy said.

"No, no, you misunderstand. These aren't for sale, at least not until my client exercises her right of first refusal. There's an ethical consideration here, an obligation on me to—"

"How much?" Fundy demanded, not the man to be put off with ethical considerations.

Suffield shook his head, kindly but firmly. "No, really, I'm sorry."

"But that particular picture isn't a nineteenth-century English watercolor," Claude pointed out smoothly, "so perhaps your obligation doesn't hold." Fundy was paying the firm's standard $200-per-hour fee for his services, so he might as well get his money's worth.

"Not a nineteenth-century . . ." Anxiously, Suffield turned his head to look at the picture. His expression cleared at once. "Oh, yes, of course; I'd forgotten. There were a few other odds and ends included in the collection. I bid on the entire lot, you see, and a few of these came with it. They're Dutch; seventeenth century." His eyes softened as he continued to look at the paintings. "It's hardly my field, but they *are* handsome little things, aren't they?"

"They certainly are," Claude said sincerely.

Fundy actually jabbed him in the side with an elbow while the proprietor continued to gaze warmly on the paintings. This, Claude assumed, was Funnie Frankie's characteristically obnoxious way of pointing out that it was not sharp business practice to tell a buyer you liked what he was selling.

"You know," Suffield said, brightening, "you're quite right. It's only the English paintings I'm obliged to hold for my client. If you're interested in this . . ." He stood up, wincing as his knees straightened, and went to the painting. He picked it up, set it carefully on a small shelf jutting from the wall, and turned on a shaded wall lamp. Then he admired the picture some more. Claude noticed for the first time that it was painted on a panel, not a canvas.

"How much?" said Fundy, who was good at sticking to a subject when he wanted to.

Suffield's eyelids whirred briefly. His nose twitched. He was doing some rapid calculation, possibly along the lines of just how much Fundy might be good for.

"Ahum," the older man said, "The, ah, price on this one is $15,900." He scratched his mustache.

"Jesus," Fundy said, "that's a pretty small picture for 16,000 bucks. It's all dirty too."

But he didn't sound as if he were dismissing the idea, something Suffield was quick to notice. "Oh, I'll have it cleaned for you, of course, at no extra charge. That will brighten it up wonderfully." He gestured at it. "It looks as if it's had a few too many coats of varnish over the years, doesn't it? Hm, unless I'm mistaken, this is the original frame."

He turned the panel over. "Seems to be some sort of—what is it, a brand?—on the back." Thoughtfully he fingered the mark. "Interesting."

Why, he really doesn't know anything about Dutch painting, Claude thought. Of course it was a brand, seared onto the wood with a branding iron and looking just like something that belonged on the flank of a steer: an interlocked *G* and *L*. It was the trademark of the panel maker; what would come to be called a "brand name" in a later age.

"There's no signature," Fundy said craftily. "Doesn't that make it worth less?"

"Oh, naturally," Suffield answered. "That's why I'm able to offer it to you at such a low price." For a man who appeared to be a little slow on the uptake, he had his wits about him.

Fundy fingered the frame, then turned aggressively on Suffield. "How do I know it's really that old? How do I know it's not a fake?"

It took a moment for the words to sink in. Then Suffield flushed deeply. "A *fake*? My dear man, really—I mean—that is to say, I've been in business at this location since—you're free to check—well, really—"

"Okay, okay," Fundy said, waving him to a halt. "Look, I want to talk to my associate here for a minute, right? In private. So how about, uh . . ." He motioned over his shoulder with his thumb.

"Of course," Suffield said woodenly. "Certainly." He didn't like being dismissed in his own gallery, no more than he liked being accused of fraud. And who could blame him? "I'll be in my office."

"Is it worth it?" Fundy asked Claude when he'd gone. "Sixteen thou?"

"I think it is, Frank," Claude said. "It's a well-done piece, and I don't think there's much doubt about its being authentic. A follower of Hals, obviously. Maybe even one of his students. You could probably turn around and sell it tomorrow for more than you're paying for it. "

"So who's Hollis?"

"Hals," Claude said with one of those tight little smiles. "Frans Hals, one of the greatest painters of the seventeenth century."

"No kidding. Write that down, will you? So I can tell Clarice." He reached up and clapped Claude familiarly on the shoulder. On the shoulder of his new—and expensive—camel's hair coat. "Okay, what the hell, I'll buy it. But I'm not paying his asking price, no way. He just made that up out of thin air." He gestured with his chin in the direction of the glass-enclosed office where Suffield sat, his back to them. "Go in there and jew him down a little."

Claude stiffened. "I beg your pardon."

"Go offer him five thousand. He'll settle for ten, believe me. Twelve at most."

"Frank, I'm very sorry," Claude said stiffly, "I agreed to advise you to the best of my ability, and in my opinion that painting is well worth what he's asking. I did *not* agree to . . . *jew* anybody down."

For a moment Fundy's froggy eyes bulged, hot and angry. Then he laughed. "What the hell, I'll do it myself. Come on, you want to learn something about human nature?"

"Thank you, no. I'll wait here."

This also struck Fundy's funny bone. "Th'nk yaw, neow," he

said through his nose. "Hey, how much you want to bet I get him down to twelve?"

"I have no doubt you will," Claude replied coldly. He turned away even before Fundy left and took off the camel's hair coat, folding it with care and laying it neatly over the back of a chair. Then he closed his eyes and leaned against an open carton of books. He was trembling with resentment. Even at $200 an hour Fundy had no right to treat him like, like . . . It was infuriating. The very fact that an oaf like that could afford to spend twelve or sixteen thousand dollars on a seventeenth-century painting (when he really would have preferred a picture of a puppy!), while he, Claude, who could genuinely appreciate the delicate, fastidiously rendered little portrait, was reduced to being a . . . a . . .

He opened his eyes. The trembling subsided. What a gem the painting was, its artistry easily apparent through the cracked, aged varnish. Far superior to the daubings on the other two panels. Yes, it had definitely been done by a follower of Hals and very much in the style of the master's middle years: limited color range; thick impasto in the face; wonderfully spontaneous *alla prima* technique; simple, monochromatic background. One might almost think . . .

No, impossible. Things like that didn't happen anymore. No, definitely not. There was that absence of a signature, for one thing, which made it almost certain it was simply a workshop piece. Possibly a copy of one of Hals's works, painted as a studio exercise. Even so, it was particularly well done. Claude would gladly have paid $16,000 for it, and done it without quibbling. If he'd had $16,000 to spare.

Fundy's brassy voice carried to him from the office. "Okay, I tell you what. I'll give you thirty thousand for all three of the little suckers, how about that?"

"Oh, no," Suffield murmured with an apologetic laugh, "I couldn't imagine doing business in that—"

"Okay, I tell you what. You interested in a giant-screen TV with on-screen graphics and sleep-timer?"

Claude shook his head and turned from the little painting. How had he come to this? Spending Christmas Eve playing second fiddle to a barbaric ignoramus? Idly he fingered the spines of the books in the carton in front of him. Art books, mostly from the turn of the century, and mostly dealing with English nineteenth-century watercolorists. Not a subject that inflamed his interest. But one book did catch his eye: *Dutch Paintings of the Seventeenth Century*, published in London in 1921 by Methuen.

He slid it out. A big book, well used and bound in olive green cloth, with translucent endpapers. An expensive book, consisting of a ten-page introduction followed by a hundred high-quality pages with handsome black-and-white photographs glued to them, two to a page. He remembered seeing (and coveting) a copy of it years before. He leafed through it idly, paying little attention, but in the act of closing it he stopped, rock-still. An afterimage of one of the prints, unnoticed when he'd flipped by it, burned in his mind. Heat prickled across his shoulders. My God, was it possible . . . Barely breathing, cradling the image gingerly in his mind as if losing it would make it vanish from the book, he went carefully back through the volume.

He found it on page forty-seven. He studied it a long time, not letting himself look at the caption yet. He was breathing rapidly through his mouth, hardly able to get the air down. Now, finally, he looked at the words below the picture:

PLATE 92. FRANS HALS, *LAUGHING GUARDS-MAN*, 1644. PANEL, $16\frac{1}{8}$ by $13\frac{1}{2}$ IN. MONOGRAM "FH," LOWER LEFT. MONOGRAM "GL" ON BACK (GERHAERT LEYSTER, HAARLEM PANEL MAKER [?]). COLL. D. SCHULDE, VIENNA.

He glanced up at the glass-walled office. Fundy and Suffield were still going at it. Hurriedly he went back to the painting. He made himself close his eyes for a second in something like prayer, then opened them, barely managing to stifle a gasp. It was the same painting! *The same!* There was a tape measure on one of the workbenches. Making sure that his back blocked what he was doing, he quickly measured the picture: $16\frac{1}{8}$ by $13\frac{1}{2}$ inches— exactly! *My God!* But the signature, Hals's monogram—where was it? What had happened to it?

Suffield and Fundy were standing up, shaking hands. Claude ran back to the book. "Monogram 'FH,' lower left." He studied the photograph, feeling as if his heart, his lungs, were bursting. Yes, there it was in the photo, dim but visible, on the cavalier's dark sleeve. Shaking, he dashed back to the painting. Why wasn't it—

But it was. If you looked hard, if you knew what you were looking for and where to look, there it was. FH. In a dull, muddy red. Painted on the ample, gray-black folds of the sleeve, made almost invisible by age and the thick, dark varnish that some fool of a restorer had coated it with. My God, a Hals! What was it worth? Jasper Johns, for God's sake, was going for $17,000,000 in these crazy days, Van Gogh for over $50,000,000! Why, a Hals—a Hals—

He jumped—literally, both heels coming off the floor—when Fundy's meaty hand thumped him on the shoulder.

The horrible little man was grinning at him. "Twelve Gs," he said proudly. He waited for a response, but Claude's mind was numb, his throat stuffed with rags.

Fundy turned to Suffield. "I'll pay in cash," he said, as Claude had known he would. Surely he was the only person in America who actually carried $1,000 bills around in his pocket twenty years after the Federal Reserve had stopped issuing them. (This from a man who screamed "Who needs cash?" at the end of every commercial.) And of course he kept them in a glittering gold-and-diamond money clip shaped like a dollar sign.

"One," he said, and plunked a bill into the goggling Suffield's palm. Fundy laughed, delighted with himself. He stuck his thumb in his mouth and slurped at it. "Two . . ."

Claude watched, sick and desperate. In his ears he heard his own breath, the shallow panting of an animal.

Claude stood erectly on the ferry's top deck, his hands on the rear railing, looking down into the black, chill waters of Puget Sound sixty feet below. Directly below, the boiling, dimly phosphorescent wake slid smoothly away into the fog.

"It's freezing out here, Mary Beth," a woman standing a dozen feet away said to a six-year-old. "Let's go inside."

"Aw, Mom, I want—"

"I'll get us some hot chocolate, how about that?"

Mary Beth paused, wavered, and made her decision. "With extra sugar?"

"You bet, honey." Hand in hand, they headed for the steps that led below.

That left only one other person on the dark, open top deck; Franklin Fundy. It was time to act.

The cleansing wind and moist, salty air had purged Claude's mind of its dithering confusion. He knew what had to be done, and he knew how to do it. He turned, narrowing his eyes against the pelting strands of his own wind-whipped hair. Fundy was sitting in one of the plastic chairs, staring happily at nothing, chewing on a dead cigar. At his side, tossed carelessly onto the seat next to him, was a large red plastic sack containing a thick cardboard package that jutted out of it. Dear God—a Hals in a plastic shopping bag!

Characteristically, Fundy had shown no surprise when Claude had suggested that he accompany his client on the ride to Bremerton. "For the conversation," Claude had said, and Fundy had affably, even generously, agreed—as if it were only natural that his conversation should be a sought-after commodity. And for once Fundy's disgusting propensity for sweaty warmth had come in handy. Claude had been delighted to follow his suggestion that they make the trip in the fresh air of the upper deck.

"Well, I wonder what that is!" Claude said loudly, leaning over the rail to peer down at the water.

"What what is?" Fundy said with little interest.

"I'm not sure. It appears to be . . ." He had given this a lot of thought. Fundy was not a man of wide interests. A seal or even a whale would be unlikely to get him out of his chair. Even a floating body might not do it. ". . . It appears to be a washing machine!" Claude exclaimed.

"A *what?*" Claude was at the rail instantly, the painting left behind. "You're nuts! Where?"

"Down there. You have to lean over a little more. Just a little more yet."

He steeled himself, sucked in a lungful of the cold air. "Merry Christmas, Frankie," he murmured and stepped forward.

When the boat docked at Bremerton, Claude stayed aboard for the return run to Seattle. Once back he put the painting in one of the 75-cent lockers at the terminal and went to a pay telephone.

"Mr. Whatcom? I'm sorry to bother you, but didn't you say Mr. Fundy would meet me at Pioneer Square at four? Well, no, he didn't, sir. I came down to the ferry terminal thinking he might have gotten one of the later boats, but the six twenty-five just came in and he wasn't on it, so . . . yes, sir, I suppose he simply changed his mind. Yes, he's certainly done it a few times before." He laughed easily along with the senior partner. "Oh, no, no trouble at all. I'll do that, sir. Merry Christmas to you too."

He hung up. How calm he was, how clear-minded. And why shouldn't he be calm? Fundy's body would not surface for days, and by then the tide might have taken it all the way to Olympia, or perhaps west to the strait and the open sea. It might never be found, and even if it was the experts would never be able to determine his exact time of death. The assumption would be that he had fallen from the boat on the way in to Seattle to meet Claude. Who could say otherwise? Mr. Suffield had been paid in cash; there was no way for him to know who his customer had been, no reason to connect him with a body that might or might not wash up in Edmonds or Port Townsend the next week. And there was absolutely no one else to connect Fundy with Claude. Nothing could go wrong.

There was just one loose end. He was probably being overcareful to be worried about it, but that was the way he was. It was not his way to leave anything to chance. He rapidly walked the three dark blocks down Alaskan Way to Washington Street and turned left to Pioneer Square. It had gotten colder. He turned the soft collar of the camel's hair coat up against his cheek.

Suffield had closed up the gallery but he was still there, working with his cordless screwdriver, stooped with fatigue but smiling.

"Book?" he said in response to Claude's question. "Of Dutch . . . ?"

Claude showed him. "This," he said casually. "I'm quite interested in the period, you know, and assuming it's for sale, I'd very much like to have it."

"Well, yes, of course it's for sale—"

"And if you have any other copies of it, I'd be interested in those too. They'd make wonderful Christmas gifts for friends."

Suffield shook his head. "No, I'm sorry, it's the only copy I have. Hardly my specialty, you see." He stood there, smiling tiredly.

"And the price?" Claude prompted.

"Oh. Well. I'll have to look it up." He glanced over his shoulder toward the office in back, and apparently decided it wasn't worth the effort. "Look, I'll tell you what. Why don't you just keep it with my compliments?"

"Oh, no, I couldn't—"

"Please. As a Christmas present. And to thank you for your help earlier."

"Well . . ." Claude smiled. "Thank you so much, Mr. Suffield. And merry Christmas to you. A merry, merry Christmas."

Mr. Suffield watched him go. Then he locked up again, went to his office, and opened a waist-high metal cabinet. Inside were his twenty-four remaining copies of the long out-of-print *Dutch Paintings of the Seventeenth Century*, all authentic. Whistling to himself, he pulled one from the shelf and leafed through it, pausing fondly at page forty-seven, and stopping finally at page fifty-two.

"Ah," he said. "Just the thing."

He lifted the telephone and dialed. "Vincent? I have another order for you." He smiled at the surprised reply. "Yes," he said, "the Hals is already gone. It was wonderful; I wish you'd been there. I'd hardly unpacked it. And the book was still in the carton!" They both enjoyed a laugh. "Not my usual price, of course, but why quarrel with serendipity? Now: Do you have a pen handy?"

He waited. "You'll like this; you're good at Rembrandt. Here it is." Slowly he read aloud from the book. "'Plate Number 101. Rembrandt van Rijn, *Portrait of a Woman Holding a Fan*. 1634–35. Panel, $30\frac{1}{8}$ by 20 inches. Signature and date, "Remb. 1665," lower right. Monogram "MG" on back (Michiel Gepts, Amsterdam panel maker). Collection—' Well, that's really all you need, isn't it?"

While Vincent went over the details with him Suffield took a scalpel from a drawer and carefully edged it under the photograph of the Rembrandt, beginning to tease it from the page. "No, no," he said, "I don't give a damn what sort of fan. What difference does it make? Something Rembrandtish. Ostrich feather, I should guess. When can you have it done?"

The photograph came up from the page. Excellent; no marring of the paper. He tore it into shreds and dropped it into the wastepaper basket. There would be a replacement soon enough. "Next week is fine. And you'll have it photographed? You still have some of the stock I gave you to print it on? You understand how important it is that it match the rest of the photographs—" He jerked the telephone away from his ear as Vincent swore at him.

"Yes, yes, of course," he said soothingly. "I know how attentive to detail you are. But one can't be too careful. You won't forget to lay some heavy varnish over the signature to muddy it up?" He chuckled warmly. "You know how much they love to think they're putting one over on me."

The man railed at him some more. Suffield let him go on. He could afford to be patient. Subtracting Vincent's fee of $1,000 left him with $11,000 profit on the transaction. And legal profit at that. *He* had never claimed it was a Hals, had he?

"Thank you, Vincent," he said amicably when the ranting had stopped. "It's always a pleasure to do business with you. Oh, and Vincent? A very merry Christmas to you."

Close to tears, Mary Beth Hasty sat up in her bed, her little face pinched with juvenile frustration. "We *did* see him," she cried. "We *did*! Coming back on the ferryboat from Seattle. Funnie Frankie! And he had a big red bag like Santa Claus, and he was with a big tall man in a funny yellow coat!"

In the twin bed next to her, her sister Amber, three years her senior and infinitely superior, smiled her condescension. "Oh, sure."

"But we did! Ask Mom. Funnie Frankie is Santa Claus, and he's coming to our house, and he's coming down the chimney, and—"

It was too much for Amber. She rolled her eyes and shouted: "Mother! Mary Beth—"

"I can hear!" Susan Hasty answered from the living room,

where she was sitting guard over the presents until the girls dropped off. Lord, could she hear. They'd been at it fifteen minutes. This was what came of getting Mary Beth overtired on the day before Christmas. "Mary Beth, honey," she called, not looking up from the newspaper, "Funnie Frankie is not Santa Claus, and he's not coming to our house."

"Ha, ha," she heard Amber say.

"But we did see him, Amber," their mother added.

"Ha, ha on *you*." Mary Beth's voice.

"Now you girls go to sleep or I won't let you get up early. I mean it now."

But Amber, on the whiny brink of exhaustion herself, padded across the bedroom floor and flung open the door. "Then why didn't we see him get off the boat when we came to get you?" she said accusingly. "Where did he go? And I didn't see any big tall man with a yellow coat get off either."

Susan was getting a little cranky too. "Amber," she said evenly, "if Funnie Frankie turns up missing, I'll be the first one to go to the police, how's that? Now get back in there and hit the sack."

"I hope he fell off the stupid boat and drownded," Amber grumbled, and banged the door closed.

"Drowned," her mother called, turning the page and yawning. "You hope he drowned."

SUSAN DUNLAP

OTT ON A LIMB

Susan Dunlap lives near Berkeley, California, where Christmas is different. Even your Christmas turkey might not be what it seems. If it's suspiciously easy to carve, it may be molded tofu.

Homicide Detective Jill Smith is no stranger to odd meals or odd places. For two years she lived on a converted back porch whose indoor-outdoor carpet became more "outdoor" after every rain. She drives an old VW that ascends Berkeley's precipitous hills only in first gear and takes the downslopes like Santa's leap down the chimney.

But this year Jill Smith has hopes of a Christmas dreams are made of: curled up with her favorite man by a roaring fire, sipping champagne.

But odd things do happen in Berkeley. So don't be surprised when Susan Dunlap interferes with Jill Smith's plans and sends her to one of the oddest spots in town.

Telegraph Avenue may be the spiritual repository of Berkeley radicalism but during the Christmas holidays it goes whole hog capitalist. The sidewalks are crowded with street artists and their displays of tie-dyed long johns, stained glass panels, and crystals of every hue for every ache, pain, or psychic need. Turbaned men offer hand massage, foot massage, or tarot readings, $8 each. A violinist plays Mendelssohn. String bands strum blue grass.

You can sip a strawberry-mango smoothie or eat a falafel sandwich as you peruse card tables of used socialist books, hand-tooled belts, Peruvian sweaters, embroidered Cambodian jackets, feather earrings, beaded earrings, earrings with dangling rubber frogs. Artists display watercolors, gardeners hawk potted pine, palm, and persimmon. And there are the ever-popular T-shirts that extol the peculiarities of the city—"Berkeley, A Radical Solution," "Berserkley" (a perennial favorite), and "People's Park Lives," commemorating the city's biggest antigovernment demonstration when then Governor Ronald Reagan (*not* a perennial favorite) called in the National Guard.

When dusk fades to night the street artists pack up their display cases, fold their card tables, and leave the Avenue as deserted as a dry water hole. And yet the aura remains and makes the darkness darker, the emptiness blacker. On Christmas Eve, Telegraph Avenue seemed like the last place on earth.

It was the last place I wanted to be. I had passed up five invitations in favor of the one Seth Howard had whispered: "Homicide Detective Jill Smith is invited to a night of champagne, Howard and . . ."

Now, at eight-thirty Christmas Eve, Howard would be sprawled in front of his fireplace with the champagne. *I* was headed through the litter of pizza plates and smoothie cups on Telegraph Avenue to the office of the Herman Ott Detective Agency.

As a nocturnal companion Howard was a "10"; Herman Ott would be a minus 6. As a nocturnal habitat Ott's office slid below the scale.

I could have done the prudent thing and avoided Ott, but he'd tracked me down at eight P.M. just as I was heading out of the station, pondering if sausage rolls and chocolate macaroon ice cream would go with champagne. Herman Ott had said the only thing that could have diverted me from both Howard and ice cream. He said, "I need a favor."

Herman Ott asking a favor from the cops was like Fidel Castro proposing to Princess Margaret.

But Princess Margaret would not have chucked the royal ball and hopped the next plane to Havana.

I, on the other hand, told Howard I'd be late, and hotfooted it for Telegraph.

Ott had established his reputation on the Avenue by never voting for anyone more conservative than a Peace and Freedom party candidate, never cooperating with the D.A., and never, never giving information to an officer of the Berkeley Police Department—unless it was unavoidable, innocuous, and he got something in return. Usually that something was money from the discretionary fund, and usually the detective he got it from was me. When I did squeeze a piece of information out of him, it was something I could get nowhere else. At least two murderers were behind bars because of Herman Ott (a fact that neither of us would ever admit). I couldn't afford to ignore his request.

And besides, I was too curious.

And I owed him two hundred dollars. It was part of Ott's code never to spend the money on himself. It was an even bigger part to make sure he got it.

Two months earlier I'd leaned on Ott till he came close to snapping. He'd bent that rigid code of his and given me the key fact that linked Angus Simpson, a slippery weasel with friends on the Avenue, to a felony assault rap. Simpson was, for the moment, out on bail; Ott's info would send him back to Atascadero. In an unguarded moment Ott had announced that Angus Simpson had just one redeeming quality: he was even more adamant than Ott in his refusal to talk to the police.

There was no way I was going to get Simpson without Ott's help. Ott knew it and I knew it. I'd promised Ott two hundred dollars from the discretionary fund. I suspected he'd planned to give it away before Christmas to salve his conscience. But it still hadn't come through. And now, on Christmas Eve, I knew that the ball would drop in Times Square before he saw that money.

I hurried past the pizza shop. It was closed, but the smell of

garlic and tomatoes still filled the empty street and made me think
of Howard downing the sausage and champagne. The door to
Ott's building had been left open again. No surprise. Between the
World Wars, Ott's building had been a snazzy address for
advertising agencies, dental offices, and groups of C.P.A.s. In the
following decades it had gone seedy. By the seventies there were
few other commercial ventures, some of which the guys in Vice
and Substance Abuse busted, some Forgery-Fraud merely
watched. But the old building had taken a good turn in the
eighties.

I, too, took a turn now, from the landing of the double staircase
to the left. The hallway formed a square around the stairs. On the
outside of the hall were two-room "offices," on the inside the
old-fashioned bathrooms with the toilet in one room and the sink
in another. In the seventies the halls had reeked of marijuana and
urine, and stepping over a crumpled body had not been a startling
experience. Now what I had to watch out for was tricycles and toy
trucks careening around corners, small legs pedaling like mad on
the straightaways. The offices had been taken over by refugee
families, and the hallway had become the Indianapolis of the
under five set. The odor of marijuana had been replaced by the
smell of coconut or peanut sauce or curry.

But tonight the hall was empty. Through the open doors in the
"offices" I could see children seated close together on old sofas, as
if posing for sepia tone family portraits. Christmas music mixed
with the smell of coconut satay. And small faces eyed cardboard
fireplaces with Woolworth's stockings.

My knuckles barely brushed the opague glass on Herman Ott's
door before it opened. Standing by the door, Herman Ott was
short enough for me to have a distressingly good view of those
limp blond strands that composed his thinning plumage. His
rounding stomach perched over thighs so thin that his pant legs
fluttered like turkey wattles. His clothes were exclusively from
the Good Will, the politically correct couturier of the sixties, and

exclusively yellow (or as close to yellow as he could find). I never saw the man without wondering if he knew how much he resembled a canary.

At first I had assumed his sartorial statement was an elaborate joke. But it wasn't. His manner of dress was not a joke; nothing he said was in jest. Because Herman Ott had no sense of humor whatever. None. He never saw the humor in any situation (an accomplishment of no mean proportions for a man with an office on Telegraph Avenue). And, of course, he hated being laughed at himself.

Which made his dress all the funnier. And had tested my self-control more than once.

"No need to scowl, Ott. You invited me," I said, walking into his small, tidy office. Never had I seen a file drawer left open here, or papers strewn on his desk. The only thing that looked out of place here was Herman Ott.

With the same appalled fascination that keeps one from graciously looking away from a wart on the nose of a friend, I glanced into Ott's other room. A jumble of blankets and pillows decorated a decrepit armchair (Salvation Army circa '66). Blankets, clothes, and newspapers cascaded to the floor. It looked like the bottom of the canary's cage. Many times I'd wondered what a psychiatrist would make of Ott's two rooms. Which was the spiritual home of the real Ott?

Now Ott perched on the edge of his mustard-colored leather desk chair and said, "I've got a deal for you, Smith."

"I'm a homicide detective, Ott. I don't do deals."

Unlike some, Ott, of course, didn't laugh. "You owe me, Smith."

I settled on the corner of his desk. "Ott, you know our files are closed. There's nothing I can run for you."

He shrugged, lifting his narrow, sloping shoulders to almost normal height. "I don't need anything from *the police*. I need it from you, just you."

I looked down at Ott. Frayed cuffs hung over pudgy hands which caressed an empty coffee cup. A forefinger traced the lip. An appalling thought crossed my mind.

I could have sworn I saw the shadow of a grin on Ott's pallid face. But it was probably just gas.

"I want you to spend the night here." He paused so long that my whole life could have passed before my eyes. "Alone."

"What is this, Ott, a test of my 'manhood'?"

Ott shifted in his chair. He glanced behind me, those pale brown deep-set eyes straining not for a view of an intruder sneaking in the office door, but for someone—anyone—more desirable than me to deal with. But that was something Santa wasn't bringing him. Ott sighed; his narrow shoulders dropped so low that it looked like he had no shoulders at all. "Smith, someone's been breaking into my office at night."

"So, have a couple of cappuccinos and keep watch."

"Don't you think I've tried watching!" He pushed himself up and walked quickly to one of the file cabinets, taking short rapid steps so that his weight was never wholly on one foot. It was a careful balancing walk, the walk of a high wire artist, or a bird on a phone line—or a detective whose bedroom floor is perpetually covered with sheets, blankets, and newspapers. Ott could probably ford the slipperiest stream in the state with the daily training he got here. He rested an ecru sleeve against the file drawer handle. "If I'm here, Smith, nothing happens. Even when I've been asleep, nothing's happened. I've tried sitting here in the dark all night; I've driven around town till I was dead sure no one was following me and then looped back and came up the fire escape at two A.M. Nothing."

"Well, why don't you have a friend stand guard? You've got to have closer friends than me. Me, a cop," I couldn't resist adding.

Ott apparently couldn't resist glancing in the direction of the Avenue. It was a small slip, and one that someone unfamiliar with the community of Avenue regulars Ott counted as his friends and clients would not have noted. It reminded me that no secret stayed secret down there. Ott crossed his arms over his chest. "You owe me, Smith."

I plopped down in his client's chair, leaned back and said, "What is it, Ott, that's so secret you can't trust your friends to find out? So secret you have to turn to an Officer of the Peace?"

Ott glared.

Usually it was me trying to wheedle something out of him. God, it was wonderful to have the trumps for a change. Trying to restrain myself from becoming too obnoxious, I said, "What is your thief taking?"

"Nothing."

"Nothing! Is this a joke? Candid Camera for Cops?"

Ott shook his head. The limp blond strands trailed the movement like a fringe from a particularly decrepit ball gown. If Ott was setting up a practical joke he was doing one helluva job. But, of course, he wasn't. To create a joke, Ott would have needed an instruction manual. "He takes nothing. He leaves something each time—an envelope, wrapped in Christmas paper."

"Containing what?"

"I can't say."

I laughed. "Ott, this is a delicacy I hadn't expected of you. Are these gifts of too personal a nature to be discussed in mixed company?"

Ott's scowl deepened. Nothing ruffled his feathers like being laughed at.

I felt like I was pulling out those feathers one by one. But I couldn't help myself. There is something so irresistible about teasing the humorless. It's like giggling at a funeral; you know it isn't right, but once you start it's almost impossible to stop. I stood up and braced my hands on his desk. "Ott, you call me away from my plans on Christmas Eve. You ask me to spend the night in your office, which doesn't even have a bathroom. I'm not going to play blind here."

Ott turned and took five short, rapid steps to the window. Looking out at the six feet of nothingness between him and the next building, he said, "It *is* personal."

I started toward the door. "Merry Christmas, Ott!"

He spun around. "Okay, Smith. Wait. It's about my ex-wife."

"Ex-wife!" There were things I had considered Ott having, many of them contagious, but a wife was definitely not one of them. "You were married!"

He hunched forward. His head lowered and tilted toward his right shoulder. I had the distinct feeling he was about to tuck it under his wing and pretend I had disappeared. "Long time ago," he muttered.

"Go on."

"I was in college."

"Ott, you were in college for the better part of a decade."

His shoulders drew closer. "It was 1969. We met in the People's Park March." That was the biggest of the antiwar era marches in Berkeley, when tens of thousands of students and residents protested the University of California's plan to turn that block of green by the Avenue into a parking lot. "We got married six weeks later. In Reno," he added as if that made his accommodation to law acceptable.

"What was your wife's name?"

"What difference does it make?"

"Ott!"

"Saffron."

Saffron! With an Olympian effort, I swallowed the urge to laugh, to say I could certainly see what had attracted him. To say that that must have been a match made in the lemon-yellow clouds of heaven. To contain myself, I had to picture Ott in the full-blown rage of being laughed at. I had to remind myself how much I needed him. I had to stare hard past Herman Ott to the window. Opening on a narrow alley three stories up, it wouldn't have been an easy one to clean, and before tonight Ott had never made an effort. But now the window was spotless. "What happened to Saffron?"

Ott began to pace, five little steps from the window to the file cabinet, turn, return. "Divorced. By the end of the year."

I nodded. I had been through my own divorce. No matter what the circumstances, it's never a pleasant experience. Still, it hardly explained Ott's mysterious deliveries. Or his clean window. "So what's in these packages?"

"Messages"—he stopped in front of the file cabinet—"with letters clipped from the newspapers, just like on television," he added in a tone of disgust.

"Messages, saying?"

Ott hesitated, then pulled open his desk drawer and extricated an envelope, a plain white envelope with no return address, and an Oakland postmark. He didn't bother to hold it by the edges. I didn't offer to get the ID tech to dust for prints. I opened it and unfolded the plain sheet of cheap paper. On it, newsprint words said, "1971 Saffron Sacramento. 1989? Have a Merry Christmas."

"After the divorce, she moved to Sacramento," Ott explained.

There were two more messages, both originally wrapped as Christmas presents. The first said, "$200 a month. Have a Merry Christmas."

"Ransom?" I asked. "Do you think Saffron's been kidnapped?"

Ott shook his head so abruptly and definitely that I couldn't doubt his reaction, or at least his belief in it. "I got a Christmas card from her last week. She's been living in D.C. since '81. She's done real well for herself. The card said she'd gotten another job there with the Interior Department. It was one of those mimeographed Christmas letters. It's not like she writes me personally."

I couldn't resist asking, "Do you send her a Christmas card?"

Ott looked at me as if I'd lost my mind. The reaction was deserved. I almost got the giggles picturing one of those red-and-gold cards embossed with "Holiday Greetings from the Herman Ott Detective Agency."

"Then if the two hundred dollars isn't a demand for ransom for her, what's it for?"

"Not ransom. I called her; she's fine. She doesn't know anything about this."

"You sure?"

"Oh, yeah. She's making fifty thousand a year. What could she want from me? Besides, she's not the devious type. That's half of the reason we got divorced." Ott almost smiled. "You know how it is, Smith, if they're not always on the lookout for an ulterior motive, they're just not very interesting."

I laughed uncomfortably. I knew exactly how it was. I wanted to ask Ott what the other half of the reason was for his divorce, but I doubted I could push him any further than I already had. Instead, I said, "Okay, if not ransom then just what does two hundred dollars a month mean?"

Ott studied his shoes, tan sneakers, the old type made when sneakers were still three bucks at Woolworth's. They must have been Salvation Army specials, too. He mumbled something.

I moved around the desk closer to him. "What?"

"Alimony," he muttered to the shoes.

I leaned closer.

"Two hundred a month for two years," he told his shoes. "Figured she needed it. Wrong! By her second year in Sacramento, she was making more than I was. But I didn't know that."

Before I could stop myself, I shook my head. It was hard to say which amazed me more, Ott opting for legal marriage in the days when mere monogamy was considered selling out, or Ott paying alimony at a time when most child-free women would have been affronted by the offer. And yet there was Ott's code. It was like Ott to do the decent thing when he felt he should, in this case the more than decent thing.

I looked back at the envelope on my lap. If Ott's first two messages might have been considered innocuous, the third certainly could not. Cut from a movie ad for *The Night of the Living*

Dead, it had the word "Life" stapled over "Night." "The Life of the Living Dead. Have a Merry Christmas." I looked questioningly at Ott. He shook his head. But there was none of the definiteness that had underlined his previous denials. Ott knew something. What I knew was that I wasn't about to get that something out of him. But I might get another piece of information in its stead. "What does this message-leaver want from you?"

"Silence."

"About?"

But Ott didn't answer. Instead he said, "You've seen what I've seen. There's been nothing else. Someone's out to ruin me."

"How?"

"By ruining my reputation."

I felt a cold wave of fear. With Ott's clientele his position was always precarious; his reputation was what kept him in business. And made him useful to me. And, well, I had to admit—to myself, never to anyone else, least of all Herman Ott—I did have a certain grudging fondness for the guy, like you do for the ugliest puppy in the litter, particularly if you know you won't have to take him home.

Another chill shook me. What could this last threat be? What would be a greater blow than merely passing the word along the Avenue that Ott had ratted to the cops? My dealings with Ott were all within the law, but publicity about them wouldn't do much good for either of us. It would hold the department up to question (the city of Berkeley expects a particularly high standard from their police), grease the already shaky ground on which Ott stood with his clientele (though Ott's client pool had few other choices), and within the police department, it would make me the receptacle of every complaint every inspector, detective, or patrol officer had about Herman Ott. Which meant that I could plan on fielding five to ten calls a day for the rest of my career or Ott's, whichever lasted longer.

I walked to the clean window and stared out. If I looked sharply to the right, I could make out a glimmer of light from Telegraph, and the one cafe open Christmas Eve. Despite my considerable hesitations about the whole setup (I could deal with those later) I said, "So what do you want from me, here, alone, all night? I'm not about to compromise a department case or find myself in one of those headlines that begins: *Off-Duty Cop* . . ."

"I just want you to stay here till the drop comes. 'Have a Merry Christmas': the last drop will be tonight. I'll be across the street in the cafe. When the package comes through the door, don't do anything but turn on the light. I'll be watching. There's only one way out of this building. The fire escape's been sealed for months."

"You can expect the building inspector Monday for that one."

"Fine with me. So is that a yes?"

I glanced at my watch. It was just after nine o'clock. I could be sitting next to Ott's mail slot till dawn, and dawn comes late in December. I walked slowly into the bedroom, glancing at book-cases that must have held every radical publication ever printed, through the cascades of blankets, taking quick, little steps like Ott's. By the window (not cleaned) was a hot plate. Next to it was an empty pan, a can of coffee, two boxes of tea, and a jar of honey that was so thick and grainy that it might have been abandoned by the office's original tenant between the Great Wars. There might have been milk in Ott's fridge, but I doubted it. On the floor was a bottle of water, there presumably to save Ott from scurrying across the hall to the bathroom every time he wanted to make tea. I poured some in the pan and turned on the hot plate. Then I picked up a stained and chipped mug and walked back across the threshold into the orderly world of Ott's office. Ott was still sitting behind his desk. It was like him to put out his offer, then just sit and wait. "Ott," I said, "I know you're not telling me everything. I'm willing to accept that. But you have to assure me that whatever I don't know is not going to screw me. If it does I'll call in every favor from every cop I've ever met, and I'll get you."

Ott's face relaxed. He looked as if I'd opened the door of the cage. "You got my word, Smith. And you'll be off the hook for the two hundred you owe me."

"Okay. I just hope this is a Christmas Eve, not a Christmas morning, Santa."

"It will be."

Holding out Ott's cup, I said, "Here, wash this before you leave. I'm going to make tea, and I don't want to face gastrointestinal collapse before Santa comes."

Ott glowered. He really did hate it when I laughed at him. Even in the form of his mug.

In five minutes I poured the boiling water over a tea bag, and watched Ott turn out the lights and depart. I let the tea steep for another five minutes—it could be a long night and I wanted the tea strong.

Counting on Ott's Santa's perseverance and ingenuity, I taped the mail slot shut. Then I made one phone call, settled next to the door, on the cold wooden floor.

At nine-thirty the heat went off. Somewhere in Washington, D.C., was a woman who had changed her name back from Saffron to Helen or Barbara. While I was here shivering in Ott's unheated office (and Howard was downing the champagne and sausage without me), she was asleep in a big bed, under a thick down comforter, dreaming of her fifty-thousand-dollar-a-year paycheck.

I leaned back against the wall, sipping my cold tea. From the hallway the only sounds were the dim rumble of televisions.

I've done my share of stakeouts, I know the games to keep boredom at bay. I can name all fifty states, alphabetically and geographically starting from Maine or Hawaii. I can name all the capitals without even the temptation to think of Louisville instead of Frankfort, or Portland instead of Salem (or Augusta, for that matter).

The games had become too easy. But that didn't matter tonight. Ott had provided me with his own game.

I thought about the first two of those three messages again: 1971 Saffron Sacramento, $200 a month. Ott had divorced Saffron by the end of 1969. By 1970 she had moved to Sacramento and hadn't needed his two hundred dollars. And the third message that threatened Ott with a living death. It didn't take a detective to guess what would be death in life for him. For Ott his reputation was life. So whatever the Santa knew was enough to destroy it.

Half an hour later my tea cup was empty, and I regretted having poured that eight ounces of liquid from it into me. Stakeouts were so much easier for men. But during that hour in the dark, I had had time to guess the contents of the final message, as, clearly, Ott already had. For anyone who knew the Telegraph scene and Ott's place in it, that message was contained in the other three. What I figured was the fourth message, the one that Ott would rather die than have circulated along the Avenue, would say that Ott had paid Saffron twenty-four hundred dollars in alimony, and it would announce exactly where Saffron had channeled that money, Ott's money.

It was just ten when I heard the footsteps tap in the hallway. I stood up and moved beside the door and shifted my revolver to my left hand. The steps stopped outside. Knees cracked. Santa was bending down. The mail slot flap pushed against the tape. I could picture him stopping, staring confused at the unbudging mail slot, then angrily trying again, which he did.

The door was locked, but the dead bolt was off. The lock would take no more than a credit card. Which was what it sounded like he was using.

Holding my breath, I waited.

The door opened slowly.

Still, I waited, till a hand, bearing a small package, crossed the doorsill. The hand was twenty or so inches off the floor. Santa was still bending to put the package on the floor.

I grabbed the hand, yanked it back and up behind him, sending him forward, head down, into the corner of Ott's desk.

I flicked on the light. "Freeze!" I yelled. "Police!"

He groaned. He was Angus Simpson, the con Ott had fingered for me. I wasn't surprised. He was about to have his bail revoked. And since Simpson was even more rigid about stonewalling the police than Ott himself, he was about to spend some more silent time in stir. He would never even admit what he was holding over Ott.

"Spread your arms wide. Spread 'em! Now! And the legs. Move!" A package, wrapped in red Christmas paper, slipped out of his hand. I kicked it behind me.

I didn't pocket the package until the backup arrived. Ott was not going to be pleased I'd called to alert the beat officers. For the moment Ott would be in the cage of one of the patrol cars, no doubt squawking up a storm. It was for his own good, but I'd never get him to believe that. Were it up to Herman Ott, I could expect a load of coal in my stocking.

But Ott of all people would understand that I, too, had my code. And he would have to be satisfied with my Christmas present to him: no one would see this last package and no one on the Avenue would ever know the threat of the Life of the Living Dead, the revelation that would make him the laughingstock of the Avenue. The message said, "Sacramento 1971, Saffron received $2400 from Herman Ott and donated it to the Ronald Reagan for Governor campaign."

ISAAC ASIMOV

HO! HO! HO!

When I sold my first mystery novel, I was lucky enough to be assigned the same editor as the writer of this story. In her office stood two tall bookcases, one to hold all the books of all but one of the authors she handled, and the other one crammed full with the works of Isaac Asimov. As almost everybody who's ever read a book must know by now, this ultra-prolific author has an analytical mind. Once Isaac gets started thinking about anything at all, there's no telling what may come of it. Not long ago, Isaac got to thinking about Santa Claus's whiskers . . .

Baranof entered the somnolent precincts of the Union Club library with a most offensive air of cheer and jubilation.

"Me-e-e-erry Christmas," he said.

To which Jennings and I responded, in perfect unison, "Bah! Humbug!" while Griswold snored very softly in his huge, winged armchair.

"No, really," said Baranof. "There's even a chance of snow predicted for Christmas Day. We may have a white Christmas."

"Goody," I said sourly. "All the little kiddies can take their new sleds and go belly-whopping in New York traffic."

"I wonder," said Jennings, "if any New Yorker gives his children a sled for Christmas."

"What," said I, "and expect them to go out in the cold when they can stay home and watch a nice warm television set?"

Baranof said, "You two disgust me. I have half a mind to ask Griswold for a Christmas story. He's bound to have something heartwarming."

I don't think Baranof was serious there, but Griswold began the process of rumbling to life.

His eyelids opened, and the ice blue of his eyes penetrated us one after the other. He took a prolonged sip at the scotch and soda he was holding in his hand, and said, "Actually, I do have a Christmas story about a friend of mine who had a particularly unpleasant Christmas season."

"Oh, well," said Baranof, "if this is going to be something dreary, no thanks. We'll talk about something else."

Since you insist [said Griswold] I will tell you the story of a friend of mine, whose name was Dan Arbutus, and who worked for me in Intelligence in the days before I was fired for the crime of being intelligent. We stayed friends, of course, when he was sure no one was looking, and then eventually, he retired on a good pension, which was more than I did, and amused himself by taking on little jobs, just to keep himself busy.

He came to see me immediately after Christmas about ten or twelve years ago, shaking his head and with a look of deep trouble on his face.

"That's it, Griswold," he said, "I'll never be able to look into the face of a Santa Claus again. Of all the bloopers I ever pulled—"

We shared a drink, then I said, "What kind of a blooper, Dan? You used to be pretty fair in the old days for someone who wasn't me."

"Those were the old days. Would you believe it, Griswold? Someone walked off with an expensive necklace from the jewelry department right under my nose, and I *think* they're suspecting *me*."

"What jewelry department is this?"

"Well, I've been doing little jobs. Just keeping my hand in. So I've been serving as a private detective at the Goodwell Department Store on the East Side. They're victimized by shoplifters, you know, especially over the Christmas season."

"And someone shoplifted a necklace?"

"Yes, but after hours."

"And this has something to do with Santa Claus? You said you'd never be able to look into the face of a Santa Claus again."

"Well, yes. —Look, Griswold, let me tell you the whole story. I'm not expecting you to supply me with an answer. There are no answers, believe me. I just want to get it off my chest and then maybe I can forget it." He hesitated. "But first, can I have one more small slug?"

I pushed the bottle in his direction and waited.

Finally, he said, "The job's routine, but I like to watch the crowds and keep my eyes open for the wiseguys who manage to slip things into their pockets or bags. I give the high sign to the store personnel who are strategically placed, and the lifter is quietly followed till he or she is just outside the street door. Then we whirl them around, bring them back and search them. You can't stop them before they leave because then they always claim they were going to pay and start raising a fuss about their good name and how they're going to sue.

"But sometimes, the department store asks me to take on something outside the shoplifter watch. For instance, a couple of weeks ago, they asked me to help out after hours during their training program for Santa Clauses."

I stared at him, "They train Santa Clauses?"

"Well, of course. Department stores have Santa Clauses in the Christmas season, and they have to have them in shifts and with replacements, because it's a tiring job, so they need quite a few and they change around. The kids don't care. With the Santa Claus suit, one person looks like another. Even if the kid comes back and there's another Santa there, he doesn't know. Neither do the parents. Neither do I, for that matter."

"What is the training about?"

"A lot of things actually. They can't eat onions or garlic, or anything too darned spicy on the job, and they can't drink or

smoke, either. That's no kidding. If their breath is offensive,
they're out on their ears. And they've got to learn how to hold
kids. They've got to learn how to tell if the child *wants* to sit on
their lap. If the kid is bashful, the kid just stands there. If you can
get the parent to put it on your lap, that's better than doing it
yourself.

"Then, too, you've got to ask the right things, and you don't
make any suggestions yourself, you don't push any products,
because that gets parents mad. You've got to repeat everything the
kid says and you've got to be cheerful and you've got to 'ho, ho,
ho,' a lot."

"Ho, ho, ho?" I said.

Dan said, "Oh, yes, that's essential. Santa Claus is very jolly.
Even aside from his costume and all the stuffing to make him look
fat, his face, what you can see of it, is pink, especially the tip of
his nose, and he's got to smile a lot, which means that good teeth
are essential, and he has to go 'ho, ho, ho.' He says, 'And what is
your name, little boy? Joey? That's a very nice name, ho, ho, ho.
And have you been a good boy this year? You have? Wonderful.
Ho, ho, ho.' And they've got to make that 'ho, ho, ho' good and
deep. Believe me, after two hours of that, a Santa Claus needs a
replacement."

"I can see that," I said.

Dan said, "The training is done after hours. It would upset the
kids to see a number of Santa Clauses walking about the store. I
sometimes wonder how many kids really believe in old S. C., but
the store has to assume they all do.

"Anyway, it was only a few days till Christmas and there were
four Santa Clauses being trained for last-minute replacements and
shifts. They had on their costumes. That's necessary, you know.
Those costumes, combined with the padding, are not exactly
comfortable and they don't feel natural. The Santa Clauses have to
get used to the feel of it as much as possible, and for that matter,

they have to be able to get into them and out of them quickly. Believe me, I learned more about Santa Clauses than they did."

I said, "Look, Dan, since this was after hours, and there weren't any customers, why did they need your services?"

Dan said, "They didn't exactly tell me. Just asked me to be there and keep my eyes open. After all, the four Santa Clauses weren't the only ones in the store at the time. There were various minor executives in charge of the training and personnel and there were other employees working after hours. It was *hinted*, without actually being said, that there had been some petty losses that might be inside jobs, so to speak, and I was there to keep an eye out for funny stuff, while pretending to watch the Santa Clauses.

"That particular night, the woman in charge of the jewelry department showed up suddenly, all flustered. She was a tall woman, skinny, with a very high-pitched voice. Everyone called her Mamzelle, but she didn't sound French to me. Anyway, she came in and said, 'There's something wrong with the warning system in my depart—'

"I glared at her, and she stopped short and turned a mottled red. There was nothing wrong with her intelligence and I suppose she realized that if there *was* something wrong with her warning system, she shouldn't be announcing it to the whole world. She scuttled away, whimpering, and I thought, well, I'd better take a look at her department after a while.

"I wandered about, trying to be unnoticeable about it. There was a small coffee break, and the Santa Clauses were standing about, talking in their natural voices. During actual instruction, they practiced their ho-ho-hos a lot and talked bass. I guess it became important to talk just to make sure they had normal voices. Then they were collected and taken on a small tour. They had to know certain places in the store so they could go to their posts and leave them unobtrusively, and for a while, as they gathered, it seemed to me there were *five* Santa Clauses."

"You mean five instead of four?"

"Yes."

"Did the store have extra costumes?"

"Oh, sure. A number."

"So that some employee could have put on a Santa Claus suit and mingled."

"Yes, but I can't say for sure. That's the point. I got a momentary impression there were five, but it was just momentary as they were leaving. I dashed after them, and then I thought, 'No, I better take a look at the jewelry department.' So I did, I rushed in and there was a Santa Claus standing there."

"The fifth one?"

"I don't know. I swear to you, Griswold, I can't tell if there was a fifth one, or if there was, if the one in the jewelry department was the fifth."

"Was he doing anything?"

Dan said, "Not by the time I came in. I was caught so by surprise that I just stared at him blankly and said, 'Ho, ho, ho.' Just automatically, you know. And he didn't answer. That was the funniest thing of all. He didn't answer. I'd have thought that it would be impossible for him not to answer with a 'ho, ho, ho' of his own. He just stared at me briefly and left in a hurry."

I said, "And you chased after him?"

"No," said Dan, looking hangdog. "I wasted time—my fault, I admit, Griswold—looking about to see if anything had been broken, disturbed. Didn't see a thing, of course, and by the time I realized I ought to be following Santa Claus, it was too late. He had gone and eventually the others came back and there were only four.

"I tell you, Griswold, I stood there thinking I was going crazy. Four? Five? I was ashamed to ask. And then just before they were going to call it quits for the night, in came Mamzelle, screeching again. The necklace was gone. It had been taken right out of its case. *I* couldn't tell, because I hadn't memorized all the things that were there.

"Mamzelle was in hysterics. There had been a short in the warning system so that it was possible to open the case without sirens sounding all over the place, and if she hadn't foolishly announced this . . . I think she thought she was going to be fired out of hand, and frankly I thought she deserved it, but I gathered she had been there from the year one and was a valued employee.

"Then I mentioned that I thought there had been a ringer in the Santa Claus department, a fifth one, and right away, everyone denied it. There had only been four. All the Santa Clauses claimed they had been together at all times and there had never been a fifth. I couldn't argue very vehemently. I hadn't actually seen five. There had only been that fugitive impression.

"So I mentioned the Santa Claus in the jewelry department, and that *really* roused hostility, because that made it look as though one of the male employees had put on a Santa Claus suit and done the job after having been alerted by Mamzelle's gaffe. Naturally, every one of them started giving each other alibis. Not one of them, it would seem, could possibly have been out of sight of all the others. So there you are, Griswold. It turned out no one could do it."

I said, "Did anyone consider that it could have been an outside job. Someone sneaking in, stealing the necklace, and then leaving the store."

"Not a chance," said Dan. "Doors were all locked and *those* alarms were working. Whoever did it had to know where the Santa Claus suits were and he had to know the warning system was out. No, it was an inside job all right. —The trouble is that I'm the one who looks bad. I had all the knowledge needed, and I was trying to muddy the waters by talking about a fifth Santa Claus and one who was inside the jewelry department. There was no one to corroborate anything I said and the natural thought, I suppose, was that I had done it. It was clear that that *was* what they thought."

"They didn't find the necklace on you, I hope," I said.

"Of course not," said Dan. "They haven't found it at all. Frankly, I think whoever it was who did it must know the store pretty well. He had a hiding place all picked out. But that looks bad for me, too. I know the store pretty well."

I said, "When you saw that Santa Claus, Dan, was there anything recognizable about him?"

"Recognizable? Come on, Griswold, you know what a Santa Claus suit is like. It covers the entire body, with padding. You wear white gloves. You've got a white wig, and a thick white beard. The only part of you that shows are your eyes, nose, and cheekbones. I wouldn't be able to recognize my brother if he were dressed up like that."

"The nose was visible, and noses are pretty distinctive. Was it a snub nose, a long nose, a crooked nose, a blunt nose."

"Griswold, I can't tell you. I explained I was caught entirely by surprise. That Santa Claus and I were together for only fifteen seconds. The only thing in the wide world I can tell is that he didn't ho-ho-ho me. It's just an insoluble mystery as far as I'm concerned, but not as far as anyone else is concerned. Everyone else thinks it's me. And even if they can't prove it, Griswold, the word will get out and I won't get any jobs anymore. Not that I need them, you understand, but I do value my reputation and that's shot."

"Oh, I don't know, Dan," I said. "It doesn't seem like a terrible mystery to me. I should think the solution is quite simple."

Dan looked up at me sharply. "Oh, come *on*."

"No, really," I said, and I explained.

His eyes opened wide, and as a matter of fact, when faced with exactly what had been done, the malefactor broke down and the necklace was recovered. What was most important was that Dan emerged without a stain on his character. In fact, he was viewed as the one who solved the mystery. —And that's my Christmas story.

"That's your Christmas phony, Griswold," I said angrily. "What solution are you talking about? How did you get a solution out of what you told us?"

Griswold, who had apparently been settling down to resume his nap, snapped his eyes open again, "I can't believe you don't see it."

He looked at Jennings, then at Baranof. "Don't you two see it, either?"

They shook their heads.

Griswold sighed. "The people I have to deal with. —Look, it seems quite clear that the Santa Claus costume hides everything about a person except the eyes, nose, and cheekbones. Right?"

"Right," we chorused.

"Well, there's one other thing it doesn't hide, you idiots. It doesn't hide the *voice*."

"The voice?"

"Absolutely. That's why the Santa Claus in the jewelry department didn't go 'ho, ho, ho.' He *couldn't*. Because he wasn't a he. He was a woman. Mamzelle was tall. She was skinny but there was padding. Everything was covered that could be covered but she had a high-pitched voice. She couldn't have emitted a bass 'ho, ho, ho' if you had pointed a gun at her, and the absence of it gave her away. She knew the warning system was off. She had gimmicked it herself. And she made the announcement concerning it and wore the suit to spread suspicion to the men."

Griswold smiled and lifted his glass, "Ho, ho, ho, gentlemen!"

MARCIA MULLER

SILENT NIGHT

Marcia Muller says she brought Sharon McCone to life as a female private eye because she herself had gained so much similar experience as a survey researcher, extracting information from people who didn't want to talk to her. Sharon has been delighting fans since 1977 . . . longer than any of the other currently active professional women detectives in the mystery field. Part of her popularity, I think, is due to the fact that she's been endowed with Marcia's own qualities of compassion and wry humor. It came as a surprise to me that Sharon has a folksinger brother-in-law who wrote a smash-hit ballad called "Cobwebs in the Attic of My Mind" . . . and I couldn't have imagined the sort of Christmas his caroling would bring to his often overworked but never undercaring sister-in-law.

"Larry, I hardly know what to say!"

What I *wanted* to say was, "What am I supposed to do with this?" The object I'd just liberated from its gay red-and-gold Christmas wrappings was a plastic bag, about eight by twelve inches, packed firm with what looked suspiciously like sawdust. I turned it over in my hands, as if admiring it, and searched for some clue to its identity.

When I looked up, I saw Larry Koslowski's brown eyes shining expectantly; even the ends of his little handlebar mustache seemed to bristle as he awaited my reaction. "It's perfect," I said lamely.

He let his bated breath out in a long sigh. "I thought it would be. You remember how you were talking about not having much energy lately? I told you to try whipping up my protein drink for breakfast, but you said you didn't have that kind of time in the morning."

The conversation came back to me—vaguely. I nodded.

"Well," he went on, "put two tablespoons of that mixture in a tall glass, add water, stir, and you're in business."

Of course—it was an instant version of his infamous protein drink. Larry was the health nut on the All Souls Legal Cooperative staff; his fervent exhortations for the rest of us to adopt better nutritional standards often fell upon deaf ears—mine included.

"Thank you," I said. "I'll try it first thing tomorrow."

Larry ducked his head, his lips turning up in shy pleasure beneath his straggly little mustache.

It was late in the afternoon of Christmas Eve, and the staff of All Souls was engaged in the traditional gift exchange between members who had drawn each other's names earlier in the month. The yearly ritual extends back to the days of the co-op's founding, when most people were too poor to give more than one present; the only rule is Keep It Simple.

The big front parlor of the co-op's San Francisco Victorian was crowded. People perched on the furniture or, like Larry and me, sat cross-legged on the floor, oohing and aahing over their gifts. Next to the Christmas tree in the bay window, my boss, Hank Zahn, sported a new cap and muffler, knitted for him—after great deliberation and consultation as to colors—by my assistant, Rae Kelleher. Rae, in turn, wore the scarf and cap I'd purchased (because I can't knit to save my life) for her in the hope she would consign relics from her days at U.C. Berkeley to the trash can. Other people had homemade cookies and sinful fudge, special bottles of wine, next year's calendars, assorted games, plants, and paperback books.

And I had a bag of instant health drink that looked like sawdust.

The voices in the room created such a babble that I barely heard the phone ring in the hall behind me. Our secretary, Ted Smalley, who is a compulsive answerer, stepped over me and went out to where the instrument sat on his desk. A moment later he called, "McCone, it's for you."

My stomach did a little flip-flop, because I was expecting news of a personal nature that could either be very good or very bad. I thanked Larry again for my gift, scrambled to my feet, and went to take the receiver from Ted. He remained next to the desk; I'd confided my family's problem to him earlier that week, and now, I knew, he would wait to see if he could provide aid or comfort.

"Shari?" My younger sister Charlene's voice was composed, but her use of the diminutive of Sharon, which no one but my father calls me unless it's a time of crisis, made my stomach flip again.

"I'm here," I said.

"Shari, somebody's seen him. A friend of Ricky's saw Mike!"

"Where? When?"

"Today around noon. Up there—in San Francisco."

I let out my breath in a sigh of relief. My fourteen-year-old nephew, oldest of Charlene and Ricky's six kids, had run away from their home in Pacific Palisades five days ago. Now, it appeared, he was alive, if not exactly safe.

The investigator in me counseled caution, however. "Was this friend sure it was Mike he saw?"

"Yes. He spoke to him. Mike said he was visiting you. But afterward our friend got to thinking that he looked kind of grubby and tired, and that you probably wouldn't have let him wander around that part of town, so he called us to check it out."

A chill touched my shoulder blades. "What part of town?"

". . . Somewhere near City Hall, a sleazy area, our friend said."

A very sleazy area, I thought. Dangerous territory to which runaways are often drawn, where boys and girls alike fall prey to pimps and pushers . . .

Charlene said, "Shari?"

"I'm still here, just thinking."

"You don't suppose he'll come to you?"

"I doubt it, if he hasn't already. But in case he does, there's somebody staying at my house—an old friend who's here for Christmas—and she knows to keep him there and call me immediately. Is there anybody else he knows here in the city? Somebody he might trust not to send him home?"

". . . I can't think of anybody."

"What about that friend you spent a couple of Christmases with—the one with the two little girls who lived on Sixteenth Street across from Mission Dolores?"

"Ginny Shriber? She moved away about four years ago." There was a noise as if Charlene was choking back a sob. "He's really just a little boy yet. So little, and so stubborn."

But stubborn little boys grow up fast on the rough city streets. I didn't want that kind of coming-of-age for my nephew.

"Look at the up side of this, Charlene," I said, more heartily than I felt. "Mike's come to the one city where you have your own private investigator. I'll start looking for him right away."

It had begun with, of all things, a moped that Mike wanted for Christmas. Or maybe it had really started a year earlier, when Ricky Savage finally hit it big.

During the first fourteen years of his marriage to my sister, Ricky had been merely another faceless country-and-western musician, playing and singing backup with itinerant bands, dreaming seemingly improbable dreams of stardom. He and Charlene had developed a reproductive pattern (and rate) that never failed to astound me, in spite of its regularity: he'd get her pregnant, go out on tour, return after the baby was born; then he'd go out again when the two o'clock feedings got to him, return when the kid was weaned, and start the whole cycle all over. Finally, after the sixth child, Charlene had wised up and gotten her tubes tied. But Ricky still stayed on the road more than at home, and still dreamed his dreams.

But then, with money borrowed from my father on the promise that if he didn't make it within one more year he'd give up music and go into my brother John's housepainting business, Ricky had cut a demo of a song he'd written called "Cobwebs in the Attic of My Mind." It was about a lovelorn fellow who, besides said cobwebs, had a "sewer that's backed up in the cellar of his soul" and "a short in the wiring of his heart." When I first heard it, I was certain that Pa's money had washed down that same pipe before it clogged, but fate—perverse creature that it is—would have it otherwise. The song was a runaway hit, and more Ricky Savage hits were to follow.

In true *nouveau* style, Ricky and Charlene quickly moved uptown—or in this case up the coast, from West Los Angeles to affluent Pacific Palisades. There were new cars, new furniture and clothes, a house with a swimming pool, and toys and goodies for the children. *Lots* of goodies, anything they wanted—until this Christmas when, for reasons of safety, Charlene had balked at letting Mike have the moped. And Mike, headstrong little bastard that he was, had taken his life's savings of some fifty-five dollars and hitched away from home on the Pacific Coast Highway.

It was because of a goddamned moped that I was canceling my Christmas Eve plans and setting forth to comb the sleazy streets and alleys of the area known as Polk Gulch for a runaway . . .

The city was strangely subdued on this Christmas Eve, the dark streets hushed, although not deserted. Most people had been drawn inside to the warmth of family and friends; others, I suspected, had retreated to nurse the loneliness that is endemic to the season. The pedestrians I passed moved silently, as if reluctant to call attention to their presence; occasionally I heard laughter from the bars as I went by, but even that was muted. The lost, drifting souls of the city seemed to collectively hold their breath as they waited for life to resume its everyday pattern.

I had started at Market Street and worked my way northwest,

through the Tenderloin to Polk Gulch. Before I'd started out, I'd had a photographer friend who likes to make a big fee more than he likes to celebrate holidays run off a hundred copies of my most recent photo of Mike. Those I passed out, along with my card, to clerks in what liquor stores, corner groceries, cheap hotels, and greasy spoon restaurants I found open. The pictures drew no response other than indifference or sympathetic shakes of the head and promises to keep an eye out for him. By the time I reached Polk Street, where I had an appointment in a gay bar at ten, I was cold, footsore, and badly discouraged.

Polk Gulch, so called because it is in a valley that has an underground river running through it, long ago was the hub of gay life in San Francisco. In the seventies, however, most of the action shifted up Market Street to the Castro district, and the vitality seemed to drain out of the Gulch. Now parts of it, particularly those bordering the Tenderloin, are depressingly sleazy. As I walked along, examining the face of each young man I saw, I became aware of the hopelessness and resignation in the eyes of the street hustlers and junkies and winos and homeless people.

A few blocks from my destination was a vacant lot surrounded by a chain link fence. Inside gaped a huge excavation, the cellar of the building that had formerly stood there, now open to the elements. People had scaled the fence and taken up residence down in it; campfires blazed, in defiance of the NO TRESPASSING signs. The homeless could rest easy—at least for this one night. No one was going to roust them on Christmas Eve.

I went to the fence and grasped its cold mesh with my fingers, staring down into the shifting light and shadows, wondering if Mike was among the ragged and hungry ranks. Many of the people were middle-aged to elderly, but there were also families with children and a scattering of young people. There was no way to tell, though, without scaling the fence myself and climbing

down there. Eventually I turned away, realizing I had only
enough time to get to the gay bar by ten.

The transvestite's name was Norma and she—he? I never know
which to call them—was coldly beautiful. The two of us sat at a
corner table in the bar, sipping champagne because Norma had
insisted on it. ("After all, it's Christmas Eve, darling!") The bar, in
spite of winking colored lights on its tree and flickering bayberry
candles on each table, was gloomy and semideserted; Norma's
brave velvet finery and costume jewelry had about it more than a
touch of the pathetic. She'd been sitting alone when I'd entered
and had greeted me eagerly.

I'd been put in touch with Norma by Ted Smalley, who is gay
and has a wide-ranging acquaintance among all segments of the
city's homosexual community. Norma, he'd said, knew everything there was to know about what went on in Polk Gulch; if
anyone could help me, it was she.

The photo of Mike didn't look familiar to Norma. "There are so
many runaways on the street at this time of year," she told me.
"Kids get their hopes built up at Christmas time. When they find
out Santa isn't the great guy he's cracked up to be, they take off.
Like your nephew."

"So what would happen to a kid like him? Where would he go?"

"Lots of places. There's a hotel—the Vinton. A lot of runaways
end up there at first, until their money runs out. If he's into drugs,
try any flophouse, doorway, or alley. If he's connected with a
pimp, look for him hustling."

My fingers tightened involuntarily on the stem of my champagne glass. Norma noticed and shook her elaborately coiffed
head in sympathy. "Not a pretty thought, is it? But what do you
see around here that's pretty—except for me?" As she spoke the
last words, her smile became self-mocking.

"He's been missing five days now," I said, "and he only had
fifty-some dollars on him. That'll be gone by now, so he probably

won't be at the hotel, or any other. He's never been into drugs. His father's a musician, and a lot of his cronies are druggies; the kid actually disapproves of them. The other I don't even want to think about—although I probably will have to, eventually."

"So what are you going to do?"

"Try the hotel. Go back and talk to the people at that vacant lot. Keep looking at each kid who walks by."

Norma stared at the photo of Mike that lay face up on the table between us. "It's a damned shame, a nice-looking kid like that. He ought to be home with his family, trimming the tree, roasting chestnuts on the fire, or whatever other things families do."

"The American Christmas dream, huh?"

"Yeah." She smiled bleakly, raised her glass. "Here's to the American Christmas dream—and to all the people it's eluded."

I touched my glass to hers. "Including you and me."

"Including you and me. Let's just hope it doesn't elude young Mike forever."

The Vinton Hotel was a few blocks away, around the corner on Eddy Street. Its lobby was a flight up, over a closed sandwich shop, and I had to wait and be buzzed in before I could climb carpetless stairs that stank strongly of disinfectant and faintly of urine. Lobby was a misnomer, actually: it was more a narrow hall with a desk to one side, behind which sat a young black man with a tall afro. The air up there was thick with the odor of marijuana; I guessed he'd been spending his Christmas Eve with a joint. His eyes flashed panic when I reached in my bag for my identification. Then he realized it wasn't a bust and relaxed somewhat.

I took out another photo of Mike and laid it on the counter. "You seen this kid?"

He barely glanced at it. "Nope, can't help you."

I shoved it closer. "Take another look."

He did, pushed it back toward me. "I said no."

There was something about his tone that told me he was

lying—would lie out of sheer perversity. I could get tough with
him, make noises about talking to the hotel's owners, mentioning
how the place reeked of grass. The city's fleabags had come under
a good bit of media scrutiny recently; the owners wouldn't want
me to cause any trouble that would jeopardize this little goldmine
that raked in outrageously high rents from transients, as well as
government subsidized payments for welfare recipients. Still,
there had to be a better way . . .

"You work here every night?" I asked.

"Yeah."

"Rough, on Christmas Eve."

He shrugged.

"Christmas night, too?"

"Why do you care?"

"I understand what a rotten deal that is. You don't think I'm
running around out here in the cold because I like it, do you?"

His eyes flickered to me, faintly interested. "You got no choice,
either?"

"Hell, no. The client says find the kid, I go looking. Not that
it matters. I don't have anything better to do."

"Know what you mean. Nothing for me at home, either."

"Where's home?"

"My real home, or where I live?"

"Both, I guess."

"Where I live's up there." He gestured at the ceiling. "Room
goes with the job. Home's not there no more. Was in Motown,
back before my ma died and things got so bad in the auto industry.
I came out here thinking I'd find work." He smiled ironically.
"Well, I found it, didn't I?"

"At least it's not as cold here as in Detroit."

"No, but it's not home, either." He paused, then reached for
Mike's picture. "Let me see that again." Another pause. "Okay.
He stayed here. Him and this blond chick got to be friends. She's
gone, too."

"Do you know the blond girl's name?"

"Yeah. Jane Smith. Original, huh?"

"Can you describe her?"

"Just a little blond, maybe five-two. Long hair. Nothing special about her."

"When did they leave?"

"They were gone when I came on last night. The owner don't put up with the ones that can't pay, and the day man, he likes tossing their asses out on the street."

"How did the kid seem to you? Was he okay?"

The man's eyes met mine, held them for a moment. "Thought this was just a job to you."

". . . He's my nephew."

"Yeah, I guessed it might be something like that. Well, if you mean was he doing drugs or hustling, I'd say no. Maybe a little booze, that's all. The girl was the same. Pretty straight kids. Nobody'd gotten to them yet."

"Let me ask you this: What would kids like that do after they'd been thrown out of here? Where would they hang out?"

He considered. "There's a greasy spoon on Polk, near O'Farrell. Owner's an old guy, Iranian. He feels sorry for the kids, feeds them when they're about to starve, tries to get them to go home. He might of seen those two."

"Would he be open tonight?"

"Sure. Like I said, he's Iranian. It's not his holiday. Come to think of it, it's not mine anymore, either."

"Why not?"

Again the ironic smile. "Can't celebrate peace-on-earth-good-will-to-men when you don't believe in it anymore, now can you?"

I reached into my bag and took out a twenty-dollar bill, slid it across the counter to him. "Peace on earth, and thanks."

He took it eagerly, then looked at it and shook his head. "You don't have to."

"I *want* to. That makes a difference."

*   *   *

The "greasy spoon" was called The Coffee Break. It was small—just five tables and a lunch counter, old green linoleum floors, Formica and molded plastic furniture. A slender man with thinning gray hair sat behind the counter smoking a cigarette. A couple of old women were hunched over coffee at a corner table. Next to the window was a dirty-haired blond girl; she was staring through the glass with blank eyes—another of the city's casualties.

I showed Mike's picture to the man behind the counter. He told me Mike looked familiar, thought a minute, then snapped his fingers and said, "Hey, Angie."

The girl by the window turned. Full-face, I could see she was red-eyed and tear-streaked. The blankness of her gaze was due to misery, not drugs.

"Take a look at the picture this lady has. Didn't I see you with this kid yesterday?"

She got up and came to the counter, self-consciously smoothing her wrinkled jacket and jeans. "Yeah," she said after glancing at it, "that's Michael."

"Where's he now? The lady's his aunt, wants to help him."

She shook her head. "I don't know. He was at the Vinton, but he got kicked out the same time I did. We stayed down at the cellar in the vacant lot last night, but it was cold and scary. These drunks kept bothering us. Mr. Ahmeni, how long do you think it's going to take my dad to get here?"

"Take it easy. It's a long drive from Oroville. I only called him an hour ago." To me, Mr. Ahmeni added, "Angie's going home for Christmas."

I studied her. Under all that grime, a pretty, conventional girl hid. I said, "Would you like a cup of coffee? Something to eat?"

"I wouldn't mind a Coke. I've been sponging off Mr. Ahmeni for hours." She smiled faintly. "I guess he'd appreciate it if I sponged off somebody else for a change."

I bought us both Cokes and sat down with her. "When did you meet Mike?"

"Three days ago, I guess. He was at the hotel when I got into town. He kind of looked out for me. I was glad; that place is pretty awful. A lot of addicts stay there. One OD'd in the stairwell the first night. But it's cheap and they don't ask questions. A guy I met on the bus coming down here told me about it."

"What did Mike do here in the city, do you know?"

"Wandered around, mostly. One afternoon we went out to Ocean Beach and walked on the dunes."

"What about drugs or—"

"Michael's not into drugs. We drank some wine, is all. He's . . . I don't know how to describe it, but he's not like a lot of the kids on the streets."

"How so?"

"Well, he's kind of . . . sensitive, deep."

"This sensitive soul ran away from home because his parents wouldn't buy him a moped for Christmas."

Angie sighed. "You really don't know anything about him, do you? You don't even know he wants to be called Michael, not Mike."

That silenced me for a moment. It was true: I really didn't know my nephew, not as a person. "Tell me about him."

"What do you want to know?"

"Well, this business with the moped—what was that all about?"

"It didn't really have anything to do with the moped. At least, not much. It had to do with the kids at school."

"In what way?"

"Well, the way Michael told it, his family used to be kind of poor. At least there were some months when they worried about being able to pay the rent."

"That's right."

"And then his father became a singing star and they moved to this awesome house in Pacific Palisades, and all of a sudden

Michael was in school with all these rich kids. But he didn't fit in. The kids, he said, were really into having things and doing drugs and partying. He couldn't relate to it. He says it's really hard to get into that kind of stuff when you've spent your life worrying about real things."

"Like if your parents are going to be able to pay the rent."

Angie nodded, her fringe of limp blond hair falling over her eyes. She brushed it back and went on. "I know about that; my folks don't have much money, and my mom's sick a lot. The kids, they sense you're different and they don't want to have anything to do with you. Michael was lonely at the new school, so he tried to fit in—tried too hard, I guess, by always having the latest stuff, the most expensive clothes. You know."

"And the moped was part of that."

"Uh-huh. But when his mom said he couldn't have it, he realized what he'd been doing. And he also realized that the moped wouldn't have done the trick anyway. Michael's smart enough to know that people don't fall all over you just because you've got another new toy. So he decided he'd never fit in, and he split. He says he feels more comfortable on the streets, because life here is real." She paused, eyes filling, and looked away at the window. "God, is it *real*."

I followed the direction of her gaze: beyond the plate glass a girl of perhaps thirteen stumbled by. Her body was emaciated, her face blank, her eyes dull—the look of a far-gone junkie.

I said to Angie, "When did you last see Mike . . . Michael?"

"Around four this afternoon. Like I said, we spent the night in that cellar in the vacant lot. After that I knew I couldn't hack it anymore, and I told him I'd decided to go home. He got pissed at me and took off."

"Why?"

"Why do you think? I was abandoning him. I could go home, and he couldn't."

"Why not?"

"Because Michael's . . . God, you don't know a thing about him! He's proud. He couldn't admit to his parents that he couldn't make it on his own. Any more than he could admit to them about not fitting in at school."

What she said surprised me and made me ashamed. Ashamed for Charlene, who had always referred to Mike as stubborn or bullheaded, but never as proud. And ashamed for myself, because I'd never really seen him, except as the leader of a pack jokingly referred to in family circles as "the little Savages."

"Angie," I said, "do you have any idea where he might have gone after he left you?"

She shook her head. "I wish I did. It would be nice if Michael could have a Christmas. He talked about how much he was going to miss it. He spent the whole time we were walking around on the dunes telling me about the Christmases they used to have, even though they didn't have much money: the tree trimming, the homemade presents, the candlelit masses on Christmas Eve, the cookie decorating and the turkey dinners. Michael absolutely loves Christmas."

I hadn't known that, either. For years I'd been too busy with my own life to do more than send each of the Savage kids a small check. Properly humbled, I thanked Angie for talking with me, wished her good luck with her parents, and went back out to continue combing the dark, silent streets.

On my way back down Polk Street toward the Tenderloin, I stopped again at the chain link fence surrounding the vacant lot. I was fairly sure Mike was not among the people down there—not after his and Angie's experience of the night before—but I was curious to see the place where they had spent that frightening time.

The campfires still burned deep in the shelter of the cellar. Here and there drunks and addicts lay passed out on the ground; others who had not yet reached that state passed bottles and shared joints and needles; one group raised inebriated voices in a chorus of "Rudolph, the Red-Nosed Reindeer." In a far corner I saw another group—two women, three children, and a man—gathered around a scrawny Christmas tree.

The tree had no ornaments, wasn't really a tree at all, but just a top that someone had probably cut off and tossed away after finding that the one he'd bought was too tall for the height of his ceiling. There was no star atop it, no presents under it, no candy canes or popcorn chains, and there was certain to be no turkey dinner tomorrow. The people had nonetheless gathered around it and stood silently, their heads bowed in prayer.

My throat tightened and I clutched at the fence, fighting back tears. Even though I spend a disproportionate amount of my professional life probing into events and behavior that would make the average person gag, every now and then the indestructible courage of the human spirit absolutely stuns me.

I watched the scene for a moment longer, then turned away, glancing at my watch. Its hands told me why the people were praying: Christmas Day was upon us. This was their midnight service.

And then I realized that those people, who had nothing in the world with which to celebrate Christmas except somebody's cast-off treetop, may have given me a priceless gift. I thought I knew now where I would find my nephew.

When I arrived at Mission Dolores, the neoclassical façade of the basilica was bathed in floodlights, the dome and towers gleaming against the post-midnight sky. The street was choked with double-parked vehicles, and from within I heard voices raised in a joyous chorus. Beside the newer early twentieth-century structure, the small adobe church built in the late 1700s seemed dwarfed and enveloped in deep silence. I hurried up the wide steps to the arching wooden doors of the basilica, then took a moment to compose myself before entering.

Like many of my generation, it had been years since I'd been even nominally a Catholic, but the old habit of reverence had never left me. I couldn't just blunder in there and creep about, peering into every worshipper's face, no matter how great my urgency. I waited until I felt relatively calm before pulling open the heavy door and stepping over the threshold.

The mass was candlelit; the robed figures of the priest and altar boys moved slowly in the flickering, shifting light. The stained glass window behind the altar and those on the side walls gleamed richly. In contrast, the massive pillars reached upward to vaulted arches that were deeply shadowed. As I moved slowly along one of the side aisles, the voices of the choir swelled to a majestic finale.

The congregants began to go forward to receive Communion. As they did, I was able to move less obtrusively, scanning the faces of the young people in the pews. Each time I spotted a teenaged boy, my heart quickened. Each time I felt a sharp stab of disappointment.

I passed behind the waiting communicants, then moved unhurriedly up the nave and crossed to the far aisle. The church was darker and sparsely populated toward the rear; momentarily a pillar blocked my view of the altar. I moved around it.

He was there in the pew next to the pillar, leaning wearily against it. Even in the shadowy light, I could see that his face was dirty and tired, his jacket and jeans rumpled and stained. His eyes were half-closed, his mouth slack; his hands were shoved between his thighs, as if for warmth.

Mike—no, Michael—had come to the only safe place he knew in the city, the church where on two Christmas Eves he'd attended mass with his family and their friends, the Shribers, who had lived across the street.

I slipped into the pew and sat down next to him. He jerked his head toward me, stared in openmouthed surprise. What little color he had drained from his face; his eyes grew wide and alarmed.

"Hi, Michael." I put my hand on his arm.

He looked as if he wanted to shake it off. "How did you . . . ?"

"Doesn't matter. Not now. Let's just sit quietly till mass is over."

He continued to stare at me. After a few seconds he said, "I bet Mom and Dad are really mad at me."

"More worried than anything else."

"Did they hire you to find me?"

"No, I volunteered."

"Huh." He looked away at the line of communicants.

"You still go to church?" I asked.

"Not much. None of us do anymore. I kind of miss it."

"Do you want to take Communion?"

He was silent. Then, "No. I don't think that's something I can do right now. Maybe never."

"Well, that's okay. Everybody expresses his feelings for . . . God, or whatever, in different ways." I thought of the group of homeless worshippers in the vacant lot. "What's important is that you believe in something."

He nodded, and then we sat silently, watching people file up and down the aisle. After a while he said, "I guess I do believe in something. Otherwise I couldn't have gotten through this week. I learned a lot, you know."

"I'm sure you did."

"About me, I mean."

"I know."

"What're you going to do now? Send me home?"

"Do you want to go home?"

"Maybe. Yes. But I don't want to be sent there. I want to go on my own."

"Well, nobody should spend Christmas Day on a plane or a bus anyway. Besides, I'm having ten people to dinner at four this afternoon. I'm counting on you to help me stuff the turkey."

Michael hesitated, then smiled shyly. He took one hand from between his thighs and slipped it into mine. After a moment he leaned his tired head on my shoulder, and we celebrated the dawn of Christmas together.